TEGAN AND THE GREEN MOONSTONE

JENNIFER WHIDDON

ISBN: Paperback: 979-8-9918270-0-3, eBook: 979-8-9918270-1-0

Book Cover by whiterosepublishingservice

Illustrations by Sienna Arts

First Edition, edition 2024

CONTENTS

Dedication   VI

Map   VII

Prologue   VIII

Chapter 1   1

Chapter 2   6

Chapter 3   12

Chapter 4   18

Chapter 5   24

Chapter 6   31

Chapter 7   39

Chapter 8   46

Chapter 9   52

Chapter 10   59

Chapter 11   65

Chapter 12	72
Chapter 13	79
Chapter 14	85
Chapter 15	95
Chapter 16	101
Chapter 17	113
Chapter 18	121
Chapter 19	130
Chapter 20	138
Chapter 21	147
Chapter 22	154
Chapter 23	161
Chapter 24	167
Chapter 25	176
Chapter 26	186
Chapter 27	192
Chapter 28	202
Chapter 29	208
Chapter 30	217
Chapter 31	227

Chapter 32   235

Chapter 33   242

Chapter 34   250

Chapter 35   258

Epilogue   267

For Maddie, the joy of my life.

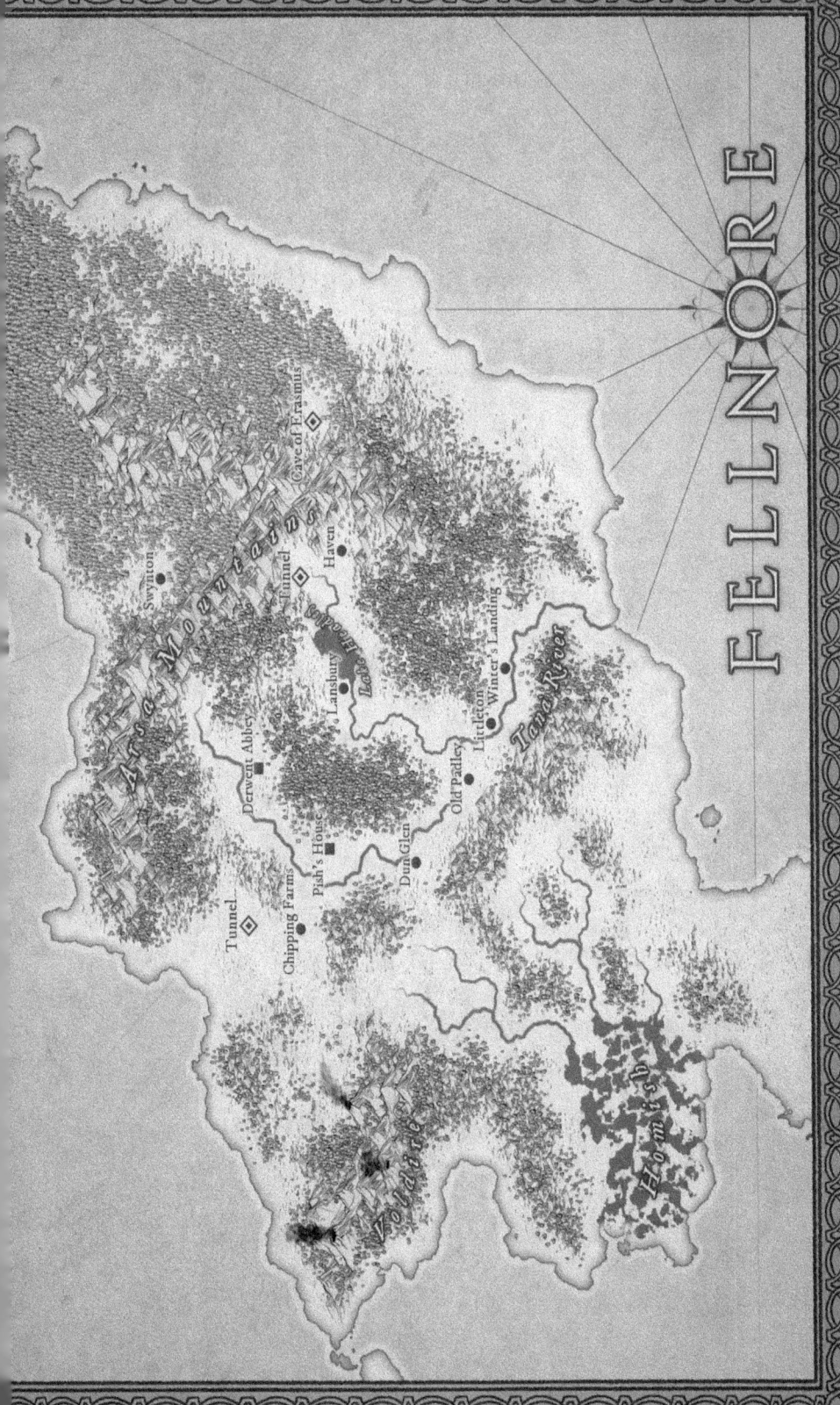

FELLNORE

Arca Mountains

Swinton

Cave of Erasmus

Tunnel

Haven

Derwent Abbey

Lansbury

Tunnel

Chipping Farms

Pish's House

Dun Glen

Old Padley

Hazleton

Winter's Landing

Tana River

Volanar

Homfield

Prologue

T he village of Haven is unlike any other.

Along the river, under the cover of tall grasses and reeds, lies what looks like a very ordinary stone. It stands almost three feet tall with ancient ogham letters etched down the front of the rock. The structure looks like it has been part of the landscape since the beginning of time. However, it was planted there hundreds of years ago as a sign that a secret foot path is merely a stone's throw away.

Down this path is an old bridge situated to the left of the hill. Plenty of forest creatures and other mystical beings have crossed this stone bridge over time. Travelers making a pilgrimage, soldiers going to war, merchants selling their wares....the bridge has many stories to tell. Its worn and weathered stone bricks positioned in the mortar as if bearing the burden of what was left of the bridge. Under the overpass, near the bank of the river, a tiny archway stands, almost unnoticeable, covered by grassy overgrowth. This door leads to the region of Fellnore...with villages like Haven within.

Dark clouds have gathered over this village of Haven as winds blow in a thunderstorm. It's close enough to smell the rain. Tiny bungalows dot the hillside with smoke piping from the quaint chimneys. Wet laundry flaps on clothes lines outside the front doors and merchants with their carts choke the narrow cobblestone streets. Tea time has come and gone, and many of those busy workers are closing their shops and heading home for dinner.

The village of Haven is unlike any other for its inhabitants consist mostly of woodland creatures like the Sombels, a miniature form of the house cat. If you've never heard of sombels, then you're not alone. These creatures live solely in the Fellnore region and enjoy a simple lifestyle of farming and close community, far away from the oppressive black rats of Voldire. And it is here, in Haven, where our story begins.

CHAPTER I

A loud clap of thunder startled Tegan awake. The little brown sombel looked around the room, trying to open her eyes. Candles remained lit in the family room, so it had to be early in the night. She sat up and pulled her dark green cloak close around her neck.

"Ma?" she whispered.

She peeked into the family room and saw several large councilmen seated around the table with her papa. A chubby one waved his paws when he talked. His name was Owen, and Papa often consulted him about business in the village.

"We can't let those rats push us around! I say we pack tonight and attack in the morning!!" Owen exclaimed.

Papa looked around the table, and then saw Tegan eavesdropping near the door. Her whiskers twitched. Ma rushed around the corner and shooed her into the kitchen.

"Tegan, come in here," Ma said.

"What's going on, Ma?" she asked while rubbing her eyes.

Ma leaned over and pulled the door close. "Something's happened to your Uncle Lewis." She turned to take the kettle off the stove and pour hot water into a tea cup. "We think the rats have kidnapped him."

Ma handed Tegan the cup, "Here, drink this. It'll help you get back to sleep."

Tegan stirred cream into her chamomile tea and added a lump of sugar. She strained to hear more of the conversation in the family room while she sipped her tea.

There were five councilmen total. Owen, the fat one, owned the bakery in the village. He wore a maroon corduroy sweater that looked like it would explode if he moved around too much.

Pish, seated beside Owen, helped down by the riverside and sold fish near the mountain trail. He had a small thatched hut he built last spring to shelter himself from the heavy showers. At times, he crafted small rafts to help the forest animals cross the river; but it had to be at the smallest point. Some places in that river were wide and rough, and don't get him started about the sea creatures!

Pish delivered the news of Lewis's disappearance. He had travelled around the mountain and through the brambles of Fellnore to bring the message to Papa himself. Though rough around the edges, Pish's heart beat truly for justice. And this, well, he was determined to do what it took to find his friend.

Ma wiped her paws on her faded yellow apron and poured a second cup of tea for Pish. As she walked out of the kitchen and into the family room, Tegan leaned over to see who the others were around the table. The dimly lit room created an amber ambience over the table. She could hear the men talking in low but stern voices.

"What do we know so far?" Sammy Fourpaws sat at the opposite end of the table.

Sammy ran a pub at the end of the main road and was known amongst the villagers for his special concoctions (including a special ale that supposedly made you shrink when you drank it). Francis, Tegan's mouse friend, tried it once, but all he got was a stomach ache and the nickname, "Bubbles."

"This morning around sunrise, a group of rats from Voldire captured Lewis as he walked toward the tunnels. Pish witnessed them forcing Lewis into a wooden cage and then carried away from the mountain," Papa replied.

"They had spears and lanterns. I couldn't see much in the mist, but I know they tied Lewis up," Pish said. He observed the capture while delivering fish to his mother in a nearby town. And good thing too. Since the seasonal storms arrived early this year, the area was devoid of travelers...and therefore, witnesses.

"I have a feeling we'll be hearing from the tribe soon," said Papa.

"Should we get our militia ready?" That was Milo, captain of the Guard's Men.

"I'd rather negotiate," Papa looked Milo directly in the eyes.

"The rats flagrantly broke the peace treaty," said Milo. "There must be repercussions for that." The captain slammed his paw on the table.

"And there will be," Papa replied. "However, we should send a messenger first."

"What? And negotiate?" sneered Sammy.

"Rats don't negotiate!" bellowed Owen. "We all know what they want, and Lewis won't budge an inch."

Papa looked at Belmar, the final councilman, sitting solemnly near the window. The older sombel listened to everyone speak and drew a deep breath as if to answer. But, instead, Belmar lifted his pipe and puffed on it. The smoke circled the room smelling of fresh clover. His wise eyes targeted each councilman in the room. He was advanced in age but still ran his own carpentry shop. Papa asked him, "Belmar, what do you think?"

Belmar stood up with the help of his knotted cane, "The rats are a tribe that go way back. Farther than any of your ancestors." He walked around the table. "There's a prophecy that says: 'when the moon turns red, the rats will lead a war against those that protect the tunnels.' And since we are the keepers of that secret, the war starts with us."

"But we've had red moons in seasons past. How do we know that this one, in a week, will be the prophecy?" asked Owen.

"We don't. Belmar heard this from Erasmus," said Sammy.

"Is that true?" Papa asked. Belmar nodded. "The crazy old sombel that lives near the mountain? Ha!" Owen mocked.

"He's not crazy...quirky maybe, but not crazy," said Pish.

"Do you remember when he dressed up like a bird wearing feathered wings?" Owen dramatically waved his arms in the air like a bird. "Then he climbed up on the ledge of his cave and frantically made squawking sounds."

"Yeah, what was that all about?" Pish started chuckling.

"He claimed he was scaring away the goblins that sneak out of the forest at night," Owen replied.

The sombels roared with laughter.

"I say he's crazy. How does he know half the things he predicts?" Owen asked.

"Magic?" Suggested Pish.

Papa turned to look directly at Owen and Pish. "Do you really think Erasmus uses dark magic to tell the future? Or do you think he *wants* you to believe that?" He paused before he stated, "Erasmus is much older and wiser than any one of us. And his main weapon is intel."

"What do you mean?" Owen asked.

"A smart sombel sends out feelers...scouts...to bring back reports from the frontlines. He uses this priceless, firsthand information to answer the questions we have....or in this case, warn us of impending war," Papa said.

The room quieted down as Papa had their full attention.

He continued, "I'm sure Erasmus has scouts all over the river banks. He also has friends in precarious places. That's how he knows so much. And we would do ourselves an injustice if we didn't seek his council." Papa returned, "So, again I say, we send a messenger to try to negotiate and remind these rats of the oath they took when they signed the treaty."

Belmar picked up on this comment and sat down again. "Friends, this is a perilous time. Negotiations are a must to keep our centuries old treaty intact. If negotiations fail, I'm afraid war will be our reality."

The men murmured among themselves. It sounded like bees humming on a warm summer day. Tegan was well aware of this treaty they mentioned. The Compromise Treaty was signed to keep the rats out of Fellnore and the villages on the east side of the river. However, the rats only signed the agreement because they lost the final battle, and their leader banished to a swamp down in the Homish wetlands. Rumor had it that small skirmishes had been breaking out all along the river just south of the Arsa Mountain range. But no one wanted to talk about that.

Tegan finished her tea and listened to the rain pouring down, splashing against the outside windows. The voices in the next room became all but a whispering sound. She stood up and wrapped her cloak around her. The weather brought a chill in the air and light frost on the ground. She walked over to the fire and added another log, then stoked the embers. It would be light in a few hours, so Tegan found a cushion near the fire and laid down, her curiously red furry tail curled around her feet.

As she settled in, Tegan barely heard the door close. The councilmen left the house one by one and agreed to reconvene in the morning. Ma talked quietly with Papa at the dinner table.

Tegan wondered where her uncle had been taken. How far off was he? And what were these tunnels they mentioned?

She finally drifted off to sleep.

CHAPTER 2

The sun finally rose in the morning and poured bright rays of light into the little bungalow. Tegan woke up as the sun splashed across her face. She sat up and yawned. Ma was busy in the kitchen, so Tegan walked in to see what she was cooking.

"Hand me that basket, Tegan," Ma said pointing to the stone counter.

Tegan looked around and grabbed the basket from the same counter as the jelly jars. Ma took the basket and placed freshly baked oat cakes in it, wrapped in linen.

"Can you take these down to Sammy Fourpaws?" Ma asked. "He's selling them in the pub now."

"Yes," Tegan replied. "I am going there anyway. Mrs. Fourpaws has a few clothes she wants me to mend."

Tegan drank a glass of huckleberry juice and went outside with the basket full of oat cakes in her arms. Even though the sun was out, the air was still chilly. She jumped out of the way of an oncoming carriage and settled behind another group of merchants taking their wares to local shops in town.

Along the main road, workers threaded leafy garlands through low-hanging tree branches. Others hammered posts into the ground to hold oil lamps for night lights and ceremonial flags. As she passed by a small hat shop, a poster nailed to the wall outside read:

"Midlands Fair,
Come celebrate with us
Food, drinks, and fun!
Everyone in Haven is welcome."

Tegan knew all about this annual fair. The villagers of Haven always looked forward to sharing their home cooked meals and drinking fresh wine and brewed ale. Their kids gathered in the grassy area near the town center to play games, like hide and seek or stick ball, until dark. Later that night, some of the elders would tell stories to the children while couples danced and sang under the magical fairy lights. It truly was the event of the year for everyone in the village, including Tegan herself.

Ma stayed up late at night tweaking her new plum and raisin oat cake recipe for the fair. She even thought about testing her acorn butter and huckleberry jam sandwiches on her neighbors...to see if those should be added to her table as well. Papa loved the sandwiches and urged her to make more for the fair. And since Papa oversaw the Midlands Fair proceedings, Ma told him that she would "think about it" and winked at him.

Past the hat shop, the cobblestone street wound around an open space of lush, carpet-like grass. Several small picnic tables sat comfortably in the middle of that opening. And female villagers huddled together, weaving small baskets with reeds collected from the river bank.

Tegan crossed over an ancient wooden bridge stretching across a creek. This particular body of water connected the older and newer parts of Haven into the north and the south sides.

From this point, the street widened and shops were plentiful on both flanks of the road. Do you want spices or herbs for your stew or bread? Ms. Haddie sold them on the left there. Inside her shop smelled amazing; and when the wind blew in the evenings, the whole block soaked up the fragrances of curry, saffron, and cinnamon.

Need to service your cart or wagon? Mr. Barton replaced wheels, aligned the steering, patched the seats, reinforced the bed, you name it! He also built custom wagons. Tegan's friend, Beckett, ordered a wagon there built like a carriage with a basket on the back. Mr. Barton's shop was under the oak tree on the right, just next to Caldwell's fruit and vegetable market.

Tegan walked past a cluster of food stalls, a pottery shop, a paper stall, and the bakery. The basket she carried was beginning to feel like a bag of rocks instead of cakes, so she sat down on a large tree log to catch her breath. She didn't have much further to go. Orchard Path turned off Main Street behind her, leading to the elementary school. And just ahead, she could see both the mill and the blacksmith shop, the last merchants before Sammy's Pub.

At that moment, a rolling cart stopped in front her. It was loaded down with pottery from plates and cups to pitchers and round cooking pots. "Tegan!" the voice rang out.

She stood up and saw Beckett in the driver's seat. "Beckett, so good to see you!" Tegan exclaimed. Beckett had longer, cream colored fur and wore a dark blue tunic with a well-worn messenger bag across his chest.

"Are you headed to the shop?" she asked.

"Yes," Becket replied. "My father finished these last week, so I'm taking them to the shop for mother to sell. Want a ride?"

Tegan nodded and handed him her basket. Beckett placed it behind his seat. "Where are you off to?"

"I'm actually headed to the pub. Ma made a batch of fresh oat cakes to deliver, and I need to pick up some clothes to mend from Mrs. Fourpaws." Tegan sat beside Beckett in his wagon. They bumped and rolled along the road until they reached the front door of the pub.

On the way, Tegan examined this amazing cart-turned-wagon that Beckett created with Mr. Barton. It resembled a cart but had a seat attached to the front with wheels, pedals, and steering like that of a bicycle. With regular goods in the cart, Beckett could pedal his way to town and back without breaking a sweat. But if he loaded lumber or iron in the back, he needed two bloxen (or other strong, diminutive creatures) to pull that wagon for deliveries.

Beckett jumped down and handed Tegan her basket.

Inside the pub, tables and chairs were crammed together with a few patrons gathered for morning gossip. Tegan noticed a rabbit wearing a white apron in the dark corner. She swept the floor with a short, bushy broom and made her way around the wall toward the door.

"Is Mr. Fourpaws here?" Tegan asked the rabbit.

"I'll get him fer ya," she replied with a lisp and a twitchy nose.

Tegan nodded and walked up to the bar to sit on a small toad stool there. The smell of barley and candles was intoxicating to her. She looked around taking in the warm, amber hues of the room. Many villagers considered Sammy's place to be the heart of the town. They gathered here to drink, celebrate, and mourn...a place to relax, a place to hear the latest news. Papa brought her many times when she was little to play with the other sombels. He regularly met with townspeople and shop owners in the main room here.

All the wooden chairs were placed on the tables so the rabbit could sweep the floor. This was the first time Tegan noticed the paintings on the dimly lit wall. Most of them depicted scenes from the Fellnore history annals: the first settlement in Haven, Sir Milford's victory over the green dragon, coronation of Princess Nora of the pixie clan, defeat of Greygor the rat king, and more.

Behind the bar, bottles of oils and spices sat on the counter as well as ceramic plates, cups, and pitchers. Sausages hung from strings tied to the roofing timber and pastel-colored linens were tucked snugly into a small shelf. Cheeses sat on the back counter among baskets full of strawberries and fresh bread, and herbs dried near the closed window.

Sammy emerged from the back room and stoked the fire in the fireplace, "Good to see you, Tegan," he said. He wore his trademark gray flannel shirt tucked into blue overalls. Tegan felt the warmth of the fire as she moved closer to the pub owner.

"Here are the oat cakes you ordered from Ma," she opened the basket and placed the cakes on the little table against the wall.

"Thanks Tegan, I'll square up with your Ma tonight."

"Is Mrs. Fourpaws here?" Tegan asked. "She has clothes for me to mend."

"She's in the shop 'round back," he replied. "You can go through there and find her." Sammy motioned toward the side door that led to the back of the pub and outside into an alley.

It was cooler in the breezeway. Tegan wandered through the alley and peeked into the side window of the fabric shop. The small room illuminated brightly from the sun shining in through the door and both open windows. Voices chattered low enough to sound like humming, and she paused near the door to hear some of the conversation:

"I heard they caught him on the way to the tunnels and tied him up...." said one voice.

"Tied him up like a pig!" said another. "Those rats are coming; you mark my words."

"Does anyone else know?"

"If they did, I don't think we'd still be celebrating. There's only six days left until the solstice."

"Why would Arthur Wells keep his brother's kidnapping a secret?" the voice asked.

"To keep the Midlands Fair on schedule."

"There's something else going on, I know it!" said one voice. "Have you heard about the skirmish near Littleton?"

"The town on the south side of the river?"

"Actually, it's one of the villages just below Littleton. Remember the wedding we attended last year when I wore that gorgeous pink chiffon dress?"

"Oh yes! I remember your bonnet was stunning!"

"Yes," she sighed. "Well, that village is Winters Landing. A group of rats just showed up one night and pillaged everything in their storehouses, and then burned down their huts."

"What?!" the voice gasped. "Isn't that where your brother-in-law lives?"

"He does, indeed."

"Did he get away?"

"He and his family are safe. They were warned just in time. But the cherry trees are gone, burned down the entire harvest."

"The whole crop? Well, there goes my spring cherry pies."

"And my cherry preserves."

There was a long pause. For a split second, Tegan thought she had been seen. But the conversation continued.

"Does Arthur know?"

"Sammy told him last night. Arthur said he plans to inform the men tonight at their meeting."

"Why isn't he doing anything about it? About his brother too?"

Another pause followed by the sound of a box hitting the floor.

"Maybe because Arthur has something to hide," a voice whispered.

CHAPTER 3

Deep in the Homish wetlands, a tribe of black, warmongering rats planned their revenge. They feverishly squabbled and bared their buttery yellow teeth, chipped from gnawing the bones of dead animals in the woods. What was once a flourishing, diverse ecosystem in the swamp was now a sickening, dark refugee camp for banished rats. Since the defeat of Greygor, the rat king, most of his rodent followers left their bleak mountain home of Voldire and joined him in the wetlands. Here, Greygor schemed and bided his time until he could attack. The once pure streams became polluted with decomposition as rat hunters brought back their dead carcasses for banquets and bonfires.

Fires burned day and night causing smog to permanently choke out the sunlight. Charred and singed, the earth lay wasted as this den of thieves built large ovens to forge and sharpen crude weapons. As scavengers, those rats in charge of food were sent out to forage nearby forests or towns for anything they could eat. Rat cooks slopped the rotten meat or spoiled fruit into cauldrons over a fire pit. And soldier rats scooped the cooked sludge out of the pot with their wooden bowls to eat....the bowls pillaged from either the gnomes or the sombel villages along the river bank.

And now, Greygor sat on his throne made from bones of his dead enemies. His Royal Guards nervously twitched at the stone table in front of him. He glared at the two with red eyes while he unrolled a piece of parchment on the table. Using several wooden cups, the rat king kept the paper lying flat for the group to see.

"This is what I'm looking for," Greygor snarled and pounded on the paper.

The guards looked at the parchment and saw a crude map with traces of familiar landmarks on it. Towards the middle, they noticed a red circle and illegible scribbling to the side.

"What is this?" the rat guard asked timidly.

"The entrance," he bellowed. "The entrance to the tunnels!"

The guards pounded the table in unison.

Greygor continued, "I've been planning this for a long time. My scouts have narrowed down the opening to this particular mountain." He pointed to the landmark on the map with his gnarly finger. "Once we're in, we'll have control."

Around them, groups of soldiers worked furiously to forge spears and daggers in the heat of the fiery ovens. The sound of those iron hammers resonated throughout the camp.

"When do we leave?" one guard asked Greygor.

"In a week. The moon will be full and I'll have an answer by then."

"An answer?"

"Yes, a personal guide so-to-speak." He smiled eerily, "your job is to get the soldiers ready. I'll take care of the scouts myself."

The guards talked feverishly to each other while Greygor studied the map. They were anxious to fight and all these preparations spurred them on. The soldiers needed weapons and wagons for war. So far, the rats completed several wagons to carry war supplies into the enemy's territory...in addition to swords, bows and arrows, and knives. The rats trained with them for weeks now in hopes of rushing out, head first, into battle.

Over a mound of dirt, boulders, and garbage scraps emerged a rat scout in the distance. He ran down the path along the barracks to the center of the camp. Greygor mumbled under his breath at the paper in front of him. And the guards immediately blocked the scout from approaching the rat king.

"Who are you?" the guard snarled.

"I'm Pel. I've been scouting for the king. I have news about the prisoner," Pel said loudly for Greygor to hear.

"Let him in," said the rat king.

The guards moved aside and motioned for Pel to join them at the table. Pel sat down across from Greygor.

"What is it?" Greygor asked.

"They have him," Pel said. "There was a witness, but they have the prisoner."

"Is he talking?"

"No," Pel shook his head. "But he is acting funny." He wrung his paws and continued, "I watched as they tied him up and put him in the wagon. Threw some sacks in there and loaded the wagon for camp."

"Did you see which direction they were headed? Which path were they taking?"

"Should be here in another day. They are heading to Cardiff Forest." "What?!" Greygor spun around. "They're supposed to go around the mountain, not through those woods! That area is completely haunted at night, and I can't afford to lose *any one* of my soldiers!"

The rat king paced while Pel watched nervously.

"You leave *now* and find the captain," Greygor said slowly to Pel. "Tell him to go around the mountain and avoid those woods, or I'll finish him off myself!"

Pel nodded and raced away to find the captain and his prisoner.

Tegan grabbed the stack of clothes piled on a rocking chair beside the open door of the shop. She didn't know what to make of the conversation she just heard between Mrs. Fourpaws and another clerk. Could Papa be hiding something? As the mayor of Haven, he knew a lot of people in town. She turned and shoved the clothes into her basket.

Beckett's wagon was parked outside the blacksmith's shop. Tegan wandered inside the hut-like structure to see if her friend was in there. Beckett stood admiring several swords that Phinn had been working on. A muscular sombel with black fur and gold eyes, Phinn wore a small tool bag around his waist and a green kerchief around his neck.

The blaze smoldered in the stone pit as Phinn hammered on a new blade. Tegan watched him flip it over again and again to get the blade even. Once satisfied, he removed it from the heat and plunged it into a clay pot full of cold water to cool the blade down. Steam hissed as Beckett leaned over to see the blade closer.

"Who are you making this for?" Beckett asked.

"Ah, this one here doesn't have an owner yet," Phinn replied.

Beckett stood in front of the fire confused. "How do you know who it should belong to?"

Phinn smiled a toothy grin, "Oh, I'll know. Once I'm finished with the handle, this sword will be ready for its new owner. And it will tell me."

"It talks to you?" Beckett asked.

15

Phinn laughed a great, big belly laugh. "Something like that my boy!" He noticed Tegan in the doorway. "Come here lass, look at this blade." He motioned to her.

Tegan picked up her basket and walked toward the table where the newly forged blade lay. It was perfectly beautiful in its shine and luster. A blade that could very well be turned into a fine sword, but also small enough for a stature like hers. She imagined herself wielding a sword like the one on the table and then sliding it into a magnificent sheath. One day she would have a sword, and she would use it in defense as her father and siblings had in the past.

"It is a beautiful weapon," Tegan said in a low voice.

Phinn laughed again, "Indeed!" He picked it up and walked to the other side of the shop. There he gathered a few knives and a long, silver iron sword to hand to Beckett. "Take these to your father," Phinn said. "He's already paid me for this order."

Beckett took the weapons outside to put into his wagon. As he stepped out, Phinn said to Tegan, "I'm sorry to hear about your Uncle Lewis. He's a good sombel. Respected in Haven."

"Thank you, sir," she replied.

"I'm waiting to hear the plan at the meeting tonight. I reckon we're going to need a lot more of these," he motioned to the swords and blades on the shelves near the back wall.

Tegan turned to walk out of the shop door. Her red tail flickered from the bottom of her cloak.

"Would you look at that?!" Phinn whispered to himself. "Her tail is red."

He disappeared into a side room used mostly for storage and poked around in a box or two. Rifling through papers, old tools, and some cloth rags, he found an archaic book buried in the mess. He pulled it out and sat down at a small desk to thumb through the pages.

Another sombel came into the room quietly while his father read in the book. Silas was tall like his mother but soft spoken like his other siblings. His dark gray fur camouflaged him in the dim lighting.

"What is it, father?" Silas asked.

"The red tail," Phinn mumbled. "That red tail. There's something about it that I read in here a long time ago." He flipped through the pages loudly. "Can you believe it? Of all the villagers here in Haven, she has a red tail!"

Silas looked at his father in confusion.

"Here it is," Phinn silently read the page, then slammed the book closed. "Silas, take over for me in the shop. I have to go out for a bit before the town meeting tonight."

Phinn buttoned up his coat and slipped out the door.

Silas picked up the blade his father previously worked on and observed it closely. Prestigious iron...it just needed a handle and matching sheath. While he selected material to hone a sword handle, he thought about what his father said.

Tegan has a red tail. What did that mean?

And why did his father act so strange when he saw her red tail?

CHAPTER 4

Arthur Wells looked at his watch. Impatient and anxious, he could not wait any longer. So he started the meeting a few minutes early. The crowded pub overflowed with villagers concerned about the rat invasions so close to their town. Sombels sat in chairs around the main table and other villagers stood behind them. Pub waiters served ale and acorn bread to the crowd as they talked among each other.

"Friends!" Arthur called out to quiet the noise. The sombels turned to listen. "Our village, our very lifestyle is in danger!" He waited until he had everyone's attention. "Some of you already know this, but our dear Lewis has been captured by those filthy rats of Voldire."

Several villagers gasped while others grumbled in disbelief under their breath.

Arthur continued, "In the wake of this very pressing news, we must unite our forces and bring my brother home." The room got very quiet. "The floor is open to suggestions."

Arthur looked around the room at the villagers, but no one spoke up. "Milo? Would you like to go first?" Arthur asked.

Milo stepped forward dressed in his black military vest, decorated with shiny metal awards from past battles. Milo and Lewis fought together in several wars, so this capture was personal. "After much discussion with our captains and military leaders, I propose sending a scout to bring back word of the captivity while beefing up our defenses here. Our units are ready for battle but we still need more weapons, arrows to be precise." He looked over at Phinn. "I need as many as you can forge. Can you do that?"

Phinn nodded, "I'm on it."

"This is the time for our village to unite and help each other in one endeavor to rescue a respected member of our community, and a trusted sombel. Everyone can contribute." Arthur looked at Owen, the baker, and said, "Even Owen over here can help! We'll need bread for the troops. Owen, you're responsible for that."

Owen gulped. He never thought he would "participate" in a rescue mission.

Belmar spoke next, "I have two wagons that you can use to carry weapons. I will bring them around tomorrow."

As the business leaders spoke, the villagers whispered to each other. The rats had been raiding cities to the south of Haven and taking all their supplies. Something had to be done to push the rats back across the river. Breaking the Compromise Treaty was a big deal and the villagers were afraid that Haven would be the next victim.

"What about the invasions to the south of us?" One villager asked. Those in the room nodded in agreement.

"There's a scout down near Littleton now," Arthur said. "We're waiting to hear back from him. In the meantime, Milo is sending a team that way to intercept the rats that violated the treaty."

"The unit left yesterday at dawn," Milo confirmed.

More grumbling and cups slamming on the table. The lanterns and candles glowed low light as shadows hung on the tired villagers' faces. Everyone knew a battle was coming. The rats took a bold step in capturing Lewis, and now they wouldn't stop until they had the exact location of the tunnel entrance. That opening was strictly a secret that only a few trusted sombels knew about.

As Chief Protection Officer, Lewis understood the importance of keeping that entrance a secret. And now, the rats had captured him.

"Does anyone else have comments?" Arthur asked. He knew the villagers were restless and worried about invasions. The fact that one of their residents had been kidnapped catapulted their fear into borderline panic. He looked each crowd member in the eye and continued, "Rest assured that I will be working closely with our leaders and with Milo to plan Lewis's safe return, and to defend our village against an invasion."

The meeting descended into villagers groaning about revenge. They talked about what they could offer to the soldiers to rescue their friend, Lewis. As they finished their ale, the crowds left the pub to go home. A few stayed behind to speak with Arthur directly and he took notes to share with business leaders afterwards.

Once all the others left the pub, Phinn approached Arthur with an old, dusty book in his hand.

"What's this?" Arthur asked motioning to the book.

"Arthur," Phinn walked closer to the table where Arthur gathered his meeting notes. "I need to talk to you about tactical plans." He shifted his weight and continued, "You mentioned sending out a scout. Have you determined which one?"

"I'm leaving that decision to Milo."

"Yes, Milo is the finest leader to plan a strategy for attack," Phinn took a deep breath, "But have you considered sending someone closer to you than Milo's candidate?"

"Someone like?" Arthur's face showed confusion and fatigue.

"Someone like.... Tegan?"

Arthur stepped back from his friend and looked him in the eye, "What?!"

"Tegan," he repeated. "I believe she's been chosen for this mission."

Arthur pulled himself together and whispered gravely, "You expect me to send my daughter to the pits of hell to spy on those rats and how they're handling Lewis? Are you crazy?!!"

"I know, I know.....it sounds crazy." Phinn waited a minute for Arthur to calm down and digest the information. "But have you heard the prophesy about the rats and the red moon?" he asked.

"Yes, of course. We all know that one," Arthur said irritated. "When the moon turns red, the rats will lead a war against those that protect the tunnels."

"But there's more," said Phinn. "Look." He opened the dusty book and flipped through a few yellowed pages. "Here it is."

Arthur read:

"When the moon turns red, the rats will lead a war against those that protect the tunnels.

And the red-tailed one will deliver the enemies into the hands of judgement." Arthur sat down silently, processing the information. Tegan was his youngest. Yes, she was an adult sombel, but how could she be key to this situation? She was no warrior. This must be a mistake.

"Just because you used to be a scholar does not mean you are right about Tegan...or the prophecy for that matter," Arthur scoffed. "I mean, it's...Tegan. She has never lived anywhere else but Haven. Shouldn't the deliverer be more, I don't know, worldly?"

"My studies specifically focused on prophesies. You know that, Arthur," Phinn replied. "I gave it up when I had a family to take care of. I needed to provide for them. So I worked a proper job."

Arthur knew this. Of course he did. He was present at Phinn's wedding, and his wife nannied Silas as a youngster. He saw the change in Phinn as he matured and gained responsibility. But this prophecy...maybe it was just a myth, and the red tail a coincidence? Could it be?

Phinn sat down next to his friend and lowered his voice, "She is capable, Arthur. Trust the prophecy and give her wings to try."

Arthur knew Phinn meant well. But Tegan? Could he be right? He read the words again. If the prophecy proved true, and he didn't prepare Tegan, the fallout could be devastating. Without a way to deliver the enemy to judgement would enable the rats to ultimately destroy Haven, and possibly, all of Fellnore. Oh, what should he do?!

"I need to think about this, Phinn," Arthur responded.

"It's also time she knew about the tunnels, Arthur, and the creatures that live there. If she's the chosen one, the tunnels and their protection will be passed to her one day anyway."

Arthur shook his head, "the chosen one? How can you say these things?!"

Phinn continued, "Take her to Erasmus, let her stand before him and ask for wisdom. Beckett can go with her, as well as a soldier from Milo's team for protection." Arthur felt somewhat comforted. Beckett was handy with a hammer as well as a loyal friend. A soldier might be overdoing it, but Arthur felt he could never be too safe. Besides, what if Erasmus dismisses this so-called prophecy? Or confirms that Tegan is not the chosen one? At that point, life could return to normal in just a few days. The more Arthur thought about it, the more he agreed with getting sage advice. He still doubted Tegan's defensive skills, so surely this topic would dissipate as soon as they examined it.

As for Tegan, well, she excelled in her fighting classes at school, but had no real-life experience with a sword or dagger. Her brothers and cousins saw action over the past years, and she admired them for that. Last year, Tegan learned to use a bow and arrow under the instruction of a talented ex-militia sombel, but she preferred the sword. If she would just practice more, her father promised to give her a weapon of her own.

"I'll talk to Tegan about this in the morning," sighed Arthur.

Phinn quietly closed the book, stood up, and turned to leave. As he neared the door, Arthur called out, "Phinn?"

The sombel turned around to face Arthur.

"I'm scared," Arthur said.

"So am I," whispered Phinn.

Phinn left the pub and walked back to his blacksmith's shop. The heaviness of the evening lingered over him and he subconsciously struggled to breathe. It had been hundreds of years since anyone mentioned this prophecy. And now it seemed like events were happening at the speed of light to fulfill it.

Once inside his shop, Phinn put the kettle on a small fire burning in a clay pit. He changed his blackened clothes and wiped his smutty face, wrapping himself up in a clean robe. Phinn lived on the second floor above the shop, away from the fires, the tools, and the iron. The winter air found its way through the cracks of the structure, but his straw bed was warm enough, even for Haven's coldest nights.

Phinn poured hot tea into his mug and sipped it slowly. His whole body began to relax now that he had removed himself from the pub crowd. He sat back and closed his eyes, thinking about all that was said at the meeting. He could hear Silas upstairs, already snoring.

The blacksmith wrapped up and climbed the ladder to his loft. Once he took his last sip, Phinn put away his mug, snuggled under his blanket, and blew out the candle next to him.

Tomorrow would be a new day.

CHAPTER 5

Tegan threaded a needle with green thread and skillfully tied a knot in the end. There were four more dresses to mend, and a cloak to hem. Each month, Mrs. Fourpaws sent gently used and well-worn garments to Tegan, and paid her to mend them. At times, Tegan received requests for new clothing. But right now, she was knee deep in sewing warm hats for Mrs. Fourpaws' shop. And with the fair only a week away, there were plenty of last-minute requests for mending dresses and hats to keep her busy.

In and out, in and out, she guided the needle through the fabric until the patch was complete. Tegan thought about what Mrs. Fourpaws said about her Papa...about hiding a secret. But Papa was not the kind of sombel to keep things from his villagers.

Papa left for work early this morning...before she woke up. But he told her he'd be home by lunch time. Tegan cut the thread and placed the garment on the stool next to her.

"What is taking him so long?" she wondered. Tegan ate a few blackberries from a wooden bowl on the table in front of her. Just then, the front door opened and Arthur shimmied in. "Sorry, Tegan, I was held up at work," he said. There was another sombel with him. Short and stocky, this sombel had a military vest and a bow and quiver of arrows strapped around his chest.

"Would you like tea?" she asked both of them.

Arthur nodded and introduced Tegan to Max. She greeted Max while he removed his bow and arrows from around his chest. Max was an officer in Milo's unit; but more importantly, he was Milo's brother. Arthur trusted this gray sombel and Tegan knew it.

She went into the kitchen and poured several cups of tea, carrying the cups back into the living room for her father and Max.

"Sit with us," Arthur said to his daughter.

Tegan took a seat next to her father and across from Max.

"How did the town meeting go last night, Papa?" she asked.

"Well, that's what I want to talk to you about," he said. "After much discussion last night, it was decided that we need to send a messenger to do reconnaissance work as well as deliver a message. With Milo's unit marching toward Littleton, and another team preparing for the retrieval of Lewis, your name was mentioned as a candidate for this mission."

Tegan sat on the little tufted sofa confused. She looked at her father and then Max. What did she have to do with anything? Why would someone mention *her* name? Max watched Arthur as he sipped his tea nervously.

"But, but what am I supposed to do?" she looked at her Papa, searching for answers in this preposterous situation.

Arthur sighed and then stood up. Uncertain as to how much information he should divulge to his daughter, he decided, instead, to remind her of her ancestry...and see where that led. "Tegan, you know our family history and how we became the protectors of the community in the tunnels." He sat his cup down and continued gently, "Well, many years ago, the black rats invaded Haven. Those rats stole every vegetable, every fruit, every grain and every nut that the villagers had stored for the winter months. They relied heavily on each season's harvest to survive. And during that raid, the rats damaged and burned our houses, and left our farmlands in ruin." He paced around the room and then stopped.

He continued, "We were all left to die. But do you know what happened?"

Tegan shook her head.

"King Fallon. Well, he wasn't king at the time, he was still a prince," Arthur corrected himself and sat down opposite of Tegan. "Fallon saw what happened to the village that week and waited until the rats left. He returned with a few of his friends, walked into our devastated village, and offered us what food they had left."

"But why would the fairies offer to help us out?" Tegan asked.

"Because they knew we would gather our forces and attack the rats with a vengeance," Arthur answered. "And that's what we did. In the end, the fairies sought our powerful protection because they realized the imminent danger from those very rats to their own lifestyle in the tunnels. And since that day, we agreed to be their sworn protectors."

"I knew we had a strong connection to the fairies," Tegan replied. "But I didn't realize how integral our partnership was to both of our clans' survival."

"The House of Wells has been established for centuries. It is respected. And it is fair," Arthur said. Max nodded in agreement. "Your ancestors served in the military to protect not only our village, but to defend our name. Your brothers fought in the civil wars. Several are in Littleton now facing the invaders from across the river."

Tegan smiled, proud of her siblings and her family name. Indeed, it was this appreciation that compelled her to openly consider the mission her Papa spoke of. Consider, yes. But actually go through with it? She did not know. Could she survive long enough to deliver a message? And what if she got caught?

Her father's face told her that the situation was dire, and he took the predicament seriously. She should do the same.

Was she hesitant? Yes. Was she scared? A little. But she had a familial sense of justice that she knew would serve her well. Several years of defense training in school might be just as useful...if this messenger responsibility proved true.

"What should I do?" Tegan asked.

"I've sent word ahead, requesting a meeting with Erasmus," Arthur replied.

"The sage that lives near the mountain?"

"Yes, we need all the wisdom we can get," Arthur said and squeezed his daughter's shoulder. " I am going with you as well."

"When do we leave, Papa?"

"Gather your things, now. We don't have long to travel before nightfall," Arthur said to his daughter.

Tegan stood up and wandered around the room, disappearing into the kitchen. Thoughts whirled around in her head; *is this really happening*? She would rather stay home, in her comfortable surroundings. Just the mention of Erasmus suggested that this trip might end in something way bigger than she could handle. She breathed in deeply and exhaled slowly. *Focus!* Tegan rummaged around for snacks to take on the short trip.

Max listened to Tegan in the kitchen and chose a safe moment to whisper, "Sir, why didn't you tell her about the prophecy?"

Arthur shook his head. "She'll find out soon enough," he said. "For now, she's better off not knowing."

The wheels of the caged wagon clunked along the rocky path, pulled by a myriad of rats. Lewis sat inside the swaying vehicle and looked out at the tall grass and rugged landscape. Not a tree in sight. Large, flat rocks outlined the pathway while small, scrubby vegetation and grass squeezed against those rocks. As the rats pulled the wagon through the meadow, blades of grass passed over the wooden spokes of the cage. The sun rested high in sky and Lewis felt the heat.

The rats marched with uneven strides; they laughed with a growl; they clicked their teeth on each other; and they smelled of rot and swamp. Several of the top-ranking rats fought for leadership as they argued about which way to smuggle their passenger.

"It's by the giant mushroom!" the particularly tall one said.

"Captain told us to go west, around the mountain," the reddish black rat shouted back.

"But that will put us back by at least two days," the tall one, the rat leader, said.

"So? Why are you in a rush?" sneered the red and black rat, soldier, second in command. "Trying to impress the Captain back at base?" He laughed maniacally.

The leader lunged at the soldier with gnashed teeth and sharp claws. They rolled around on the ground kicking and scratching and biting at each other. The rest of the rats moved in and encircled the two fighting for their pride, enjoying a good conflict. Shouting started and the group of twenty or so rats leapt into the madness. They kicked up dirt and patches of grass into the air.

The loud growling noises covered the sounds Lewis was making. The sombel used a small dagger, concealed in his belt, to cut into the bars of the cage holding him captive. Sawing quickly back and forth, back and forth, he grunted and pulled on one of the bars. As he tugged on it over and over again, the wagon itself began rocking.

Lewis looked up and saw the crowd of rats still pushing and knocking each other over. A few more slices into this bar and it would sever. He continued to work feverishly, while the rats were distracted, to free himself of this prison.

Once the bar loosened, Lewis grabbed it with his paws and shook it violently. Almost free, he gave it one final yank towards his chest. The bar broke loose from the frame and smacked Lewis on the chest. The force threw him to the backside of the cage. Because Lewis was a heavy and stocky sombel, his weight forced the cart over. The wagon fell on its side with a noisy THUD!

The battling rats looked up from their brawling pit and scrambled to the overturned cage. They squealed and screeched as they looked in to see their prisoner still inside. Lewis laid very still. The dagger he used landed somewhere in the fall, and he needed to find it fast. He scanned the ground and ran his paw over the grass sticking in between the cage bars.

"He's there!" Snarled one of the rats.

Others laughed nervously and twitched their furless tails.

"Push it up! Push it up!" The rats surrounded the wagon on all four sides and proceeded to pull and push the frame. The timber creaked and one of the wheels was lodged in between two large stones.

"Move it," the rat leader shoved several rats to the side. "Let me see the problem."

A few of the rats moved away so the leader could get a closer look at the wheel. He ordered four soldier rats to dig out the smallest of the stones, then gave orders to the others to push the stone out of the way. The rats struggled and strained, but finally gathered enough muscle power to slide the stone away from the wheel frame.

Lewis shifted his weight around the cage and noticed the sun shining on the dagger's shiny steel. It had fallen in the corner near the ground and had wedged itself in the wood during the fall. He grabbed it and pulled quickly, and the dagger broke free. He shoved it into his belt just in time for the cart to be turned upright.

The leader dusted off his oily black fur and turned around to face his unit. He eyed them with an icy glare and yelled, "Line up, all of you!"

The rats scrambled around the cage and grabbed the ropes. Others amassed behind the wagon as lookouts. Each of the rats in the front carried long spears as they scurried ahead.

"This is the plan and I am your leader," he stared directly at the second in command. "I will say where we go, and you will do as I say."

The rats remained quiet.

"My plan is to take the shortest route," the rat leader said. "Half a day's walk to the ruby mushroom and from there, we'll take the shortcut. Then we'll head toward Littleton and watch our soldiers continue their destruction there."

"Watch what destruction?" questioned the second in command. "All the wreckage, the burning and stealing will be finished by the time we get there."

The rat leader walked toward him and stood uncomfortably close.

"Not if we take the shortcut," he hissed.

CHAPTER 6

Tegan strapped on her messenger bag and pulled the door closed. Stepping out, she crossed the road to catch up with her father and Max. It was a short walk to the mountain to meet Erasmus. His house consisted of a small room carved into a cave that already existed in the side of the mountain. She'd only been there once before; her parents made the journey years ago when her older brother sought much needed wisdom from this sombel.

Arthur and Tegan led the way with Max walking behind them.

"Let's turn here," Tegan said to her father. "I want to see if Beckett is in."

Tegan rounded a bungalow with a light blue awning and peeked into the window. She smiled; Beckett was inside, so she opened the door and went in. He turned around with an arm full of clay plates straight from the fire.

"Need help?" she asked with a laugh.

"Sure," he replied. "Bring those cups with you too. I need to load the wagon for a delivery."

Tegan stacked the cups and followed Beckett out back to his wagon. As they walked, she told him about what her father had and the need to visit Erasmus.

"Is your Papa sure of the prophecy? I mean, villagers have been talking about it for years."

"I thought about that too. Papa seems very serious."

"Well," Beckett scratched his head, "when are you leaving?"

"We're going now," Tegan said. "I need a friend with me. I'm not sure I can swallow all of this."

"Scared?"

"Terrified." Her eyes pleaded with him. "Will you come with us?"

"Well, I don't have to make this delivery until tomorrow," Beckett wiped his face with his sleeve. "So, yeah, let me grab my bag and I'll join you."

Tegan felt relieved. She needed a friend to help her make sense of this, and Beckett was a close companion. The two walked up to Arthur and Max sitting under an oak tree. "We're ready," she said.

For over an hour, the sombels trekked a small footpath on the outskirts of Haven. They crossed over rocky stones and under tall grasses, jumped over small creeks, and ambled through mushroom forests. The four stopped near a clearing to snack on oat cakes and huckleberry juice. It was at this point that Tegan first heard the very faint jingling of bells.

She turned her head but couldn't figure out where the sound was coming from. "Do you hear that?" She whispered to the others.

Tegan stood up and walked toward a ravine. Tree logs and green overgrowth had conquered this strip of land over time. She held onto a sturdy tree trunk and leaned to her left. There, she saw something moving down below. Tegan's eyes focused on the object and her paws gripped the tree even harder.

The object moved closer and closer until she realized it was a tinker, dressed in sashes of deep red and blue. The tinker held a walking stick that she used to scale the ravine wall. Tegan couldn't see her face yet; a dark green cloak covered it. As the tinker climbed with slow, study steps, Tegan noticed that the sound of bells was actually a cape full of metal wares she was likely selling. All of the metal clanking together caught Tegan's attention. Now the tinker stood before her; Tegan took a few steps back.

Removing a thin scarf from around her head, the tinker revealed herself... an old raccoon with bushy fur and claw like paws. She pulled a bag over her shoulder making more jingling noises, and her cloak wrapped closely around her for warmth. She embellished it with a black knitted shawl. Her walking stick contained intricate carvings and designs as the tinker clearly travelled to distant lands in her time.

Tegan watched her move and studied her face. She had never seen a tinker before, but learned about conducting business with them from her Ma and Papa. "Good day," she said to the traveler.

The tinker walked past her, turned around, and replied, "Good day, child."

Her voice rasped when she talked. Nothing that a good pot of tea and honey couldn't cure!

She continued, "Would ye like to see my wares?" The tinker opened her bag and proudly displayed a few metal items. She showed off her talismans, utensils, plates, cups, shiny buckles and mirrors. There was more in the bottom of the bag, but Tegan waved her hand to signal that she wasn't interested.

"Maybe it's a dagger you need, eh?" she cackled.

33

"Oh no! We're not out here to fight," Tegan looked over at Max, who observed the interaction with a protective eye. "We're looking for a friend's house."

The tinker leaned in and asked, "Would this friend be a wise man?"

Tegan looked at her nervously, "Indeed, we are on our way to meet a wise man. How did you know?"

The tinker howled with laughter until she quieted down with a cackle and a cough. "I know a lot of things, child," she whispered to Tegan. She dug around in her sack and pulled out something with her claw. It was a paw sized item wrapped in soft, brown paper.

"Here," the tinker handed Tegan the object. "You'll need this."

Tegan took the wrapped gift hesitantly and asked, "What is it?"

"Your wise man will know," she said in a low voice and then smiled.

As Tegan looked at the paper offering in her paw, she heard the tinker walk off, singing in a high-pitched voice.

"woe to the enemies
Woe to you under the red moon,
the red-tailed one is coming for you
and she's coming soon....."

The tinker whistled the tune again as she approached Arthur, Beckett, and Max. Tegan heard the voices faintly behind her as the conversation went from polite greetings to a showcase of wares. She looked out over the ravine again and wondered what this old raccoon meant by giving her this gift. Tegan unrolled the paper slowly and saw three sprigs of some sort of herb with green leaves and yellow flowers. She also recognized a small, circular green stone.

"Tegan!" Beckett called out.

Startled, Tegan turned around and rolled her gifts back into the paper. She stuffed them in her messenger bag and headed back to where the others were sitting.

Tegan looked around for the tinker, but she left. No sign of her anywhere...just like she vanished into the air.

By the time the sun was beginning to sit lower in the sky, the rats turned near a flowering tree and stood before the ruby mushroom. It towered above them with the white fleshy part only visible from below. The top of its umbrella glowed a deep ruby red color, where the fungi got its name.

The rats wheeled Lewis's wagon underneath the massive mushroom and dropped the ropes. The rats out front turned back to their leader for instruction. The leader, himself, circled Lewis and observed his cage. "Sit tight," he said mocking Lewis. "We're not there yet."

The large red mushroom marked the boundary into an expansive forest with magnificent fern like trees and craggy rock formations. A wooden sign at the entrance of the forest, near a small path, read "Cardiff Forest."

Many years ago, the area was used as a quarry for mining stone. The remnants of the machinery could still be seen beyond the trees on a hill inside the forest. Over time, the need for stone dwindled and residents moved on, leaving their small shacks, convenient stores, and water wells to be repossessed by the overgrowth.

But more than this, Cardiff Forest had a reputation for being haunted at night. Some say the shrinking demand for stone did not drive the residents out; the goblins living there did. As night creatures, the goblins sabotaged machinery, attacked farm animals, and even slipped inside cottages to frighten families in the early morning hours of dawn. It wasn't until things got worse that word spread about the hauntings.

Hunters sometimes camped in the forest, spending the night in a tent under the stars. During those times, incidents occurred where the goblins attacked the hunters...sometimes for food, sometimes for trinkets, and sometimes just for fun. One hunter said he woke up in the middle of the night with a goblin's claw like hands around his neck, trying to strangle him.

There had been creatures to survive the forest, but they suffered terrible nightmares and traumatic episodes after emerging from the other side of the woods. Villagers often questioned the survivors about their experiences in the forest, but they typically refused to verbalize anything about their time there. It's rumored that one individual talked briefly about his experience in a pub, but no one knows his name or where he lives now.

And this forest was the shortcut.

The rat leader shouted to the rats in the front of the line, "We're going through there." He pointed ahead with his sword toward the small, single foot path near the front of the forest. The rats looked back at him with fear. "Forward march!" He commanded.

The rats with spears slowly moved forward with hesitant steps. At the opening of the forest stood several fallen trees with vines all intertwined in them. The growth formed a rough archway for the crew to step through. Lewis felt the temperature drop as soon as his wagon rolled under the arch.

The overgrowth blocked the sun's rays so it seemed like nighttime while on the path. Lewis looked around the forest and felt eyes watching him. He could hear the crunch of fallen branches under his wagon as it rolled over them. Along the path, Lewis strained to look out through the trees that surrounded him. He searched for something familiar.

"There," the rat leader stated. "Stop in that clearing."

The path opened briefly to an abandoned shack with the roof caved in. The leader propped his sword against the dilapidated porch railing and sat down on the first step. Pulling a map from his vest, he read over it quietly. There was a fork in the path ahead and he needed to decide which way to go. He stood up and walked to the front of his unit to survey the split in the road. Both paths seemed daunting, but the trail to the right appeared to wind in the right direction. And according to his map, it was the shortest route.

"This way," he pointed.

At the same time, a massive shadow passed over the group, darkening the light above them. Flapping noises and a huge gust of wind whooshed across them. The fur on Lewis' neck stood up as he watched the rats turn around and around, looking at each other for any indication of what to do.

The sudden burst of wind blew through the group causing the leader's sword to fall from its perch, and make a loud banging sound as it ricocheted off the porch stairs. Startled, all the rats turned toward the structure where the noise came from.

Then, in the quiet and the calm, they heard scratching and scrambling noises coming from inside the shack. Lewis also heard hushed laughing and growling sounds emanating from the remnants of the building.

"What was that?!" one soldier whispered to another.

No one responded. The air stood eerily still.

Spooked, the rats froze in place. They all looked at each other and then at the leader. The rat leader swallowed hard and commanded, "Go now! Move!"

As the wagon started rolling, something jumped out of the overgrowth and lunged toward the cage. It was hideous...with soul-less black eyes and orange, snaggled teeth. It scrambled around the bars, reaching in with its claw like hands and growling at Lewis.

The rats closest to the wagon backed away quickly as they watched the creature in horror.

The sound of rustling in the overgrowth suddenly got louder and louder. Small, horrific creatures launched out of the side of the shack with a scream and leapt on the rat soldiers. The monsters grabbed and bit the rats' ears and necks, causing absolute chaos among the unit.

Lewis moved from one side of the cage to the other to avoid the creature's claws. He looked closely at the creature and saw its large green ears, shaggy eyebrows, oversized nose, and felt its ghastly breath. He recognized the monster before him.

"Goblins!" Lewis shrieked. "It's the goblins!!!!"

CHAPTER 7

"It's just ahead," Arthur said as the others gathered up their bags and weapons to hike again.

The four approached the base of the Arsa mountain range and rounded a rock formation jutting out from the side of it. The mountain consisted of black rock and very little vegetation, except around the base of the mountain and near the cave. The travelers cautiously watched their footing amongst the slippery rocks and boulders.

A spring of water trickled down the path toward the mouth of the dark cave. Tegan observed twisting vines and knotty tree roots covering the opening, and dark green moss clinging to the massive rocks around the cave. As they approached the home of Erasmus, they saw a flickering light inside; a small fire glowing in the cool darkness.

Arthur led the group over a path of stepping stones and a hand-made bridge to the entrance of the cave. A large gray cloth partially covered the opening. He approached cautiously and called out, "Erasmus?" The sound echoed throughout the cavern.

Out of the corner of her eye, Tegan noticed a figure advancing from the back of the cave. The figure was covered in a gray cloak with a hood and carried a cup in his paw. As he got closer, the sombel put down the cup and opened his hood to expose his large green eyes. He had a kind but guarded face.

"Arthur?" he asked slowly.

Arthur nodded and smiled. "Hello, my friend."

The two greeted each other warmly and exchanged a few pleasantries. Then Arthur introduced Max, Tegan, and Beckett to the wise man.

Erasmus motioned for everyone to follow him towards the fire in the center of the main room. A sizeable rug with numerous colorful cushions and wool blankets covered the floor. The visitors made themselves comfortable on the little pillows in front of the warm fire.

Tegan noticed several stacks of books piled like columns all the way to the top of the cave.

Unusual curios like stones and talismans decorated the shelves along the wall, behind which hung a red tapestry, detailing the Arsa mountain range.

Erasmus carried a pitcher of ale and cups from the shelf and offered drinks to his friends.

After a sip of the cold beverage, Arthur began, "As you know, we've come to seek your guidance about an issue with my brother, Lewis."

"Ah, the one captured by the rats," Erasmus replied.

"Yes," Arthur hesitated. "What do you know about his kidnapping? Is it connected to the conflict in the north?"

"Greygor has been restless for many years. My scouts tell me they have been forging weapons for quite some time with the plan to strike soon," Erasmus took a sip and put his cup down. "The rats are scavengers, as you know. They don't plant farms or store food like the rest of us. They invade and take what's not theirs in order to survive."

"And Lewis?"

"Well, he is the protector of a valuable secret, isn't he?" He looked at Arthur with a hushed tone. "And Greygor has scouts himself. I've seen them up and down the river looking for vulnerable towns and stored supplies. Lewis must have crossed paths with some of them."

"Or, maybe, he was the target all along," Arthur interjected.

"Maybe."

Arthur chewed on those words in silence. He changed the topic slightly, "The prophecy says that when the moon turns red, the rats will lead war."

"That prophecy has been around for a long time," Erasmus took a deep breath. "But we may indeed see it come to fruition sooner rather than later."

Arthur laughed nervously, "Fifty years ago, I would've told you that you're crazy. That the prophecy was a farce." He hesitated, "but I'm seeing the signs now, and they are ominous."

"Certainly, the breakout fights in the south alone are causing tension around Fellnore," Erasmus noted.

"The conflicts near Littleton have me concerned too," Arthur said. "My captain's guard has a unit scoping out the area to see if we need to set up a defensive stance. I am preparing terms of surrender now for a messenger to deliver to the rat king."

"And you are aware that the rat king will most likely *not* sign this document?" asked Erasmus.

"I am," Arthur replied. "But we must initiate contact. As governor of Haven, I cannot just sit back and wait for the day when these rats decide to ransack our village. The rat king signed the treaty with our representatives, so it must be our contacts that follow up with him. Greygor *cannot* continue to ignore the terms that protect the creatures of Fellnore from his mercenaries. If the prophecy is true--"

"IF—that is the whole point. We do not know if these events confirm the prophecy," Erasmus stated. "You may be sending a messenger to their doom."

"A messenger must be sent whether the prophecy is true or not. They have Lewis! And if they make Lewis talk, they can access the tunnels," Arthur emphasized.

Erasmus nodded and held up his paw in a friendly motion. He centered his thoughts and focused on what Arthur said to him. Lewis was now a prisoner of the black rats; and those rats recently broke the terms of the Compromise Treaty on several occasions. Erasmus felt a heaviness with this visit. He thought about these two events happening so close together, but why? And the reason filled him with trepidation.

"If Lewis is the intended target, then this is bigger than just Haven," Erasmus stated. "You need support from all of Fellnore."

"So, what is your counsel?" Arthur asked.

"Talk to King Fallon and ask for his help," Erasmus replied. "If the prophecy is true, those tunnels and his home will be under attack soon. And we both know why..." He raised his eyebrows at Arthur and grunted.

"The moonstone, yes," Arthur replied. "Only the most powerful gem in all of Fellnore."

Erasmus nodded and said, "You could get to King Fallon by tomorrow, if the weather cooperates."

"Thank you, Erasmus." Arthur hesitated, "One more thing..."

Erasmus looked at Arthur and then at Tegan. She placed her empty cup on a small table and sat back down near the fire. As she rested there, her tail curled around her by the burning timber, showing off its amber red color.

Erasmus noticed Tegan's red tail and marveled at it, "It's true then?" He stood closer to the sombel to get a better view. "I heard from my intel that the red tailed one was near, but I didn't realize...."

"Yes, that's what I wanted to see you about," Arthur said. "The prophecy mentions a red-tailed deliverer." He looked over at Tegan, "but she is just so young!"

"The deliverer," Erasmus whispered, recognizing the significance of the red tail.

This was the first time Tegan heard about the prophecy. Her eyes widened and her heart raced. She was just a messenger, which was scary enough. But a deliverer? They had to be mistaken. Tegan looked at Beckett who was obviously confused.

Tegan couldn't fight, she could barely hold a sword. And isn't that what deliverers do? Fight? She turned to her father and questioned him. "Are you sure about the prophecy? I am not a fighter, much less a deliverer."

Her Papa softly answered, "Tegan, I cannot undo what is foretold by the prophet. But I can send those to help you on your quest."

"I don't want to go! Can't someone else be the deliverer?" Tegan asked frantically.

Arthur's heart ached for his daughter, but he tried not to show it. "Don't be afraid, my dear, you will surely succeed in the face of danger." He hugged her tightly.

Tegan wanted to cry, but she swallowed back those tears. *Why was she chosen for this task? She was ordinary, not specifically talented in any one thing. What could she offer? What could she do to deliver her clan from the clenches of evil? Wouldn't another sombel be better qualified for this task?* She felt overwhelmed and alone.

"Tegan, you can do this," Beckett whispered to her.

"Beckett, I need you to accompany her," Arthur replied. "And find others to ensure a safe journey."

Erasmus straightened his posture and said, "Tegan, go and deliver the terms as mentioned in the prophecy." He turned to Arthur, "Take her to King Fallon. He will provide protection to make it to Homish safely. This must be a swift and effective mission."

In the heaviness of the moment, Tegan remembered the gift the tinker gave her...the green stones. But instead of asking Erasmus about it, she decided to hide it from the others. *Was it moonstone?* she thought. *And if so, what powers could the gem possibly hold that the rats would kidnap her uncle for?*

Greygor scanned the horizon for any signs of his soldiers. The smoldering fires all over camp contrasted against the blackness underneath his feet. He paced back and forth along the north wall, watching for movement.

"Captain! Captain!" shouted one of the rats.

Greygor turned around, "What is it?"

"Come see," motioned the rat. "It's finished."Greygor walked around to the back of a hut with a large shed attached to it. And there it stood. A massive, wooden structure designed for war...a menacing trebuchet. The rats put several more finishing touches on the machine and stood back to admire their work.

The structure contained two large wheels attached to a platform where an enormous arm stuck straight up in the air. The basket that held rocks and debris for catapulting into enemy territory had been shackled to the trebuchet's arm for stability.

The rat king stood back rubbing his chin and admired the machine before him. He smiled eerily and commanded, "Show me how it works."

A few rats scurried around the platform pulling at the basket and the ropes. A large stone was placed into the basket and others yanked at the ropes to steady the platform. One rat shouted out commands as the others pulled back the arm. On his command, the rat in charge counted down and then shouted "Go!"

The wheels creaked and swayed in place as the large arm rotated forward, slinging the huge stone over an immense pile of blackened rocks and ash and into a gravelly pit. Greygor squealed at the destruction caused by the massive stone; it smashed into the ground and created a giant crater. He remained motionless, contemplating the destruction that this one machine could cause.

The rats waited for a sign from their leader. "Yes!" he finally exclaimed, and they sighed in relief. The rat king walked around the machine and observed the structure in detail. "Yes, yes," he murmured under his breath. The rats cheered at their own success.

Pulling at the ropes, Greygor looked up and touched the wooden arm, and then peered into the basket. "This is exactly what I need," he said to himself. "Once I have the moonstone, this will be the most formidable weapon ever and no one can stop me."

CHAPTER 8

Screams pierced the darkness and absolute chaos ensued. Rats jumped and scrambled and climbed over each other to backtrack down the path from which they came from. Goblins scratched and bit the rats, causing high-pitched shrieks and growls from the hysterical rodents.

In the pandemonium, the rats abandoned the cage with Lewis crouching down in it. That is until the rat leader, himself, grabbed two soldiers by the tails and flung them at the wagon. "Pull the cage you idiots! Pull!" He commanded.

A gruesome goblin jumped onto the rat leader's back with a howl and embedded its teeth into his neck. The leader fell down and grabbed the creature with his claws, pulling it off his neck and throwing it onto the ground. The leader reached for his sword, which had been trampled in the stampede, and quickly sliced through the goblin still charging toward him. He used the sword to pull himself up and climbed up and onto the back of the wagon.

As the rats pulled the cage in terror, the wheels clamored over the rocks along the slim trail, bouncing Lewis all over the place. He looked over at the leader who clasped his neck as he held on to the back of the wagon, wounded but still conscious of the situation.

"Go! Go!" The leader yelled at the soldiers, watching the goblins lunge at the cart. He held his sword with the right paw and swiped at the monsters as they gnashed their teeth and chomped at the rolling wagon. Lewis laid low at the bottom of the cage and kept his wide eyes on the path ahead of him. He searched for an opening to the forest, a light at the end of the trail, the sun or the moon, or anything besides these menacing creatures biting at the bars.

Then Lewis noticed a glowing light in the distance. Faster and faster the wagon approached the illumination. As the group rounded a huge overgrowth, they saw a blaze in an open field brightening the forest. It stretched high up in the night sky and flickered off the boulders nearby.

The wagon turned sharply away from the fire and shimmied down another trail. The rat leader struggled to stay on the cart as it weaved quickly through the forest, bumping and banging over the rough footpath. Lewis watched as fewer and fewer goblins chased after the wagon until the monsters finally tapered off.

He took a final look behind him and noticed a number of smaller fires starting where they had just been. A large black shadow eclipsed one of the flames and Lewis strained to see what it was. But the rats had finally approached the forest opening and the wagon was out of the thicket before he could figure out what he saw.

"Why haven't you said anything about these tunnels?" Tegan asked her father as soon as they left the cave.

"It wasn't important...until now," Arthur responded. "Many creatures know about the tunnels and the inhabitants there, but the entrance has always been kept a secret."

"Why?"

"The pixie community that lives there protects a very powerful gemstone. It can only be mined in the tunnels. If it falls into the wrong hands, the power can certainly be destructive."

Tegan recalled her father talking with other council members about the pixies during meetings, but didn't realize that they were, indeed, the actual inhabitants of the tunnels. Her Uncle Lewis was on the council and had been entrusted with protecting the tunnels for as long as she could remember. Lewis was the liaison for the pixie clan and all the other creatures living there.

Tegan, Beckett, Arthur, and Max hiked back on the small foot-path they previously walked on. It was almost completely dark, and the moon peeked out from behind a distant hill. Arthur stopped in a clearing to light a few lanterns that Erasmus gave him for the journey. He placed a lantern on opposite ends of a branch and then balanced that branch on his left shoulder. The light was just bright enough to see underfoot as well as watch for danger a short distance before them.

Silence among the four allowed Tegan to meditate on what her father said earlier. *Powerful gemstones? What power did they have? How could they be destructive? And where was this magical tunnel entrance?* She listened to her footsteps as they made their way through the meadows and the forest.

"Where are we headed?" Tegan asked.

"The tunnels," Arthur said. "You and Beckett will finally see what all of Fellnore wishes they could see."

Beckett perked up. "We're going to the entrance?" He asked with excitement.

Arthur paused and turned to Beckett, "You have grown up with our family since you were a kitten. Your family's name is just as important to the foundation of Haven as mine." He hesitated in the dark, "I have watched you over the years and determined that you can be entrusted with this secret. The outcome of this quest depends on it."

Tegan looked over her father's shoulder and noticed lights in the distance. She took one of the lanterns from the branch Arthur held and walked a few steps forward to get a better view. The lights reminded her of fireflies showing off their lights at dusk. They flickered with a yellow glow that contrasted against the dark night sky.

"Is that Haven?" She asked.

Even though her father had been talking, the night was quiet. Only a soft breeze blew through the leaves. She shivered a little and pulled her cloak closer around her neck.

"Yes," he replied. "We're close to the outskirts of the village. But we need to keep going. There's a clearing up ahead where we can find shelter for the night and start again in the morning."

The group trekked across a grassy field and then climbed up stepping stones to the top of an outcrop of rock. There they gathered under a natural shelter made of fallen tree logs that had been a victim of stormy winds. Beckett and Max gathered hay nearby to make soft beds, and Tegan hung her cloak at the opening to block out the cold air.

Inside the shelter, a little clay pot proved that a previous inhabitant cooked there over a small flame. Max emptied the ashes from the pot and added kindling to start a fire. Since the shelter was small, the tiny fire heated the area quickly and the group enjoyed the cozy warmth.

"Papa?" Tegan asked. After some time. "Tell me more about the gemstone."

"What do you want to know?" he asked.

"Why is it in the tunnels?"

Beckett added, "And why is it so special?"

Arthur chuckled, "Well, maybe I should start at the beginning."
Tegan and Beckett nodded their heads vigorously.

"Thousands of years ago, the rats inhabited the tunnels under the Arsa mountain range. Their interest is genuine in that they want the tunnels back for themselves. But it is not for nostalgic reasons. The tunnels safeguard a very precious gem that they covet to dominate the world. The gem is called green moonstone and there is a story behind it.

In the early days of the tunnel formation, there was a lovely pixie named Rowan. She had long red hair and fiery blue eyes. But more importantly, Rowan could sing so beautifully that all the creatures in the forest would stop and listen to her. Even the spirits would lean over from the heavens to enjoy the melodic sounds coming from deep within her soul.

But not everyone admired her exquisite voice. In fact, there was a particular fairy that envied her talents so much so that she struck a deal with the rats. If they captured Rowan and imprisoned her in the tunnels, then she would show the rat scouts where the fairies stored their harvest.

The rats accepted the offer and ambushed Rowan one morning while she was singing by the riverside. They captured and imprisoned her in the tunnels underneath the mountain so no one could hear her voice ever again.

In the days and years that followed, Rowan cried out for help. She wept for so long and so hard that her tears accumulated into a pool in the bottom of the cavern. Over time, she began singing again, just to comfort herself. And in the darkness, she heard a monstrous sound.

A dragon had been flying near the mountain and heard the faint sounds of a lovely voice singing out for help. His heart immediately melted and he searched for the entrance of the tunnel to rescue her. As the rats saw the dragon creeping in the opening, they began attacking it at once. With their long spears, they sliced the monster's legs and jabbed at its eyes and mouth. The furious dragon drew in a deep breath and out propelled a stream of fire that obliterated the entire rat community in those tunnels. A few rats survived, however, simply because they had been out scavenging at the time.

The fiery blaze scorched the cave walls and blackened the rock all around it. The cave smelled of smoldering ash, seared wood, and singed remains. All traces of the rat settlement permanently removed in an instant.

As the dragon moved through the darkness, he heard a quiet voice squeaking out a soft song. He crawled toward the sad sound and observed Rowan swimming in the pool of tears. To his relief, she was untouched by the flame. But the cavern walls all around her had been blasted by the fire, and in a magical transformation, her sorrowful tears miraculously became green moonstone.

Now, this gem is said to hold power for those with a pure heart and even change color to emanate fire like a dragon. However, no one has ever witnessed that. Unfortunately, if the gems get into the wrong hands, they can be a sinister force to reckon with.

In the end, Rowan successfully escaped the tunnels with her liberating dragon. She returned to her village and led a force to find and capture her traitor. Legend has it that this conspirator was taken to Fealltoir Hill and hung on the gallows with a silver noose. The structure remains on the hill to this day.

In order to protect the green moonstone and the power it possesses, the pixies moved into the tunnels to safeguard it. The clan has lived there ever since."

CHAPTER 9

The rats sprinted out of the forest and into the open field, swiftly tracing their steps back to the ruby mushroom. Lewis bounced around in the cart and watched as black smoke rose from the fires within the woods. *What is causing those fires?* He wondered.

The rat leader jumped off the wagon and limped to the front line to speak to the soldiers. The second in command spoke sarcastically, "I guess we're going with the original plan now."

The leader growled and walked back toward him, pointing his sword at the commander's throat, "We're heading south, around this cursed forest." The leader glared into the commander's eyes and then sheathed his sword. He rubbed his sore shoulder, wincing at the pain.

Straightening his shoulders, the leader stepped up onto a tree stump and addressed the group by shouting, "Does anyone else have something to say?" He examined all the soldiers but none of them spoke up. "Good, then we're all in agreement," he said smugly looking at the second in command.

But the commander would not let the leader have the last word. "What about Littleton? I thought we were going to watch all the destruction when we got there?" He half chuckled.

The leader tightened his fists and roared, "Do you know why I am leading this group and you are *not*?" The rats ceased talking and listened in fear.

The commander quieted down, "Why?" He asked nervously.

The leader composed himself and took a deep breath. "Because you're one comment away from being eradicated," then he screamed, "by me!"

He turned and walked slowly to the front of the line again and ordered the soldiers to march south, around the forest. The rats picked up their spears and marched on, the others pulling Lewis on the cart as they moved.

The convoy traveled around the edge of the forest for several hours on a well traversed path. A bright moon pierced through the darkness. Lewis napped on and off throughout the night catching glimpses of trees, burning lanterns, and soldiers with spears in between his slumbers.

By early morning, the group reached the edge of the river. Tree roots and overgrowth lined the banks near the water. Besides the rushing water, the rats could hear noises in the distance and smell fish cooking over a fire.

One of the high-level soldiers asked timidly, "What is your plan, sir?"

"Wait here," the leader said annoyed.

Walking through the grass, the leader crossed over several giant tree roots until he came across a fallen rock. He climbed on top to pinpoint the noise.

Along the river sat several huts built on stilts. The height allowed excess water to roll under the structures without flooding them (in case heavy storms blew through). On the shore, in front of the nearest hut, a sombel rested in a chair. He held a stick as he cooked several fish over a flame in a firepit. The sombel wore a straw hat and a black vest with knitted gloves.

The rat leader also noticed a shack containing two water rafts, stacked and leaning against the side wall. Fishing supplies like fishing poles, bait, a bucket, and nets lay on the ground near the building.

The sombel pulled the cooked fish off the fire and placed them on a plate. His whiskers twitched so he paused and turned to look around. Something in the dawn's moist air didn't feel right. Afraid he'd been seen, the leader quietly backed down the rock and returned to the group of rats.

"We're going down the river!" the leader stated bombastically as soon as he saw his group of soldiers.

"Why?" asked several of the rats. "We hate the water, you know that!"

"And rats don't swim," the commander sneered.

"We need to make up for lost time," replied the leader. "Taking a raft down the river will get us to the marsh quicker than marching on land."

Grumbling among the rats didn't help the leader's state of mind. "Line up soldiers!" He ordered, "We're raiding this settlement and taking their rafts!"

Tegan and her father sat on a log in front of a campfire outside the wooden shelter. The group slept through a wind storm during the night, and woke up to scattered leaves and small branches covering the area they now gathered in for breakfast.

Beckett propped together a few branches to hang some fish over the flame. He dug around in the ashes to stoke the fire. Max handed Arthur a kettle with coffee, still warm from the embers.

"I see you found breakfast," Arthur laughed.

"Where did you go?" Tegan asked, still rubbing the sleep from her eyes.

"Max and I went fishing in a pond just over the hill," Beckett replied.

Taking the kettle and pouring coffee for herself, Tegan yawned and asked, "Where'd you find this?" She held her cup up to Beckett.

"There was an abandoned shack near the pond. We went inside to see if anyone was home, but it was empty. Several cooking utensils lay on a shelf near the stove, so we borrowed them," Beckett replied. "Including this coffee."

Tegan gently removed her fish from the fire and ate it, washing it down with coffee. As the group finished their breakfast, Max extinguished the fire and put his bow and arrows over his shoulder. The rest of the group packed up their belongings and set out on their journey to the tunnels.

To cover their tracks, the four traveled alongside a creek that ran through the woods. Over large boulders and under fallen, moss-ridden trees, the sombels walked mostly west for at least two hours. Then Arthur and Max approached an area overlooking a deep ravine. The creek flowed over the edge of a rock and down into the ravine. Tegan and Beckett caught up with the other two and stared out over the clearing.

Scanning the landscape, Max said, "Over there." He pointed to a rope bridge connecting their side to another boulder hanging precariously over the drop.

The travelers jumped over random stones and slowly approached the bridge. Standing at the opening of the overpass, Beckett examined the landscape all around him and said, "Looks like the only way to get across."

Arthur agreed and grabbed onto one of the ropes, tugging at it to test its durability.

"I'll go first," Beckett said with a curious tone in his voice. He pushed ahead and grabbed each side of the rope bridge with his paws. One foot in front of the other, he walked cautiously across the bridge, staring down between his steps at the earth beneath him. He turned his head around and motioned for Arthur to follow him.

Arthur stepped out and walked some ways before Beckett reached the other side. Then Max followed behind him. By the time Arthur reached the other end, Tegan started out on the bridge. As she moved forward, the ropes moaned and creaked, complaining of the weight that they had supported for so many years.

Halfway along the bridge, the weakened section under Tegan's feet snapped. She immediately dropped through the rope, catching only a piece of it hanging from the structure. As she held on tightly, her messenger bag slipped. Tegan kicked around and managed to catch it with her right foot. As she struggled to hold onto the rope piece overhead, Tegan screamed for help.

Max, who had nearly reached the other side, froze in his tracks (in case his weight caused more problems). Beckett and Arthur shouted "HOLD ON!!" Whimpering, Tegan nodded briefly and Max turned around very slowly.

"Tegan, stay very still and I'll pull you up," said Max. He motioned for the other two to stay on the boulder. Max gently tiptoed toward Tegan and lowered himself to his knees. He grabbed his vest and pulled out the leather strap holding the pieces of cloth together. Wrapping one end around his paw, he leaned forward to toss the other end to Tegan. In that moment, a crow flew overhead and let out a bloodcurdling screech. Max jerked his head toward the noise and the bridge ripped again, dipping lower and lower towards the ravine.

With the sudden motion, Tegan wiggled around to keep her balance, and caused her bag to fall down the side of the ravine. It flipped over and over again until it finally stopped, dangling on the branch of a fallen tree.

Tegan's legs moved back and forth as she struggled to take hold of the leather strap. Arthur and Beckett shouted to her to stretch up her arm, encouraging her to hold on and to not look down.

She reached up again and again, barely missing the strap each time. Max was scared to lean over any further in case his weight caused the entire bridge to separate and fall.

"One more time, Tegan," Beckett shouted. "You can do this!"

Tegan, petrified of falling, closed her eyes and took a deep breath. As she opened her eyes, her whiskers tingled and she reached up with all her might. She finally caught hold of the strap! Beckett and Arthur breathed an audible sigh of relief.

"Now let go of the rope, Tegan, and I'll pull you up," said Max.

Tegan shook her head.

"Look at me," Max instructed. "You have to trust me."

Without breaking her eye contact with Max, Tegan slowly and tentatively released the rope and grasped the leather strap with both paws. Max braced himself against the remains of the bridge and hoisted the scared sombel up to him. Once she reached the footholds of the bridge, Tegan patted her shoulder and hips and realized her bag was missing.

"Oh noooo!" She wailed.

She looked around and spotted her bag on the side of the ravine. All she could think about was the gift the tinker gave her still wrapped in that bag.

Max scooped her up and scurried across the rest of the bridge to the boulder on the other side. Arthur grabbed his daughter and whisked her away from the edge of the ravine.

"I need my bag!" Tegan whined and put her head in her paws.

"Stay here," Beckett told her. He surveyed the bank of the ravine and scrambled down a footpath to look around. He spied her bag under a tree branch and reasoned it could be rescued if he put a few resources together. Beckett climbed back up and said, "I think I can get it; I just need a few things."

Tegan smiled and watched him search the ground and nearby bushes for useful tools, "Let's use the leftover rope." Beckett pulled the rope and detached it from the bridge. He then wrapped one end around his waist and knotted it, handing the other end to Max and Arthur.

"Wrap this around that tree," Beckett instructed. Max clutched the rope under his arm and encircled the trunk of the tree. Both Arthur and Max held on to the rope while Beckett headed toward the edge of the ravine.

Beckett trekked carefully down the short footpath. Then, as the ravine grew steep, he changed his position to rappel down the side, staying very close to the ravine wall. He passed over clumps of grass, jagged rocks, and tree roots; the smell of earth deep in his nostrils. Finally, he lowered his foot and scooped up the bag by its strap. Once he had the bag secured around his chest and shoulder, he tugged the rope, a sign for the others to pull him back up the ravine.

Max shouted, "Pull!" as he and Arthur tugged at the rope. Tegan ran to the edge to watch for her friend as the others slowly hauled him up from the ravine.

As Beckett neared the top, he handed the bag to Tegan.

"Thank you!" she said wholeheartedly.

Beckett brushed off all the dirt and grass he accumulated on the ascent. He said to himself, "I hope that's the last of our close calls."

Chapter 10

The rat leader ordered four soldiers to stay behind with Lewis. "The rest of you, fall in line and follow me," he commanded.

Back over the tall grass and bumpy tree roots, the rats marched single file. They passed the fallen rock and reached the edge of the grass covering, just before the hut. The leader held up his sword as a sign for the soldiers to stop. He paused as a strong wind gusted over and past them.

The sombel near the hut picked up an unfamiliar scent and his whiskers tingled. He pointed his nose up in the air to get a better sniff. He recognized the smell...it was rot and death.

The rat leader swung his sword toward the hut, "Go!" he commanded his soldiers.

Several rats ran towards the sombel and subdued him on the ground. They grabbed his arms, pulling him away from the fire, and tied him to a tree, his paws behind him. The rest of the soldiers hurried toward the rafts stored in a nearby shack. They tugged at the structures until the rafts toppled over and landed with a thud on the ground. Several soldiers spread out and grabbed the corners of one of the rafts, dragging it to the river bank.

The rat leader whistled loudly for the others to join him. The soldiers pushed Lewis and the wagon through the grass and around the tree roots until they reached the clearing near the water.

Lewis could see the rats swarming the hut to lift the second raft. They struggled with it until it came loose and then hauled it to the bank, placing it alongside the first raft.

Both rafts were positioned precariously near the edge. The rat leader walked around the rafts and studied their construction. The rafts consisted of wooden planks covered in places with strips of bark. He walked on top of them and jumped up and down, testing their sturdiness. Satisfied, he ordered the soldiers to bring Lewis's wagon closer. Lewis held on to the bars of his cage as they wheeled him over the rocky shore.

Lewis stared at the river anxiously. *How long would this trip be? Will the raft be safe enough?* He scanned the bank and noticed the sombel tied to the tree. Their eyes met and he immediately recognized him.

It was Pish.

Lewis waved and Pish's eyes widened in surprise. They both exchanged looks of panic and helplessness.

The soldiers pushed the first raft closer to the water and then rolled the wagon with Lewis onto it. The rat leader and several soldiers accompanied the wagon, securing it to the raft. Other soldiers pushed the raft onto the water with their rudimentary oars.

The rest of the rats boarded the second raft and pushed it off the bank with their oars. One soldier threw a rope to the first raft and the leader caught it, tethering the platforms together.

The rafts floated slowly down the river following a gentle current. An uneasiness among the soldiers filled the atmosphere. They twittered and fretted along the rafts' edges as they watched the shore pass by.

Lewis breathed in the cool air and thought about Pish tied to that tree. Surely another sombel would check on him soon. Pish was resourceful. Lewis remembered the time Pish got stuck in a tree trying to retrieve his hat. A strong wind blew both his hat and bag of bread right out of his paws. After he gathered all the loose barley rolls into his bag, Pish scurried up the tree to retrieve his hat.

As luck would have it, a sombel was cooking fish over a fire close by. Once Pish reached the branch holding his hat hostage, another gusty wind blew past him, and sparks carried from the blaze caught the leaves on fire just below his feet.

Pish panicked and looked left and right. He grabbed a few vines and braided them together. Taking a deep breath, he closed his eyes and swung from his branch to the roof top next to him. He jumped up and down when he landed, celebrating his crazy success. Somehow, in the excitement, the blaze engulfed the tree and weakened it to the point where it collapsed...just after Pish evacuated it. Lewis smiled at the memory of Pish swinging on that vine.

The rafts floated down the river. Soldiers used their oars to help the rafts dodge dangerous boulders and tree stumps, sometimes making the rafts spin around and drift backwards. The more the raft bobbed up and down on the water, the sleepier Lewis became. He settled down in the cage ready to nap when he heard the sound of rushing water. *Where was that sound coming from?* Lewis popped his head up and noticed bubbling water ahead.

The boulders on either side of the river resembled a gate ushering the rafts into turbulent waters. Lewis braced for impact. The rats squealed as they neared the boulders, terrified of the stormy water.

The rafts picked up speed and spilled down a short downhill current into a bubbling pool. Something was in the water. Lewis could see a tail splashing around from one side of the bank to the other. The soldiers readied their spears while others paddled furiously.

The rat leader pressed ahead, disguising his fear. All the rats huddled closer together in the center most part of the rafts.

And then, the head of the creature surfaced and Lewis gasped in horror.

Tegan's group moved swiftly under the mid-day sun. Arthur assured them that the tunnels were close, but the travelers felt fatigue from the voyage. Arthur and Max plodded along the grassy path in front of them. Birds called out to each other and the breezes blew gently, rustling the leaves in the trees. Tegan and Beckett laughed together as they pulled up the rear.

And then the scenery changed. It changed from normal, everyday shrubs, trees, and foliage to gigantic ones. The four stopped and looked up. Trees as high as the sky with leaves as big as blankets! Tegan's mouth stayed open as she took the scenery in. *Did they shrink?! Why was everything so enormous?*

"Welcome to Mor Landing," Arthur smiled at the others.

They stood inside a mushroom ring full of yellow and white fungi the size of Fellnore's trees. Beckett ambled around kicking at leaves on the ground.

"Look at this!" Tegan shouted as she clasped an elongated flower petal. She held her face up to the sun and wrapped the yellow petal around her shoulders like a shawl and curtsied. Arthur laughed and clapped. Beckett reached for a blue bird feather as tall as himself. He held it like a flag as he marched around waving the feather in front of him. Tegan giggled.

Tegan then jumped over a mound of fluffy moss and scampered to the other side of the fungi ring. Beckett and Tegan stomped on giant leaves making them crunch and crumble under their paws. Amidst their merriment, Arthur and Max caught up to them.

Beckett flopped belly first on top of a red, round berry. "Watch this!" he cried out as he rolled around and then fell off the tomato-looking ball of fruit. Arthur tried his paws on a huge leaf. Standing with crouched knees, he pretended to surf, but instead, slipped and landed right on top of Beckett.

Tegan laughed and held out her paw to help her Papa up. Then they both grabbed Beckett and lifted him off the ground. It felt so good to laugh again!

"Who lives here?" Tegan asked incredulously.

"More like *what* lives here," Beckett replied.

They stood quietly side-by-side and drank in the enormity of the woodland features around them. Giant trees, huge leaves and flowers, enormous berries, massive piles of moss and lichens, colossal mushrooms, and who knows what else!

Arthur motioned for Beckett and his daughter. He pointed in the direction of a slowly declining slope, "There it is," he said.

The two saw a grassy hill descending into a flat area marked by trees at the base of a mountain. There was nothing spectacular or even unusual about the scenery.

Tegan looked at her father confused, and asked, "the entrance to the legendary tunnels is located down there?"

"Yes, Tegan. I will show you," replied Arthur. "But we need to get down there first."

Tegan spotted an object out of the corner of her eye and nudged Beckett with her elbow. They walked over to inspect it.

"It's the top of an acorn!" Beckett shouted.

"An acorn hat?" Tegan laughed.

"It's as big as our bath tub back home!"

Tegan breathed out excitedly, "oooh, I have an idea!"

She pulled at the acorn hat and flipped it over. "Hand me your knife," she said to Beckett. With his knife, she hacked off the stub in the middle, making the surface as flat as possible. Then she turned the acorn top back over and jumped in. "Hey, it's a perfect fit!"

Tegan sat in the middle of the acorn hat and held on to each side, "Papa, I'll meet you down there," she chuckled. "Beckett, push me!"

Beckett backed up and then ran towards Tegan, shoving her newly made sledding saucer down the hill side. "Wait for me!" Beckett found another acorn top, chopped off the stub, and jumped in it himself. Both sombels bumped and bounced all the way down the hill, the wind blowing their fur as they neared the bottom. Beckett's top spun around and bumped into Tegan, toppling them both on the forest floor. The young sombels stood up and brushed themselves off, teasing one another and laughing at each other's faces during the slide.

Arthur was not in the mood to ride an acorn hat down the hill. So, he and Max descended the old-fashioned way and eventually met Tegan and Beckett at the bottom.

"Papa, I still don't see the entrance," Tegan said.

"It's there," Arthur replied. "Sometimes the most exquisite treasures are hidden in plain sight."

CHAPTER II

The sea beast lifted its head and showed a mouth full of sharp, pointy teeth. Black, slimy beasts with long eel-like bodies, these creatures were parasites in the river systems. And Lewis counted three of them in the water before him.

"What are they?!" screamed a soldier.

"Meripeto," said Lewis grimly.

Lewis knew these creatures all too well. He fought them years ago alongside his unit in the last battle of Fellnore. In order to cross the river safely, the soldiers fought for two days just to kill one beast. Lewis shivered a little.

The beast circled the rafts, popping its head out of the water long enough to get a good look at the rats on board the platforms. Increasing its speed, the monster circled the rafts over and over again until the structures started spinning slowly around and around.

The rats clung to the planks and to each other. They squealed and shrieked, "we're surrounded!" and "we're going to die!"

Two meripeto creatures swam over and dove under the rafts, causing bubbles to rise up through the planks. The rats cried out as the bubbles washed over their feet. They stomped around and howled in fear as they tried ridding themselves of the foamy bubbles.

One sea beast lifted its head out of the water and growled a foul and menacing roar. Its breath smelled of death; its gold, blazing eyes stared down the rat leader and his commander. The soldiers readied their spears. Even Lewis had his paw inside his vest, cradling the knife he smuggled in there.

It was a terrifying moment of watching the monsters dip in and out of the water, while waiting to see what they would ultimately do. Then, in a flash, one meripeto widened its disgusting jaws and chomped onto the corner of the raft. Lewis watched in horror as those rats nearest to the corner tumbled toward the beast, some lost in the water.

"Cut the rope!" screamed the rat leader amidst the chaos.

One of the soldiers used a spear tip to hack at the rope tethering the two rafts together. He finally succeeded and the rafts floated apart. Several rats jumped from their compromised platform on to the raft with Lewis and the rat leader. The monster descended again on the first raft, biting another chunk of the float and splintering the planks that struggled to remain intact.

Lewis watched the destruction as the creature demolished the first raft with ease. Still aggressive, the creatures now focused on the second raft, full of rats and the wagon. Lewis abruptly shouted to the soldiers, "Paddle to the shore!"

The soldiers looked at him in skepticism and vexation. They turned to their leader for a decision. "Do it!" the leader reluctantly agreed.

All the rats lined up near the raft's edge and rowed feverishly with their oars. They managed to push their shaky platform over to the right a few feet. But a meripeto cleared a wave and lunged at the leader, who then used his oar to bash the creature in the head. "Keep rowing!" he screamed to the others.

Another sea beast plunged under the raft causing it to rock from side to side. The water washed over the top of the platform, through the sides of the planks, and back into the dark water. The momentum remarkably shoved the raft towards the shore. Lewis could see they were getting closer and closer. His heart beat wildly with treacherous anticipation. *"If we can just get close enough to jump to shore,"* he thought.

Then the creature lifted its mighty tail and thrashed it around, slamming the side of the raft with a great pounding. One rat tumbled overboard and the others screeched in terror. The creaky platform rose up in the water, catapulted sideways a bit, and finally landed with a *thud* on a boulder near the shoreline. Planks separated and washed away down the river.

The wagon that held Lewis overturned and smashed on the boulder. Lewis pulled at the loose bars until they tore off the cage. Finally sensing his freedom, the sombel wiggled out of the opening, stood up, and walked free for the first time in days.

The soldiers leapt from the remnants of the raft onto the large boulder and then to the sandy shore. They waited for their leader with spears drawn, defending the shoreline.

The rat leader noticed the smashed wagon and desperately searched the landscape for Lewis. Spying him just inside the shoreline, the leader scrambled after him with his sword. Tackling the sombel and pinning him down, the rat leader asked him sarcastically, "Where do you think you're going?" He motioned for the commander, who dashed over and tied the sombel's paws together with the only thing he could find, a vine.

"Get up!" the leader commanded and stuck his sword tip into Lewis' shoulder blade. Lewis winced at the pressure. "You're still our prisoner and I <u>will</u> deliver you to the rat king!"

Arthur ambled over and put his paw on a very unassuming tree trunk. The tree stood near the base of the mountain, surrounded by other, more glamorous trees with flowing branches and leaves. But the tree before them was stumpy and had a few knots. There were no leaves growing on it, so it appeared to be dormant.

"This is it?" Beckett asked.

"The tree before you marks the entrance to the tunnels in the mountains over there," Arthur pointed over his shoulder.

"But I don't see an opening," Tegan said. "Or a door?"

"There is a key," Arthur replied. "Let me show you." He leaned over and examined the branches of a tree next to him and broke off a small twig. Ripping the leaves from it, he snapped the twig in half.

"This forest houses a special tree called the Hollow Spruce. If you break off the smaller twigs and look inside, you will see that it is hollow--like a small tube." Arthur showed his hollow twig to each one in the group.

Then he lifted the twig to his mouth and blew it like a whistle. For something so small and elementary, the sweetest sound emerged from the shoot and twirled through the air. Beckett and Tegan glanced at each other amazed.

Arthur blew the twig again, but longer this time. He stopped and listened to the wind. Tegan looked in the same direction as her father. And then she heard rustling in the grass next to them, a fluttering of wings.

"What is that sound?" she asked.

Arthur turned around and smiled. "It's the gatekeeper, I believe."

"Hello?" he called out. "Is there anyone there?"

A small figure with long, brown hair and a set of translucent wings peaked out of the grass. She examined Arthur first and then flew to the lowest branch of the spruce tree to get a better look at the group.

"Who calls?" the beautiful little pixie asked.

"I'm Arthur Wells, friend of King Fallon."

"Speak your purpose." The pixie stared at each sombel suspiciously.

"My friends and I have come to talk with the king. We seek his help."

"Arthur...from the House of Wells clan?" the pixie leaned closer.

"Yes. I am here on official business—"

"For Lewis, I imagine," she interrupted.

"I am pleased that you heard the news about my brother."

The pixie jumped from the branch and flapped her wings, floating down to the ground. She wore a short, blue dress that looked like it was crafted from a cloud, and tiny blue shoes. Little yellow flowers were entangled and twisted into her hair and she carried a brown satchel around her neck and shoulder.

"It is clear that you all are on a journey. Do you seek the advice of King Fallon?"

"We are here because of the prophecy," Arthur glanced at Tegan, "and for your wise king's advice."

The pixie's pinkish eyes focused on Tegan and spied her red tail. "Tegan Wells?"

Tegan stepped forward and curtsied, "I am Tegan from the House of Wells."

"Come with me," the pixie motioned to her.

"What about the others?"

The pixie looked over Tegan's shoulder, "They may come too."

She lifted herself with her wings and placed her tiny hand on top of a circular shape etched into the trunk of the bare tree. An outline of a rounded door emerged on the surface, complete with a door handle.

The pixie paused and said, "I can only take you to the entrance. Another will guide you once you are inside."

Tegan studied this curious little creature and asked, "What is your name?"

"I am Ree," she answered and pushed the door outlined on the tree trunk. The trunk divided into two halves and an opening appeared at the base of the tree. "Now, step inside, quickly!"

Ree corralled the group inside the opening and then the tree closed behind them. "Here, everyone take one of these." She held several torch sticks and waved her hand over each one to set them ablaze. The torches provided just enough light to see that they were definitely inside a tree. The smooth wood and smell of sap gave it away.

"Follow me," the pixie directed, "and watch your head."

The group followed behind Ree. *How could we be inside a tree?!* Tegan wondered. She noticed the shadows from the torches seem to dance along the walls. There were knots and scorched patches all along their walk. They ambled slowly down a dimly lit path, stopping only to turn right and then climb a set of stairs. No one said a word.

Ree finally halted. "Here we are."

The sombels crowded around the pixie as she continued, "Follow this hallway to the last door."

"That's it?" asked Beckett.

Ree nodded, "I must get back to my post. Good luck."

With that, she turned to leave the travelers. Tegan watched as the pixie disappeared back down the stairs.

"Tegan," Arthur called her gently. "This way." He put his arm around her shoulders.

They crossed the hallway without even a whisper, their footsteps made the only echoing sounds. But something wasn't right.

In front of them stood a door, the one the pixie mentioned. Arthur noticed something .... He leaned in closer with his torch to see what was moving next to the door. He shrieked in fear.

Arthur jumped back and fell on the ground, still holding his torch.

"What is it, Papa?" Tegan asked alarmed.

"T..T...Trolls..." Arthur stammered.

Two trolls holding spears stood guard on either side of the tunnel entrance.

CHAPTER 12

Lewis's paws were tied tightly behind him but at least he could walk on his own. The second in command held him close as they climbed onto a flat rock behind the shoreline to rest. The rat leader gathered the other soldiers on the rock to catch their breath as well. They shook the water off their fur and inspected their weaponry. Four soldiers lost in the river; but spears, still functional, and prisoner, still alive.

"Looks like we're on foot from here," one of the soldiers mumbled.

"Where are we anyway?" Another soldier asked.

"From the look of that craggy rock formation, I would say we're near Old Padley," a soldier muttered.

"About a half day's journey south to Littleton then," the rat leader mused.

"What now?" the commander shouted at the leader.

The rat leader covered his eyes with his paw and swiped down his face in exasperation. He turned and pulled out what was left of his map. Studying the still legible lines, the leader turned to the commander and asked, "Which way is southwest?"

The commander pulled out a pocket compass and held it in front of him.

"That way," he pointed.

The leader faced southwest and grunted. "Do you see that wall in the distance?"

Rat soldiers looked in the same direction as their leader. Along the horizon stood a stone wall. Its beautifully hewn stones placed perfectly in alignment by skilled workers a long time ago. Over the years, weathering and wars robbed the architecture of its original stature. Missing rocks and growing moss had taken its toll, but the wall still held itself together, maintaining an unmistakable landmark contrasted against the sullen sky.

One of the soldiers heard rustling in the grass and turned to investigate the noise. He suddenly shushed the crew, including the leader.

"What is it?" asked the commander.

"There," the soldier said pointing to the area of disturbance. "The sound came from over there."

The commander leaned over to take a closer look; the crew, silent with trepidation.

"Show yourself!" shouted the rat leader to the patch of grass that now lay still.

A small rat emerged from the leaves. It was Pel, the rat king's scout.

The leader growled, "What are you doing here?"

"He's spying on us," sneered the commander. The soldiers mumbled in unison.

"It's true," Pel hissed, his gravelly voice barely audible over the sound of the leader's huffing around. "The king commanded me to follow you to ensure the safe transfer of the prisoner."

"What? Like a babysitter?!" the leader asked infuriated. He walked over to Pel and stuck his finger in his face. "Let me tell you something. I do NOT need a sitter. I will transfer the prisoner to the king and receive all the glory myself for his safe delivery!"

"<u>ALL</u> the glory?!" the commander balked. "So, you captured and transported the prisoner all by yourself? How autonomous of you."

"I am in charge here!" the leader seethed.

"Soldiers," Pel responded. "You are to keep your orders. I am simply observing and reporting to the king."

"Well report this," the leader hissed. "I am on schedule and the prisoner will be dropped off by my orders."

"So, no more hiccups?" Pel asked sarcastically and leered.

The commander laughed boisterously. "Cardiff Forest. I warned you to stay on course!"

"Cardiff Forest is off limits," Pel said. "The king sent me to directly warn you about veering off course."

"If he doesn't trust my decisions," the leader threatened, "then he can come get the prisoner himself!"

The soldiers grumbled, restless from the tension between these three.

"Shall I report that to the king then?" Pel asked.

The rat leader rubbed his chin and smirked, "Yes." He continued in a slow, poised tone, "Tell his majesty to come see the prisoner for himself. In Old Padley."

"Are you crazy?" the commander wailed. "He will kill you for that!"

"Only if the prisoner escapes," the leader responded dryly. "Command the soldiers to build a throne for me so I will have a proper place to wait for his majesty. Oh, and make sure the prisoner stays put."

A troll stood guard on each side of the wooden door. Holding long spears, they looked like small elderly men with large ears and long pointed noses. Not the handsomest of creatures by far. Tegan observed the creatures clothed in poorly made, leathery vests, wide furry belts, and burlap-like pants through the dim light.

The trolls caught sight of the group and positioned their spears in front of them, ready to defend the sacred entrance. Their eyes twitched back and forth between the visitors.

"Who are you?" One troll growled.

Arthur stated carefully, "I'm Arthur, from the House of Wells. I'm here on official business to seek the counsel of the king."

The troll lowered his spear and looked closer at Arthur. Tegan could smell his foul odor and beastly breath. "What business?" the creature scowled and stared into the sombel's eyes with his own creepy yellow ones.

"The rats captured my brother, Lewis, several days ago. Erasmus suggested we seek the king's council. We left his cave yesterday and have only just arrived here."

The second troll moved closer to the first one and whispered something in his ear.

"House of Wells, you say?" the first troll grimaced and motioned to the other. "Go tell the clerk that we have a visitor for the king. A visitor from the Wells clan."

The second troll kept his eye on Arthur until he walked through the thick, wooden door. The first beast licked his lips and ambled around the group, inspecting their clothing with his grimy hands.

"We don't get a lot of outside visitors down here," he laughed eccentrically. "Well, not from your clan at least." He circled Tegan and caught a glimpse of her red tail. "What's this?" He stopped and asked.

Tegan remained quiet, unsure of what to say and too frightened to open her mouth anyway.

The troll continued, "A red tail.....surely that's unusual, even for a sombel?" He cackled and wheezed. "Maybe it's worth something? Like a nice gold coin or two??" The troll laughed again, raucously and unremorseful.

The door opened quickly and the second troll called to the first. "Let them in." He held the door wide so the group could step just inside and then shut the door completely.

Tegan scanned the darkness but couldn't see anyone, much less the clerk mentioned by the troll outside. Their torches provided the only light inside this cave-like room. She breathed deep and stepped forward. Arthur, Beckett, and Max followed closely behind in a single file line. They descended a path down several primitive stairs until it stopped along a small body of water.

Beckett noticed a series of tiny boats secured with rope to a rudimentary pier. Every few feet, a tall timber pole held a fiery lantern for light. The shadows flickered on the water making it look like fish dancing just beneath the surface. Beckett tapped Tegan on the shoulder and whispered, "What is this place?" All Tegan could do was shake her head.

"Step aside," a voice close to them stated. "Are you the visitors from the House of Wells clan?" The tall figure asked.

Arthur nodded. He had forgotten how pale and unconventionally beautiful these creatures were. The elf before him wore a long, pale green tunic that contrasted with his lengthy, yellow blonde hair. His arms were sleek but muscular, and his boots were well worn from expeditions. He stood before them and motioned to the boats, "Please step in."

"Yes!" Beckett replied eagerly and hopped into the wooden dinghy closest to the elf.

The others boarded behind him. The small boat contained several planks for visitors or inhabitants to sit on as they traveled to and from the tunnels. Since the dinghy floated low in the water, Tegan reached overboard and felt the cold water with her paw.

Once everyone was seated, the elf grabbed one of the lanterns and stepped into the boat. He placed the lantern in a holder near the front and stepped up onto the bow.

"Stay seated and hold on. This is a short transport." The elf lifted his arms and grasped a rope overhead. Tegan's eyes had now adjusted to the dark and she suddenly noticed the labyrinth of ropes above them. The elf propelled the small boat along the pond of water using these ropes, an unusual conveyance system. Hand over hand, the elf forced the little boat toward its destination. Tegan was fascinated. She had never seen anything like this before.

The water rippled smoothly as they glided in the dinghy. A cool, gentle breeze wafted over the group as they drifted along in the water. As the cave walls began to narrow, Tegan noticed tiny, shimmering dots covering the roof of the cave. It reminded her of the open sky at home on a bright, starry night. The dots twinkled and glowed as she floated underneath them.

"What are those glimmering lights?" Tegan asked the elf.

"Worms," he replied. "We have a special group of inhabitants that live in this part of the cave. We call them glow worms."

"Why do they glow?"

"The worms produce light when they eat a particular alga found only in this cave environment," the elf stated as he pulled on the rope. "This symbiotic relationship benefits us here in the tunnels. We use their luminescence as a guide to the village."

Tegan watched the twinkling lights in silence. Only the lapping of water against the boat could be heard in the quietness. The dinghy turned a corner and firelight brightened their path. The elf steered the boat toward another rustic pier where several creatures waited for their ride. He floated to the pier and jumped off to secure the boat with rope.

The dinghy rocked a bit and the travelers grabbed the sides of the vessel to steady themselves. The elf motioned for the visitors to disembark and stated with open arms, "Welcome to the village of Tollan."

CHAPTER 13

Tegan stood up in the wobbly boat and stepped onto the pier. As the others followed behind her, the elf said, "This is my stop, I have others to transport. A pixie will meet you here and take you to the king."

The group thanked the elf for his assistance and walked toward the lights and the sounds. The narrow path opened into a main chamber followed by a series of small cave openings to the right and the left. Torches and lanterns attached to the cave walls provided sufficient light for the energetic community living here. And a large sign posted in the middle of the room simply read:

"Tollan
Population of many."

Everywhere she looked, Tegan could see creatures bustling about. Pixies in the main chamber carried wares like vegetables, blankets, and even weapons for sale. Each of the small cavern openings housed a stall for displaying those wares. To the right, a textile market offered colorful woven blankets, scarves, sweaters, and hats. The next business showcased vegetables farmed from nearby fields, including potatoes, carrots, tomatoes, and leeks. She even spotted bins full of small mushrooms.

Pixies swarmed the market tables and the sounds of shoppers haggling for bargains filled the air. Wagons rolled through the crowds carrying tools and pulled by gritty gnomes. Laughter broke through the humming of business and negotiations while smells of cooking rye bread and vegetables consumed Tegan's senses.

"Where do we meet our guide?" Beckett asked. He wandered off before he could hear the answer, distracted by the smells of food cooking all around him.

"The last time I visited, a pixie met us in the maps area," Arthur replied. "Let's go and state our business there."

Walking in a single line, the group made their way through the middle of the community market. Tegan passed a merchant selling fish on the left and another offering milk and eggs next door. She observed the movements of the inhabitants as they went about their daily lives. Pixies wearing shoulder bags full of food, kindling, or blankets glided back and forth over the smooth cavern floor. Each coming or going somewhere. Each representing a family living under the protection of the warm, well-lit tunnels.

Moss and shrubby vegetation grew in patches overhead. In the corners, baskets hung from the walls holding flowering plants, herbs, and garden mushrooms. Tegan was captivated. She could see black areas where the story of Rowan proved true....the roof and walls scorched by the dragon's fiery breath.

Tegan followed her father around a pottery merchant and a wool vendor until they reached a stall on the left, covered in large parchment maps. She approached the parchments and felt the material in her paws, smooth and a bit grainy. As Arthur conversed with the stall owner, Tegan's attention turned to the unique wares in the booth beside her. Bright bursts of colorful fabric hung from ropes strung to shelves behind the merchant's front table. Stacks of fabric swatches cluttered the shelves and tabletop. And a pixie dipped cloth into a giant clay pot of simmering water, stirring with a wooden paddle.

Tegan watched as the pixie plunged the cloth up and down in the pot, and then slopped it onto a wringer. The pixie turned a handle to push the wet cloth through several rollers and squeeze out any remainder of water from the fabric. As the water spilled onto the floor, Tegan noticed it was, in fact, a blue-ish color. The pixie then shook out the fabric and draped it over a rope to drip dry near a small pit fire.

"Can I help you, miss?" the pixie realized someone was watching her work.

"I can't help but admire your beautiful fabrics," Tegan replied.

"Oh, but these are no ordinary fabrics," the pixie pulled her hair back exposing the sweat on her face. She wiped her slender hands on her stained yellow apron and approached the sombel behind the table. "Your cloak there. It's made of wool, yes?"

Tegan glanced down and cringed. Her cloak had definitely seen better days, more like better years....especially since that near death experience on the rope bridge. It had been patched and hemmed, and then patched again. Actually, Tegan hadn't thought about how her cloak looked until the pixie questioned it.

"Yes, it is wool," she replied and brushed off some debris from the front of the garment.

"I see," the pixie nodded. "Well, this fabric is made from a special thread produced by the Sioda butterfly."

"Is it like silk?"

"Stronger than silk, and softer." She held up a red swatch and said, "Feel this."

Tegan's paw glided over the velvety fibers of this magical cloth. She smiled and giggled a little, "It feels like a cloud!"

"Each of these fibers comes from a butterfly cocoon and is woven into a fabric using a special spinning machine."

"A butterfly? What in the world do they eat to produce such smooth fibers?"

"They feed on honeysuckle flowers that grow in the fields above our tunnels."

Tegan let that sink in. "And that clay pot back there?" She asked and pointed over the pixie's shoulder.

"That is the color process. I dye each one of my fabrics by hand," the creature smiled. "The one drying over there is blue."

Tegan's eyes explored the many shirts, cloaks, and other garments hanging on hooks to the side of the stall. Each of the pieces handmade, hand dyed, and hand embroidered with sioda thread. She immersed herself in visions of wearing such beautiful clothes, an emerald green cloak with her name embroidered in gold. A striking raiment with resilient, sturdy fibers. What a magnificent sight she could be at the Midlands Fair if she showed up wearing that!

Arthur noticed his daughter's interest in the handsome fabrics and smiled despite the gravity of the situation. "Tegan," he called for her warmly. She returned to reality and joined her group at the maps stall next door.

Parchments were stacked on the table before her, each outlining different areas in Fellnore for those traveling throughout this land. Next to the maps lay smaller squares of parchment paper, most likely used for notes and cards. Small ink pots and writing brushes dotted the shelf behind the table as well.

Arthur rolled a small parchment and handed it to Beckett. "The terms of surrender," he said. Beckett placed the scroll in a pocket inside his tunic. His other pocket stashed several meat pies purchased from a vendor.

"I apologize for making you wait," an exquisite pixie said as she approached Arthur.

The creature addressed Arthur with a slight bow that accentuated her petite frame. She wore a long yellow dress with short sleeves, exposing her brilliantly pale skin. White, glossy hair entangled in golden thread flowed past her shoulders and her beautiful smile eased Tegan at once.

"Princess Nora," Arthur greeted her with a kiss on the cheek. "It has been a while! You look magnificent!"

"And you haven't aged a day since I last saw you," she replied.

Arthur chuckled and turned to Tegan, "This is Princess Nora."

The princess bowed to Tegan and Beckett as her father introduced his daughter and friend to the pixie. Beckett brushed crumbs off his face and smiled sheepishly.

Princess Nora motioned for the travelers to step into a small room away from the noise of the market. "My father is in a meeting, but will be here soon. I understand you are here to seek his council?"

"Indeed. We spent time with Erasmus earlier to discuss the prophecy."

"I see," the princes replied. "So, what requests do you have for my father?"

Arthur fidgeted a little and then said, "I need the king's favor to garner troops for a potential war."

"The prophecy? Is that why Tegan is here?" she asked.

"Yes, she is marked by a red tail," Arthur looked at Tegan's tail and sighed. "It seems we will see the prophecy come to fruition after all."

"And what is your quest?" the princess asked Tegan.

"I am to deliver the terms of surrender to the rats of Voldire," Tegan replied. She had never spoken those words out loud until now. It felt like a huge weight had been placed directly on her shoulders. Her throat constricted, making it hard to breathe.

Beckett recognized her panic, "You're not alone in this," he said to her and placed his paw on her shoulder.

Easy for him to say, Tegan thought. While she appreciated the gesture and nodded to him, Tegan was now afraid of the quest before her. All she had to do was deliver the message. But how could she do that without getting captured herself? Could she even make it through Fellnore to trudge through the dreadful swamplands? What was the plan? She now felt like she was falling apart.

Trembling, Tegan looked at Beckett. He, on the other hand, actually looked forward to this ominous journey. A natural action seeker, he was ready to dive in. Ready to resolve conflict. He thrived on it. But why?? At least Beckett would be with her so she would not have to travel alone.

Princess Nora held Tegan's paw and the sombel quickly calmed down. Nora said to Arthur, "she will need resources for the journey. I can take care of that."

The princess paused for a moment and then continued, "Arthur, meet us in the chamber. Tegan, Beckett, come with me."

CHAPTER 14

Princess Nora led Tegan and Beckett across the main thoroughfare and under an archway to additional stalls. "These are the finest merchants we have," Nora said as she approached the first vendor, a bakery. The princess requested two loaves of rye bread and cheese, paying with small, green coins. The vendor curtseyed and handed the goods to her.

As they ambled from stall to stall, Princess Nora picked up other supplies and handed them to Tegan including kindling, blankets, candles, and fruit. As they headed further down the hall and away from the noisy market, the torches flickered tirelessly showing a dark, damp and empty pathway. Black, scorched walls and the faint smell of smoke filled the air.

As their footsteps echoed in the passageway, a low growling sound reverberated through the tunnel, horrifying Tegan and Beckett. The two crouched down in fear and looked at each other with wide, petrified eyes as the terrible noise surrounded them.

"What is that?!" Tegan shrieked.

Princess Nora stretched out her fair hand, "Come and I will show you," she encouraged them.

Tegan's heart pumped wildly. She timidly stood up with Beckett and fell in line behind the princess. With watchful eyes, she tiptoed softly, listening for any clues that might reveal the source of the frightening noise.

The princess strolled with royal poise; her wings tucked behind her and her steps steady and graceful. She turned to see the group behind her and smiled to reassure them.

"This way," Princess Nora reached the tunnel opening and stopped. Behind her burst a red orange blaze of light, the flare so hot that Tegan's whiskers burned and her eyes watered. She covered her face with her paws and gasped for air.

"Tanwyn, stad *(stop)*!" Nora shouted into the opening. She ducked under the archway and disappeared into the dimly lit cavern.

Tegan tiptoed closer and peeked into the room. Under a beam of daylight bursting from a crack in the ceiling, Princess Nora approached a scaly and lean dragon. The dark gray beast reclined against the cave wall growling under its smoky breath.

"Oh, why are you so grumpy today?" the princess cooed at the creature. She reached up towards his mouth and scratched under his chin. The dragon's growl transformed into more of a low guttural vibration, almost a purr, as he stretched his head out for Nora's touch. She stroked the furry cheeks while the beast closed his huge, green eyes.

The princess motioned for Tegan and Beckett to come closer. "Meet our resident dragon, Tanwyn," she said.

Neither of the sombels had ever seen a dragon in real life, at least not this close. Sometimes at dusk, Tegan had witnessed the beasts flying overhead, their wings contrasted against the setting sun and darkening sky. But those sightings were unusual.

Tanwyn rested on his belly, but his shoulders, neck, and head still towered over Nora. His sleek, scaly body reflected the light while his muscular tail wrapped around his claw-like feet.

"He's still very young and in training," the princess rubbed his nose and patted his head.

Intrigued, Beckett moved closer to the dragon, admiring the beast from head to tail. Tanwyn shifted his head to take a closer look at the sombel, his eyes glowing a glorious green. Beckett felt the dragon breathing him in, a gentle suction of warm air. Then the dragon snorted bits of ash and turned his head back to the princess.

She laughed heartily, "He approves." Beckett chuckled nervously and wiped the ash from his face and shoulders.

Tegan's fear relented long enough for her to join the other two in front of the dragon. She breathed in nervously and stared into his eyes. Tanwyn turned and looked directly at her. He sniffed and then laid his head down on the cavern floor. Hesitant, Tegan cautiously leaned over and touched his nose with her paw. It was cold and rough, but she could not help but stroke it. The beast lifted Tegan's paw with his nose so she could pat his head. There was something about his eyes that Tegan found different. Though this creature was enormous and frightening, his large eyes were gentle. This captivated her.

"I think Tanwyn likes you," Princess Nora smiled at Tegan.

"What kind of dragon is he?" Beckett asked.

Nora answered, "Tanwyn is a fire breather. He is a direct descendant of Rowan's dragon in the legends."

"THE Rowan?" Tegan asked incredulously.

"Yes, she tamed the dragon that rescued her so that its progeny could protect the tunnels for future generations."

"Does Tanwyn live here?"

"He stays here sometimes, but comes and goes as he pleases."

"So he's not secured with chains?"

The princess laughed, "No, Tanwyn is a restless creature, but he is trustworthy."

"Wait," Beckett spoke up, "He comes and goes? How does he enter this cave?" He twirled around and eyed the door to the cavern. "Surely he doesn't ride the boat like we did, and then march through the market?"

"No, there is a portal hidden within this cavern that Tanwyn uses to enter and exit," Nora explained. "Many of us in the royal family use it as well."

"Does anyone else know he lives here?" Beckett asked.

"Do they see him come and go?" Tegan asked.

"The inhabitants know Tanwyn lives here, but they don't see his coming or going. They are too afraid of the dragon to venture this far into the tunnels," the princess answered.

She rubbed the dragon's chin and kissed him on the nose. The great beast shook his head and lifted his front claw as the princess giggled at his antics. "Come with me," she said to the sombels. "It's time to meet Arthur."

King Fallon, along with another pixie, paused in the main chamber to speak with Arthur. His long blue tunic embellished with gold leaf threading contrasted against his flaxen skin. The king also had long pale hair but he wore a simple crown on top of his head decorated with green gems.

The king introduced his companion to Arthur, "may I present to you my youngest son, Prince Callum."

The boy resembled his father in physical appearance and in posture. He wore a long brown tunic with a small messenger bag wrapped around his neck and shoulders. His facial features appeared sharp but gentle, a kind face, but it could easily turn war like if necessary. Prince Callum stood a few inches taller than his father, and respectfully allowed the king to continue his conversation without interruption.

"This is the safest place in the tunnels," King Fallon said to Arthur. "We can speak here in confidence."

Indeed, the immense cavern sparkled with green gems coating every inch of the cave walls. As sprinkles of natural light pierced through cracks in the high ceiling rock, the sun bounced off the gems to create a greenish glow throughout the room. In the back, a small pond of water mirrored the twinkling reflections of the gems. Torches blazed in holders around all the massive walls and the sound of hammers echoed from a small hallway in the corner.

Arthur noticed a wooden wagon in the distance with several gnomes chopping at the walls with their hammers. The king explained, "The gnomes work here. We employ them to harvest the gems during certain times of the year."

The gnomes wore red vests and brown pants, both covered in soot from hacking the walls of the cave. Their hats were dirty and faces smudged in ash. They sang simple songs in an unknown language as they pushed their wagon and whacked at the green stones lodged in the walls and the roof.

"King Fallon," Arthur began, "I seek your council and support for an impending war against the rats of Voldire." He took a few steps and turned around, "and Lewis is in trouble."

"I've heard about the skirmishes and the treaty violation. I regret that Lewis is caught up in the middle of this; but you have our full support."

"Thank you," Arthur replied. "I beg you to summon the clans to fight with us...to rescue my brother and bring him home safely."

"Have you sent the terms yet?" the king asked.

Arthur hesitated. "No. It's just....the prophecy. I have to send my own daughter to deliver the terms of surrender. I'm, I'm....."

King Fallon put his hand on Arthur's shoulder, "The prophecy, yes." He continued gently, "My clerk tells me she has the red tail."

Silence ensued as Arthur appealed to the king with his eyes.

"Arthur, I will send out the order for our pixie clan to mount arms and fight with your units. Elves will scout and accompany your daughter to deliver the terms of surrender. If this turns into war, I'll notify the tribes on the outskirts of Fellnore to unite in the quest."

Arthur relaxed a little. "What about Lewis?"

"Let me speak with our military captain. I'll assign him to your unit to develop a strategy for rescue." The king paused for a moment. "But Arthur, I just left a meeting with our scout who reports seeing Lewis and his captors near Old Padley. Apparently, they traveled down the river toward Homish and crashed on the rocks after an attack. My source tells me the rats are setting up camp there."

"In Old Padley? Why would they just stop?"

"It appears to be a power struggle."

"And now Lewis is caught up in the middle of an inner battle for dominance," Arthur mused.

"Old Padley is now our point of rescue," said King Fallon. "If those rat soldiers are stationery, then Greygor will likely catch up with Lewis there." He paced a bit with his fingers stroking his chin, contemplating the next move. "We must appoint troops to siege the area and bring back Lewis before they have the chance to question him properly."

Arthur sighed, "Then Tegan must travel to Old Padley as well." He looked at the king and concealed his anxious thoughts. "We also have a unit near Littleton. I'll ask Milo to reassign those soldiers to this location at once."

At that moment, Princess Nora, Tegan, and Beckett entered the main chamber through a tiny door on the right side of the cavern.

"Ah, there they are," announced the king.

The three approached the king. Tegan and Beckett turned around and around soaking in all the beauty of the sparkling gems. Mouths open, eyes wide, they searched every inch of the cave, mixing legend and reality in front of them.

Tegan pointed in disbelief, "That's the pool of tears," she whispered to Beckett.

"And look at the scorched wall underneath the gems!" Beckett replied. "It's really true! The dragon created all these stones out of Rowan's tears!"

Tegan turned to Arthur, "Papa, you would not believe the dragon we saw in the cave next door!"

Her father chuckled, "Yes, Tanwyn is a robust beast. I remember his mother, Dragmar, the chamber's protector many years ago."

Prince Callum laughed, "That truly has been a long time ago."

Arthur introduced his daughter and Beckett to both King Fallon and Prince Callum. The young sombels both bowed to the king and the prince.

"The red tail," the prince whispered to his father.

"Tegan," the king started. "Your father and I have discussed the plans for the delivery of the terms. I have information that the rats are holding up in Old Padley. The message you carry must be presented there."

Tegan took a deep breath and said, "I will complete the quest you have assigned to me."

"The king has promised to send aid with you, so you will not be alone," Arthur said. "I am travelling back to Haven with Max to inform Milo of the recent news of Lewis' capture. The troops will meet you in Old Padley."

With that, Arthur hugged and kissed his daughter, and then whispered gravely to the prince, "take care of her." He didn't want to leave his daughter at all. But if she didn't fulfill her duty, the village, the kingdom might fall into the hands of the black rats. *'It's her duty,'* he told himself, *'her duty to protect us.'* Arthur swallowed hard and gritted his teeth.

Both Arthur and Max left the chamber in a rush to get home. They had to warn Milo and the villagers of the looming battle.

King Fallon reassured the sombels. "Take this," he said and handed Tegan a small, fabric pouch. She gently took the gift and opened it. Inside were several green gems, the same ones that covered the cave walls.

"What's this?" she asked.

"Green moonstone," he replied. "You will need protection along the way, and these gems can provide that."

"What can they be used for?" asked Beckett mesmerized by the gems.

"The stones, in fact, boost the powers and abilities that one already possesses. They are powerful and must be applied responsibly," stated the king. "Having said that though, the moonstone gems have mostly been used in powering machines, aiding weapons, and boosting farm growth when crop output is low." He paused, "Of course, there are official military applications and royal functions that the gem is used for, but those implementations are confidential."

Tegan remembered the gift that the tinker gave her and pulled it out of her bag. She showed the gems to the king, "I received this from a tinker in the woods. Is it a green moonstone gem as well?"

The king analyzed the stones she held, "Yes, it appears to be our gem," he replied. "Tell me again, where did you get this?"

"I was approached by an old tinker in the woods on our way to visit Erasmus."

"I wonder if that was Sabreena, the one that travels through Fellnore?" The king looked at his son.

"I haven't heard from her in a while, but it is possible," the prince replied.

"She also gave me these dried herbs," Tegan showed the shriveled leaves and stems to the king. "What are these?"

King Fallon touched the leaves and inspected one of the stems, "These look like Athru berries. Well, the stalks and leaves do. Oh, there are a few berries in there, I see them now."

"What are they used for?"

"Athru berries are mood changers," Prince Callum answered. "The leaves are brewed into a tea but the berries can be eaten in pies or stew."

"Why would the tinker give me dried Athru leaves?"

"Good question," the prince replied. "But be careful," he poked at the leaves, "the berries change your mood to the opposite feeling you currently have. So, for example, if you are happy and you eat the berries or drink the tea, your mood changes immediately to feelings of sadness or anger."

Tegan wrapped the stones and dried Athru in the packaging and placed them back into her bag.

Clearing his throat, the king asked Beckett about his weapon. "Let me see your sword." Beckett pulled out his sword and handed it to the king. He turned it over and lifted it up, the light reflecting off the blade, "Yes, this will do." The king handed the weapon back to him.

"Tegan, do you have a sword?" the king asked.

"No Sir, not yet," she answered.

The king whispered to the prince and the prince left the chamber. A few minutes later, Prince Callum came back in with a small weapon in his hand. "This is for you," he presented Tegan with her very own sword.

The beautiful blade fit perfectly in her paw. Its ornate handle and grip were just the right size for both control and precision. She admired the workmanship of the long metal blade as it glistened in the light. The sword itself was shorter than Beckett's but contained more detail. She even noticed a circular space just above the grip, which was enveloped with gold filigree.

Overwhelmed by the gift, Tegan exclaimed, "Thank you! It is so beautiful!"

"Please accept this present as our promise of support to the House of Wells," the king replied, and then smiled. "And before you set out on your journey, I have assigned a pixie to accompany you. He will provide direction and help protect you as you fulfill your quest."

"You have been most kind, King Fallon," Tegan replied. "On behalf of my father and myself, I deeply thank you for all your support."

The king embraced Tegan with fatherly compassion. Completely caught up in the moment, Beckett rushed in and hugged the two himself. Embarrassed, he awkwardly stepped back and asked, "Who is accompanying us?"

The king looked at the sombels, "I am sending my son, Prince Callum."

CHAPTER 15

Greygor let out a bloodcurdling scream.

"How DARE they defy me!" he roared at Pel.

The rat king picked up a scorched log lying next to him and hurled it into the air. Pacing quickly back and forth, Greygor growled and hissed. "Old Padley, huh?"

The scout retreated from the king, "Yes, sir. They are now stationed in Old Padley." He bowed low and backed away from the steaming monster in front of him.

Greygor's rage skyrocketed. He picked up a torch and flung it into a nearby shack used for forging weapons, watching as it caught fire. Kicking the walls, the stones tumbled and the blaze engulfed the small hut.

Motivated by the wreckage, the rat king seized more torches and set other hovels on fire. The campsite quickly overrun with scorching flames, the king retreated to his throne and threw himself into it. He watched with morbid satisfaction as the fires raged and the soldiers rushed to collect their belongings from the carnage. Black smoke billowed from the remnants of the Homish encampment. Greygor slumped in his royal chair, laughing at the scene before him.

"So, my army leader thinks he can outsmart me...outmaneuver me? ME??" Greygor mumbled under his feverish breath. "I'll tell you what is going to happen...I will march to Old Padley. I will. And I will bring a mighty force with me to subdue this mutiny once and for all."

He shouted to the nearest soldier, "You! Go round up the strongest soldiers we have and meet me here." He thrust his arm forward and pointed, "Go!"

The rat soldier grabbed his spear and scurried off to carry out this new order.

Greygor continued, "And as for Lewis, well, we'll see how fast he talks when I get a hold of him."

The king's royal guards, breathless and confused, spotted Greygor on his throne and scrambled over the smoking debris to get to him.

"Sir! What are you doing?" One shrieked. They circled around the stone table and jumped up and down panicking.

"I am relocating," Greygor shouted at the guards. "This place does not suit me anymore."

"But the treaty—"

"What treaty? A piece of paper? Ha!" he scoffed. "We broke that agreement years ago."

The guards looked at each other in resignation. "Then you are prepared for war?"

"I am always ready for war!" the king rebuffed his guards. "And I never cared for this place anyway."

Prince Callum led Tegan and Beckett back into the chamber where Tanwyn was sleeping. His giant head lay nestled in his claws. He snored so loud that Tegan had to put her paws over her ears to muffle the noise. She laughed a little as they walked past the slumbering beast. For such a fierce creature, Tanwyn almost looked endearing as he slept. His great, round belly rose up and down as he breathed in and out. The dragon's silvery black scales and a bit of fur outlined his elongated face and sleek body.

"This way," the prince motioned.

They approached a small wooden bridge that stretched over a trifling stream. Large, round river rocks peppered the shallow water. The air felt warm and a breeze swept through the area, signaling an opening in the cave somewhere.

They walked up to a crevasse in the cavern wall, the rock blackened and smooth. It was a very unassuming portal. And behind the crevasse, a wooden door stood between the tunnels and the world outside. Prince Callum opened the door and the three stepped through the portal.

On top of a mountain now, Tegan adjusted her eyes to the daylight. The afternoon sky lazily held the sun just above the tree line. She took a few steps and looked around. Forest as far as she could see. The clouds above her, the green grass and shrubs beneath her feet....she breathed in deep and surveyed the countryside below. "It looks so peaceful," she thought. "And yet, it is the calm before the storm."

"Where are we exactly?" Beckett asked as soon as he emerged from a squatty, stone dolmen.

"Look over there," said Prince Callum as Beckett joined him. "The mountains across the forest...Those are the tunnels we just left."

"Over there? But...but, how?!" Beckett asked dumbfounded.

The prince just smiled and pointed over the sombels' heads, "Do you see that river in the distance?"

97

Beckett and Tegan scanned the horizon and noticed a sliver of water in the distance. It curled and wound around the trees and craggy rock formations, just like a slithering snake.

"We need to head that way," the prince stated. He held a compass in one hand and a map in the other. As he tucked them away in his bag, he heard a noise in the trees. Startled, the prince paused in a state of alert. He raised his hand, "let's go!" he commanded. "Take cover in the forest."

Tegan and Beckett trotted down the footpath and into an overgrowth they found near a rock formation. Prince Callum remained as lookout. He patrolled a small opening near the forest entrance with his bow and arrow drawn. It remained silent. The three travelers listened intently for the strange noise to reoccur. Satisfied in the quietness, the prince finally lowered his weapon and crept near the sombels.

Just then, a whooshing sound swept through the leaves of the trees overhead. A creature's shadow darkened the hiding spot where the three crouched under a rocky slab. It was a Crann owl. Its giant wingspan blocked the sunlight, so all they could see were huge, golden eyes.

The owl swooped down and landed on a log near the travelers. Its white feathers practically glowed in the daylight. The beautiful bird lowered its head and tucked its majestic wings behind its back. Tegan watched as it bobbed its head from side to side and gripped the log with its scraggly, black talons. Opening its pointy beak, the owl screeched a high-pitched noise that pierced through the forest.

"Lenah?" Prince Callum asked. "Is that you?"

The bird hopped off the log and waddled over to the prince. "Yes, my prince. I am Lenah."

Tegan and Beckett exhaled in relief, unconscious of the fact that they had been holding their breath for some time.

"How are you, my friend?" the prince asked.

"I am well, and you?" she asked.

"My family is well also," he answered. "But why are you here?" Prince Callum reached out to smooth a wayward feather.

"I've come to inform you of events I've witnessed down the river," she replied.

"Yes, that is where we are headed," the prince said.

"Beware, the rats are building a settlement in Old Padley...and they have a prisoner," Lenah warned.

"My Uncle Lewis," Tegan stepped out from her hiding place.

"It's a sombel, yes," Lenah replied.

"My apologies," the prince said. "Allow me to introduce my new friends: Tegan, from the House of Wells, and her friend, Beckett."

The two nodded to Lenah and she said, "Pleased to meet you."

The prince continued, "My father asked me to accompany these friends to Old Padley to deliver the terms of surrender to the rat king. Can you tell me anything of the situation there?"

"Is my uncle safe?" Tegan inquired softly.

The owl turned to the sombel, "He is safe...for now." She looked back at Prince Callum, "the rats are forming new campsites and even building a giant oven to forge weapons. I smelled the burning embers and heard the hammering this morning."

"How many are encamped there?"

"About twenty. But it's hard to judge from high in the trees. There may be more rats depending on if the leader sent out scouts."

"Thank you, Lenah. Please inform my father so he can disperse messengers to Haven. Our clans can use this information for battle preparations as well," the prince stated.

The owl extended her magnificent wings and flew off toward the dolmen.

"She's beautiful," Beckett commented.

"Lenah is a Crann owl. They are couriers as well as informants. The species, as a whole, is secretive, however Lenah is special to our family."

"If the owls are so elusive, how did you befriend her?" Beckett asked.

"My brother and I came upon her as an owlet when we were scouting in the forest years ago. She had fallen from her nest and hurt her leg. I bandaged her leg, fed her a few worms, and put her back in a nest near the tree where she landed." The prince laughed a little, "We camped there overnight hoping to see the owlet reunited with her family. But after hours of watching the sky, we finally fell asleep. In the morning, my brother woke up first and told me that the owlet was gone. We panicked. We searched for any sign of her and found only a few small, shiny green stones piled near our sleeping area. I later learned that the Crann owls leave small tokens as their way of showing appreciation for acts of kindness."

"So her mother found her?" Beckett asked.

"Yes, she told me some years later that her mother found her and flew her back to the family's nest high in the tree. I learned about the tokens of appreciation at the same time."

Beckett thought for a moment. "I watched her walk and didn't notice a limp?"

"Her leg healed quite nicely. In fact, she has been a very helpful liaison with other creatures in the forest since then." Prince Callum commented. "I don't see her as often as I would like. Crann owls are observers, monitors of the forest. But Lenah assures me that she sees me way more than I see her."

"Can you call on her when there is a problem?"

"I have never tried to summon her," the prince said and then paused. "But I've never really needed to."

Beckett added solemnly, "I have a feeling that might change."

CHAPTER 16

Prince Callum, Tegan, and Beckett picked up their bags and continued down the footpath. The quiet surrounded them as the sun blazed overhead. Moss grew over the surfaces of rocks that outlined the well-worn path. Large leaves of grass towered overhead, and white flowers speckled the foliage in front of them.

"I have a friend that lives down by the river," Prince Callum said. He was the first to break the silence. "We can stay with him tonight."

"Is that where we're headed?" Tegan asked.

"In a way. But first, I want to stop in the next village and ask about a scout there."

The travelers rounded a scrubby forest on the left and stepped into an opening on the right. A sprawling view of a small town lay ahead. As they neared the rows of shabby stores on each side of the main path, they could see the twinkling of lights in the windows of homes just past the buildings. Spirals of smoke trickled out of tiny chimneys and the aroma of fish and potato slices roasted over fire pits. Tegan's stomach growled. She had to taste that fish!

The prince and his companions passed a pub where noisy laughter and boisterous shouting spilled out onto the street. Two ferret-looking creatures crashed through the pub's door, rolling right in front of Beckett and Tegan. A small crowd gathered outside to witness the imminent fight and cheered the two creatures on. But Prince Callum drew a small sword and shoved one of them to the side and out of the way. Witnesses booed and grumbled as the ferret-like beasts looked startled by the interruption and walked away from their fight. The crowd and the troublemakers eventually made their way back into the pub once the scuffle was over.

Tegan felt uneasy. These creatures appeared to be different than what she was used to. And where did Prince Callum hide that small sword he just pulled out? She leaned into Beckett, "I wonder if the prince has any other weapons he's hiding?"

"I thought about that too," he replied.

Tegan touched her sword with her paw and felt the filigree, "You know, it's been a while since I took fighting lessons." She looked at the groups of villagers lurking in front of stores as she passed them. "And considering my circumstances, I think I need to dust off my skills."

"Did you take defense lessons in school?" Beckett asked.

"Yes, but that was a few years ago. Besides, I have a new sword now," she smiled briefly, then cringed as panic crossed her eyes, "I have a new mission too."

A fox-like animal smoking a large pipe spit tobacco juice on the ground near Tegan. She jumped sideways and ran to catch up with Prince Callum, who stopped under an awning and motioned for the two to join him inside.

"Come on, let's get some food first," Beckett said. "Then we'll see what moves you remember."

The three travelers entered a shoddy tavern, called the Boar's Nest, through a round, splintered door. Inside, the smell of fish and barley flooded their senses and tempted their stomachs. Village patrons, imbibing ale and debating loudly, crowded around circular tables seating four to six at a time.

The interior reminded Tegan of Sammy's pub back home, except the walls of this tavern were covered in large tapestries with unusual but colorful designs on them. The room was surprisingly soundproof given that she hadn't heard the noise from the street. Over the bar, an old map outlined the area of Fellnore and several villages along the mountain range and riverside. One in particular was highlighted: Chipping Farms.

Tegan asked her friend, "Are we in Chipping Farms now?"

Beckett looked at the old map, "It appears so."

Prince Callum approached the bar where another fox served ale to her customers. She wore a black apron with two sizable pockets over her reddish fur. Her wiry glasses held close to her nose and her furry ears lay folded like fancy dinner napkins. She wiped down the bar top with a handkerchief-like towel and chatted with other foxes across the table.

The prince waited for a chance to say something to the barmaid, listening to the sporadic conversations happening around him. When he got his chance, he said, "Excuse me, I'm looking for Edwin. Is he here?" The barmaid cackled, "Why would he be *here*?"

"My father, King Fallon, told me to ask for Edwin here at the Boar's Nest in Chipping Farms. I'm in the right place, am I not?"

She analyzed him, looked the prince up and down. Then she motioned to his companions and asked, "Who are they?"

"My friends have come with me to ensure my safe travels."

She turned her head to look at the fox seated across from her and then leaned over to the prince, "If you are indeed King Fallon's son, then you need to meet with Reginald, not Edwin. And the only way to meet Reginald is to attend tonight's ceremony in the oaks."

"We are not staying here long, miss. I only need to ask him a question."

She straightened up. "Well, you're out of luck then...until tonight," she said with a laugh. "Reginald has been gone for a week and won't be back from his trip until this evening. Drink?"

The prince nodded and flashed three fingers. Within moments, the barmaid brought over drinks for all three travelers and eyed Tegan and Beckett from top to bottom. The sombels drank their ale quickly without saying a word. They strained to hear the prince's conversation, hoping to make sense of this pit stop.

Prince Callum contemplated his options. He could stay here, eat a little stew, and wait until the ceremony begins, or leave and try to locate Reginald on his own...or find someone else that knows him. Hungry and opting to wait for the ceremony, the prince ordered fish and potatoes for his companions and stew for himself. They all sat down at a table to eat.

"What are we doing here?" Beckett asked the prince.

Prince Callum started to reply but paused as the food was placed in front of them by the barmaid. As soon as she left, the prince leaned in and lowered his voice, "Before we left the tunnels, my father instructed me to visit this town and find a proper scout to get us into Old Padley...without being seen." He looked around the tavern and then continued, "You see, there is a tribe of brown bush rats that live near that village and they have scouts everywhere. All it takes is one of those beasts to see us and run to the black rats. Once they tattle on us, our plan is compromised." The prince pounded on the table, "We will present those terms of surrender under our conditions, without being trapped as prisoners and handed over to the enemy."

A short, stocky fox walked up behind Beckett and asked the prince in a gravelly voice, "Can I join you?"

The prince motioned for Beckett to move over so the fox could pull up a chair. "I overheard you talking at the bar. You interested in speaking with Reginald?" he asked.

"Yes, I am. Do you know when he will be here?"

"I might."

Prince Callum pulled out a small silver coin and pushed it across the table to the fox in front of him.

The fox grinned and put the coin in his pocket, "Good ol' Reggie is due back in town around four o'clock. That's when the shipments arrive from across the river."

"Where can I meet him?"

The fox shifted in his chair, "He will most likely stop at the barn first, behind the blacksmith shop."

The prince asked gingerly, "Where is this blacksmith shop?"

"Just a few buildings down," the fox said and drank the last of his ale, slamming the cup down.

"And then?" Prince Callum pressed on.

"Well, you heard the barmaid," the fox straightened up in his chair. "Maeve says he'll be at the ceremony tonight under the oaks."

The prince looked confused.

"The oak trees in the meadow...behind the barn," he barreled. "They're easy to find. Town folk have been setting up all day for the banquet."

Prince Callum looked at Tegan and Beckett, who were watching the villagers sitting at tables around them. The villagers appeared to be mumbling to each other, pointing at the sombels and the royal pixie. The prince realized this as his cue and quickly thanked the fox for his information. Then he excused himself and the sombels from the table and left the tavern in a flash.

On the street, Tegan shivered. Not only was it getting chilly, but she needed to shake off the stares of the residents in this community. She had rarely travelled outside of Haven and the farmlands of sombel society. Now, she stood on the side of main street in a distant commune of fox inhabitants. Her father told her about these creatures years ago, to watch what you say, to be careful of your business with these cunning beasts, and to never pay for services or goods all at once. There were just too many stories of deceit and guile when dealing with this fox population.

The travelers headed down the street while several foxes lined up near the path to watch them leave. As soon as Tegan, and Beckett, and the prince cleared the tavern, Beckett started up, "So, how about we find that meadow and get to work on your sword fighting skills?"

"You mean defense skills?" Tegan asked nervously. "I have no plans to attack anyone. I will leave that job to you," she laughed uneasily.

"Come on, I see the clearing up ahead," Beckett said, running ahead of the others.

They neared the blacksmith shop and turned down the path beside the building. Out back stood a small shack with an open door. Villagers walked in and out carrying tablecloths, flower vases, candle holders, large bowls, and other decorations for the banquet. Chairs and tables were already set up under the oak trees for the party. Off to the side were fire pits where large pots of stews and vegetables cooked, and fish hung on spikes smoking over the smoldering embers.

Tegan and Beckett found an opening near the side of the barn, away from the hustling, to focus on practicing technique with their swords. She laid down her bag and unsheathed her sword. The metal glistened in the sunlight as she held it up over her head. Lowering it to her waist, Beckett showed her how to hold the weapon and defend herself against basic blows. Over and over she practiced...up stroke, down block, swing it around....out to the side, in near the chest, swing it again. It all sounded like a song. But slowly, her mind recalled most of the moves she learned previously in school. Though still rusty, she considered this refreshing exercise.

"Bring the sword up like this," Beckett showed her and held his weapon near his chest. "If you see that they have a sword, or any weapon, then bring your sword down like this." He turned his hip and slashed with the blade.

The sunlight caught the blade and it grazed Tegan's eyes, a rainbow of colors splattered everywhere, and a lingering green streak captivated her attention. Her thoughts wandered to the moonstone in her bag. *The moonstone! Could it help her somehow?*

"Wait," she called out to her friend and ran to her bag. Tegan unwrapped the moonstone the tinker gave her and analyzed it under the sun light. It was beautifully green and clear; she could see through it even though there were a number of cuts in it. Viewing it closer, the sombel noticed something unusual, a design, a swirl. She had seen this design before, but where?

Beckett looked over Tegan's shoulder. She turned to show him the gem and asked, "Do you see it?"

He leaned closer to the gem and said, "It's lovely, isn't it?"

"Yes, but do you see the design?" she asked.

He squinted his eyes and nodded.

"Where have I seen this before?" she asked herself. Collecting her sword from the lawn, Tegan inspected the blade and then the handle. She gasped, "Here!"

On the gilded grasp, the center filigree design, was the same swirling symbol. Tegan played with the gem and wiggled it into the space just below handle. It was a perfect fit. Amazed, she said to Beckett, "I can't believe it....the tinker knew.....!"

"It is meant to be," he replied. "Now, let's see what that gem can do!"

Beckett lifted his sword and initiated a pretend fight. Tegan held her sword with the moonstone in the ready position. Beckett swung gently to her side, and she met the blade with hers. As soon as the impact happened, Tegan's sword glowed a dull white color and she felt a vibration in the handle.

"Whoa!" Beckett exclaimed.

"That felt powerful!" she shouted.

"Let's do it again!" he said.

Beckett extended his sword and asked Tegan to hit harder. He swung to his left and Tegan lunged, connecting with his blade. Her sword glowed white again, and left a trace of light. She then held the blade up and slashed around in the air, watching the trail of light as it illuminated with each action.

Again, she clashed swords with Beckett, to his left, to her right, over her head—she tightened her grip, feeling the gentle ridges of the handle in her paw. As she gained confidence, the sword felt lighter and her strikes became more and more precise.

Beckett sparred with this friend in complete amazement at the weapon she possessed. There was something about the gem that boosted power in Tegan's sword. But what could it do?

The two friends danced around as they practiced with their blades...hopping, plunging, and swirling around, like a musical in a magical forest, and they were the main characters. Suddenly, Beckett stepped on a rock and fell unexpectedly towards Tegan, his blade swiping just next to her arm. Tegan instinctively blocked his blade with her sword and watched as a small dome of protection manifested around her. It was brief. The lining of the dome wavered and then disappeared.

"Oh, Tegan, I'm so sorry!" Beckett blurted out.

"Are you alright?" she asked her friend.

Beckett nodded and dusted himself off.

Tegan laughed, "Did you see that?!"

"The shield of protection?" he asked incredulously. "Yes I did!"

Tegan helped her friend stand up. He wiggled his foot and stretched his shoulders; the pain was minimal, but he needed to rest them for a while. The two put away their swords and settled on several wooden chairs, pushed up against the side of the barn, to catch their breath.

Activity hustled in and out of the barn. Servers holding large bowls and baskets full of fruit, vegetables, and bread, or pitchers brimming with ale, carried their bundles carefully to the tables across the field.

With all the comings and goings, Tegan suddenly wondered where Prince Callum had been. She strolled around the side of the barn with Beckett and peeked inside the open door. No sign of him in there. Beckett trotted to the other side of the building and disappeared. After a few precarious moments, he called out to Tegan, "Hey, come see this!"

The two sombels stood facing the main road and viewed a caravan of wagons in the distance. A couple of foxes with large horns blew their instruments in unison, signaling the return of Reginald and his loot. The discordant noise echoed over the field until every villager stopped to observe the wagons. They shouted with praise and laughter to welcome their leader home.

As the wagons rolled closer, the contents looked more like home goods than supplies, like the tavern fox suggested. A giant purple tufted chair with matching cushions, and a couple of tables sat in one cart. Another contained a few simple chairs, some dishes, pots and pans, and crates of flour, acorns, barley, sugar cane, and more. *Where did all this come from?* Tegan thought. *It seemed like this group was relocating to a new homestead, instead of stocking up on essential supplies (well, except for the food of course).* Next, a carriage with clothing and blankets rolled past her, complete with a few hammers, axes, and shovels.

The wagons pulled up near the barn and stopped so the drivers could disembark. Each of them walked over to join a particularly regal-looking fox dressed in a dark blue robe. One of the drivers pulled out a set of stairs and moved away so the robed fox could step off the wagon.

"That must be Reginald," Beckett said.

"Yeah," Tegan scoffed. "The fluffy robe gave it away."

The foxes gathered into the barn leaving the carts, for the most part, unattended. Beckett tugged on Tegan's cloak to follow him.

She covered her head with her hood and trailed behind him. They nonchalantly slipped past a few villagers talking amongst each other near the barn door, and then gradually approached the cart farthest from the building.

"Just a quick peek," said Beckett. He stepped up on the wagon wheel, looked around, and then glanced at the contents in the cart with the furniture. "Pretty sure the purple chair is for his majesty." He dug around in some boxes placed around the chair. "Books....boring!"

"Beckett, be careful!" Tegan whispered loudly so as not to be heard by the others in the barn.

He motioned to her, "Check out that wagon."

She passed Beckett and casually walked up to the cart containing the blankets. Tegan wasn't nearly as brave as her friend, but temptation, and more importantly, curiosity, was getting the best of her right now. The contents in front of her consisted of household things...used household items, but from where? And why did they show wear and tear?

Tegan rubbed her paw along the edge of the wagon and quickly pulled herself up on the edge. She lifted a few of the blankets to see what was underneath....more clothes. On the other side of the wagon was a few pillows. She moved them over, catching a glimpse of a wooden box underneath. It was long and wide, the top secured with a metal lock. However, that lock was conveniently unfastened. Tegan stole a look in both directions before gently lifting the lid.

Beckett noticed Tegan fiddling with the box and ran over. "What's in there?" he asked., his hot breath in her ear. They inspected the inside together. Metal swords of all shapes and sizes lay in the box. She noticed a few daggers too. Something didn't feel right.

"Oi!" a voice shouted out.

Tegan dropped the lid and the sombels spun around in a panic. A huge, burly fox holding a giant club barreled toward them.

"What are you doing?!" the fox shouted.

"Nothing....uh, just looking at your, um, successful and...and...lucrative haul," Tegan made it up as she went along.

The burly fox harrumphed, pleased with himself, and threw his club over his shoulder. "This, my dear," he patted the cart with a heavy paw, "is the result of a week's long raid down the river."

I knew it! she thought.

Beckett continued with the ruse, "Did you score this loot all by yourself?"

"I would like to say that I did. However, I had a little help," he rubbed his chest and sighed.

"Reginald?" Tegan ventured.

"What? No!" the fox roared. "He doesn't do anything but bark out orders."

"I'm sorry," Beckett diverted his attention. "Did you say where the raid was?"

"I didn't say-----"

"Pardon me, sir." It was Prince Callum. "I need these two right away." He motioned for the sombels to follow him and said to the fox. "We will see you at the banquet."

The three travelers scooted away quickly. As soon as they were a safe distance away, Tegan exclaimed to the prince, "Where have you been?!"

"Back at the field," the prince replied.

"But you left us!" Tegan wailed. "Alone!!"

"I needed to ask around about Reginald. Besides, you have Beckett to keep you company," he responded.

"Tegan's right. We're only here in this town because of your father. She is the one we need to look after. She is the messenger," Beckett said. "From now on, we stay together."

111

The prince hesitated, confused by the outburst. He was unwilling to deviate from the topic, so instead, the prince answered, "Fine, fine." He continued, "As I was saying, I spoke with one of the villagers and she pointed out the caravan coming into town. Reginald rode in on one of the carts, so I know he is here somewhere."

"I think we saw him," Beckett said.

"Yes, we saw him go inside the barn with a few of the drivers," said Tegan.

"I just passed by the door and there was no one inside," the prince said. "They must have left. Guess we'll just have to catch up with Reginald at the banquet."

"When does that start?" Tegan asked.

"Yeah, I'm hungry," Beckett blurted out.

"One villager told me that the tradition is to wait until sunset," said the prince.

"Soon then," Tegan mused. "Very soon."

CHAPTER 17

T egan, Beckett, and Prince Callum sat off to the side of the meadow, under a scraggly, little oak tree. Listening to laughter and watching the villagers chat with each other, the ale flowed as freely as the tales of raids down the river...told by the drivers and hearsay alike. Multiple rows of exquisitely decorated tables were centered in between the oak trees. Villagers feasted on fruit, stews, and breads while bonfires blazed on either side of the celebration.

The last of the sun settled behind the distant mountains. Tegan watched as the day came to an end and the evening began. From their position, the three scanned the festivities to locate Reginald among the carousing villagers.

"What are they celebrating anyway?" Beckett asked the prince.

'From what I've heard, this banquet is not just to commemorate the return of Reginald," he replied. "It is a celebration to remember the victory at Braddock Hall."

Tegan perked up, "What happened at Braddock Hall?"

Prince Callum stood up and the sombels followed suit. "This is a sticky situation," he replied. "The fight broke out between the Redlan fox tribe and the rats of Voldire." The prince drew in a deep breath and slowly let out a giant breath of air. "The problem is .... during those times, our clan sided with the rats."

"What?!" Tegan and Beckett exclaimed simultaneously.

The prince quieted the two and continued, "It was strictly a business decision back then. I mean, we are talking hundreds of years ago. The rats had resources we needed, so we dictated an agreement for trade. The Redlan fox clan wanted in on the transaction but the rats would not budge. War ensued and within a week, the foxes won."

"Wow, I had no idea," Tegan said.

Beckett spoke up, "Where does your clan stand now?"

"We no longer side with either the rats or the Redlan tribe. In the past, we have negotiated a basic trade with these foxes when deemed necessary for our clan's survival. But that's only been a couple of times and many years ago. My father simply does not trust them."

Tegan opened her mouth to say something, but a fox dressed in a tunic walked up to the prince and said, "We have a place set up for you and your friends."

"We are grateful; however, we only need to speak with Reginald for a moment. Then we are on our way," Prince Callum replied.

Undeterred, the fox said, "You may speak with him when he is ready. For now, come with me."

The prince looked at Tegan and Beckett, and then back at the fox. The creature's white tunic contrasted against its reddish-brown fur; and the sharp teeth and black eyes absolutely frightened Tegan. The fox led the three down to the center of the celebration, around a few tables and a blazing fire.

"There," the guide said. "Sit there until we come get you."

Prince Callum, Tegan, and Beckett took a seat at a wooden table directly in front of a makeshift stage. Tables with villagers were all around them, on both sides and behind them. There was nowhere to hide, and they all felt uneasy in the front. Beckett grabbed the bowls of stew in front of him and ate as fast as he could. The other two nibbled on the fruit offered by a smaller fox as she passed by their table on the way to another table.

A loud sound of pounding drums interrupted the merriment. Beside the stage, several foxes beat simple drums in a rhythmic melody. Slow, then fast, fast, faster! The sound was almost a doldrum in their ears, but then it stopped as quickly as it started. The robed fox sauntered onto the stage and motioned to his aid with a snap. The aid pulled the purple tufted chair, originally from the wagon, and centered the piece of artisan furniture on the stage. Reginald sat down on the chair and then quieted the attendees by motioning with his paws.

"His majesty's throne, I knew it!" Beckett whispered loudly.

"Friends," Reginald started as if delivering a life changing monologue. "Here we are, once again, gathered to commemorate the victory of Braddock Hall. We gather to remember the brave foxes within our tribe that so courageously fought against those evil rats. We gather to remember the brave foxes that fell at the paws of those dirty rats."

The robed fox stood up and dramatically walked around his purple chair, making eye contact with the prince. The villagers cheered. "Some might say that we were on the wrong side of the war....that we should *not* have fought at all...that we should have given in...." He waited and the crowd booed. "But the Redlan tribe is a resilient group...we are a clever group, and we are a victorious band of foxes!" The villagers, again, howled and banged their cups on the tables in agreement with their leader.

Reginald waited until the commotion died down before he started again. "Did you know that the rats of Voldire did not act alone?" Grumbling ensued among the audience members. "It is true. The pixie clan sided with our enemy!!!" He looked right at the prince, "Isn't that right?"

The crowd shouted boos as Prince Callum squirmed in his seat. "Ah, but do not worry my friends. We have made up and are now friends again." Reginald laughed fiendishly before sitting back down. He waved to a fox holding a pitcher and pointed to the prince's table. "Come, let us drink to our new friendship and to our victory!" The crowd roared with excitement and villagers began talking and laughing again, filling their cups with ale.

The fox carrying the pitcher came down to the prince's table and poured three drinks for the travelers. "Drink," he commanded.

The prince and the sombels hesitated. So the fox stated again, "You must drink this."

The sombels followed orders and took a sip each. The ale was on the bitter side but overall tasty. The fox looked at Prince Callum and said, "If you want an audience with Reginald, you must drink this to show your support."

The prince clasped the cup with his left hand and gulped down the entire amount of liquid while keeping his eyes fixed on the fox. Then he slammed the empty cup down on the table and said, "Now, I want to speak with Reginald."

The fox smiled and walked away. Both Tegan and Beckett took a few more sips and watched the fox amble over to Reginald and whisper something in the leader's ear. As the merriment continued, the sombels grew restless. Each of them wondered, who is this Reginald? And when would the prince finally get the chance to speak with him?

The bonfires began smoldering and the noise quieted down. Tegan watched as villagers collected their belongings and cleaned up the tables. A fox came over to where the group sat and said, "Follow me, Reginald is ready to see you now."

The travelers followed the fox through the dissipating crowd to the barn. He motioned for them to sit on several chairs just inside the wooden door. "Stay here and Reginald will be with you soon," the fox stated.

Once the prince and the sombels were alone, Tegan asked, "Who is Reginald? Is he their king or something?"

"I'm guessing he is," the prince replied. "But the last contact we had with him was almost fifty years ago. At that time, he served as the main council for the Redlan leader."

"Looks like he got promoted," Beckett said dryly.

"Yeah, I wonder what happened to...." The prince mumbled to himself.

Suddenly, the door flew open and Reginald himself stood in the entryway. His chest puffed up as his dark blue robe was cinched tightly around him. He smiled as he walked into the barn, "Well, well, well...if it isn't royalty we have amongst us." Reginald's two sidekicks (and bodyguards) sauntered in and closed the door behind them. One of the foxes lit a few candles and placed them on a small table nearby for light.

"To what do we owe the honor of your presence? A royal pixie from Fellnore?" the robed fox asked.

"We are in need of a scout," Prince Callum said, determined to keep this discussion strictly business. "Can you recommend a scout that knows Old Padley?"

"A scout, huh?" Reginald mused. "Why Old Padley, specifically?"

"We have business down there."

"So it has nothing to do with a new rat camp and prisoner then?" Reginald was enjoying this.

The prince didn't back down, "As a matter of fact, it has everything to do with that!"

Realizing his temper was misplaced, he regained his composure and began again. "My father, King Fallon, sent me here to ask about a scout in good faith, knowing the sticky history between our clans. If you do not have this resource, I will beg your pardon and leave this instant so as not to waste your time anymore."

The prince stood up but one of Reginald's bodyguards pushed him back down into his chair.

"I didn't say you could go," said Reginald. "Now, if we have this so-called resource you want, what do I get in return?"

"I am willing to pay silver to the scout. I only need a reference—"

"Silver to the scout?!!" the robed fox roared with laughter. "Oh, but what about me?!" He feigned sadness and put his paw over his forehead dramatically. Then he said gravely, "You walk into my village and want my help but do not offer anything in return?" He paused before saying, "Negotiations are now over. You must stay here."

"I am willing to negotiate on behalf of my father," the prince retorted.

"Your father!" the fox laughed. "The last time we saw your father, he helped the rats...the *rats*....against us!"

"And that was simply business. We set up trade with the rats already. You knew that, but still invaded anyway," the prince said firmly.

Silence ensued between the two.

"Let us talk about trade then," Prince Callum started. "If you draft a contract between the Redlan tribe and the pixie tribe to establish trade again, I will personally ensure that my father considers the partnership. I give you my word."

The fox scratched his chin, "Hmmm, I *would* like to see more food supplies, and maybe a little moonstone? Yessss," he hissed, "green moonstone."

"You know we don't trade for moonstone." The prince felt tingling in his feet and fingers.

"We will see about that." Reginald motioned to his bodyguards as he made his way to the door.

Prince Callum tried to stand up but could not move his legs. Both Tegan and Beckett were stationary as well. They panicked and strained to move their limbs.

"What...what did you do to us?" Beckett shouted. His mind was foggy but he managed to push out those words.

"Should we tie them up with rope?" one of the burly body-guards asked.

"No, they will be out in no time," Reginald responded. "Why bother?"

Tegan sat motionless with wide eyes. Her arms and legs felt lifeless, her thoughts darted all over the place. Was it the fruit? The bread? The ale? She looked at Beckett. He jerked and rocked in his chair, struggling to grasp his sword.

Reginald rested his paw on the door knob and turned to his guests, "So glad you came to visit us. Sleep well my friends." He opened the door and left, allowing the guards to lock up with the visitors incapacitated inside.

"What is going on?" Tegan slurred her words. She felt like she was inside a dream world where everything moves ridiculously slow.

It was at this point that Prince Callum lost his temper and growled under his breath, "You will pay for this! Wait and see, Reginald, you will pay for this indeed!"

"Something....in the food, the drink. We've been drugged. Was it in the ale?" Beckett asked. "I thought it tasted a little bitter and ...." His words dropped off. The sombel struggled again in the chair, even though he wasn't tied up. The side effect paralyzed his extremities and he looked like a ragdoll flailing in a rainstorm.

The prince relaxed his shoulders and stopped forcing his body to move. "Yes," he sighed. "The ale was poisoned. I've seen this before with some of our scouts." His words slowed to a mere crawl. "On remote quests, they came across ale contaminated with wild Pairilis. The herb can sour and cause temporary...." The prince passed out.

"Paralysis," Tegan finished his sentence. "Oh my head....." she moaned.

"Mine too," Beckett echoed. He kicked the prince's chair with his floppy feet.

The candles smoldered and thick traces of smoke rose from the burnt wicks. The smell found its way to Tegan's nose and she cringed.

"Why us?" she whispered out loud. "Why do they keep us?"

The room began spinning and her eyes drooped. So drowsy. So weary. Colors faded and the light extinguished. The last thing Tegan remembered was Beckett mumbling something about mushrooms.

Then in the blackness, she fell asleep.

CHAPTER 18

Scratching sounds came from the bottom of the door. It wasn't morning yet, but a dim light flashed under the opening, followed by silence. Tegan's eyes were still foggy and her head pounded from sleeping in a weird position. But she could definitely tell someone or *something* was outside trying to get in. More scratching and wiggling the latch on the door piqued her interest.

"Beckett!" she pushed him with her feet trying to wake him up. "Beckett! Someone's here!"

He groaned and struggled to open his eyes.

"Prince Callum!" Tegan whispered as loud as she could. "Wake up!"

The prince shook his head to try and shake off the grogginess he felt.

"There's someone outside," she muttered to her companions.

Beckett and the prince perked up their ears to listen. *Scratch, scratch, scratch, clink!*

The wooden door slowly creaked open just wide enough for Tegan to see the dark sky and the sliver of the moon outside.

"Who's there?" she asked.

"Shhhhh!" A voice broke through the darkness. "I mean no harm."

A figure slid into the room and held a small torch in front of its face. A petite fox wearing a brown cloak placed the torch in a holder on the wall. The slim fox pulled the hood off her head and her furry ears popped out. She held her finger in front of her mouth, motioning to the others to keep quiet.

"I am Kenna," she said softly. The small fox had dark auburn fur, silky and short, but with white markings on her paws and snout. Her black eyes flashed in the torch's flame, and her whiskers twitched as she spoke. "Follow me. I'll get you out of here."

Beckett, Tegan, and Prince Callum forced their legs to move and stood up. Still wobbly, Tegan leaned on Beckett while the prince held on to the door frame to steady himself.

"Now!" Kenna scurried out of the barn and the others limped behind her in the night.

The moonlight was the only illumination they had. Darkness covered the oaks and the small shops along the street. The group scrambled around the blacksmith shop and followed the street until they reached a store front with a square-shaped awning. There was no sound except the pounding of feet on the dirt as they ran.

Once they stopped under the awning, Kenna said, "Wait here." She pushed through the revolving door and disappeared inside the building. The three outside could hear the fox moving something heavy inside. After a few long minutes, she popped her head back out and said, "I'm ready, let's go."

"Wait," Beckett paused. "Who did you say you were?"

"My name is Kenna."

"But tell us why are you here," Prince Callum demanded.

Kenna smoothed down her fur and said, "You need a scout, right?"

"Yes, but......."

"You need a scout and, well, I need the money," she replied pragmatically. "Speaking of which, do you have the silver?"

The prince patted his bag, "I do, but how do we know we can trust you?"

"You don't," she stated. "But if you wait until morning and Reginald interrogates you, there's no guarantee he'll let you go."

The prince stared deep into the fox's eyes and then looked at Tegan and Beckett. They both nodded to the prince. "Alright," he said to Kenna. "Do you know a way to get into Old Padley without being seen?"

"I lived there for a while, before moving back here," she replied as she put her backpack on. "So, yes. Come on, let's talk about it on the road."

The four travelers grabbed their bags and followed Kenna out of the village. They kept silent as they passed through the dense forest littered with giant trees sprouting palm-like fronds. No one knew what to ask their new scout. Kenna walked in front of the group with steady steps and purposeful motions. Near an outcrop of ferns, Tegan stopped and pulled on Beckett's arm. There they stood long enough to watch the sun as it peeked over a hill in the distance; its rays illuminating the little patch of woods beneath it.

Kenna turned to the group, "Do you want to rest here?"

The prince and the sombels sat down on a long tree log that had fallen years ago. Kenna joined them on a toad stool. "We are almost to the creek," she said. "Once there, it's only a short distance to the river."

"I have a stop to make near the river," Prince Callum stated. "I want to check in with a friend."

He turned to Kenna and stated, "We were headed there before we became prisoners in your village."

"I do apologize for that," she replied. "We were not always so inhospitable."

Beckett had been studying Kenna. The way she talked seemed a bit course and gruff, her clothes appeared well worn and needed attention. He asked the question everyone was thinking, "How did you know we needed a scout?"

"I knew that was coming," she laughed a little and played with a blade of grass. "Do you remember the guards that accompanied Reginald last night?"

"The ones in the barn with us?"

Kenna nodded. "One of the guards is a dear cousin of mine. He came to our house last night and told us about your inquiry for a scout."

"Won't he be punished for helping us escape?"

"Reginald doesn't know we are related." She smiled and stood up, prompting the others to do the same.

Prince Callum took the lead this time as the travelers continued along their journey. Over rocky ground and around bushy shrubs, the group trekked throughout morning until they finally reached the creek and washed their faces in the cold water.

"We're making good time," Kenna remarked as she judged the position of the sun. "Now we just follow the creek until we reach the river. We should be there by dark."

The prince suddenly looked alarmed.

"What is it?" Tegan asked. In the silence, she froze and time stood still.

The prince put his finger over his lips to shush them and pointed to the trees across the creek. The branches bowed low trying to support the weight of several large, monster-like bird creatures. Their black, slick feathers and crusty, brown beaks looked terrifying from where the travelers stood. The beasts flapped their scraggly wings and shrieked at such a high pitch that Tegan covered her ears with her paws.

With one push, the three birds launched off the tree branches, swooped low, and flew towards the creek. The group panicked and darted into the woods, attempting to outrun the prehistoric-looking creatures. Overhead, the birds circled and squawked, flying closer and closer to the tree tops.

One beast tucked its wings behind it and dove down through the branches, barely missing Beckett. Prince Callum pulled out his bow and arrow and shot over and over again at the aggressive bird, which stood twice as high as the prince. He walked backwards while aiming the arrows at the attackers. One arrow and then another whooshed past the creature's head.

Then, the end of a bird's wing struck the prince's back, throwing him face down onto the ground. The blow knocked the bow out of his hands, a few feet away. Dazed, the prince sat up and turned around gradually. As he stood up and lunged for the bow, the bird landed in the area between the weapon and the pixie, blocking the prince from retrieving his weapon.

Two more birds swooped down and narrowly missed the fox and the sombels; Tegan and Kenna dove into a bush and Beckett rolled under a fallen rock. The enormous birds landed with a thump on the ground, their claws digging into the scrubby grass and soil. Turning their heads from side to side, the birds watched for movement, ready to pounce at any motion. The three beasts cackled in a low gurgling sound as they communicated with each other, their beaks opening and then closing as the gruesome sound echoed from their gullets.

From the bush, Tegan could see Beckett's face and front paws peeking out from under the boulder. He pushed his sword out and waved it around. The blade radiated the sun's rays and caught the eye of the nearest bird. The creature turned its head and squawked, raising its ugly claws to walk toward the boulder. Realizing the bird's intentions, Beckett backed into the crawl space and waited with his sword drawn, hidden from sight.

Kenna pulled out her dagger and nudged Tegan. The sombel reached for her sword and held it close to her chest. Her heart pounded and she felt dizzy, but somehow, she managed the courage to take a defensive stance.

Prince Callum stared down the beast in front of him. Its brown beak opened and lunged for the pixie; the prince rolled to his left side to avoid impact. The bird lifted its claw and stomped down just as the pixie scooted backwards. The prince managed to stand again, but felt a pain in his back, on his right wing. He drew his dagger anyway, ready to fight.

At the same time, Beckett was cornered under the boulder, his back against the rock. As soon as he saw the beast, Beckett jumped up and slashed at its giant beak. A bashing sound confirmed it was a solid hit and the bird stepped back in shock. It shook its head, screeched to the others, and lunged at the sombel. Beckett kneeled and thrust his sword upwards, slicing the underbelly of the beast, sending it howling and flying away.

Tegan ran toward her friend, bearing her sword. Kenna followed close behind. Both birds now stood with full attention on the prince.

Tegan hurried to Beckett, "Are you alright?" she asked.

He rubbed his shoulder with his paw, "Yes," he said in a low voice. "Just shaken up."

The sombels and Redlan fox could see the prince struggling with the two beasts. He danced around keeping his eyes on each of the birds, trying to stay out of the reach of their deadly claws and pointed beaks.

As the group ran toward the prince, one of the birds turned and faced the attackers. Tegan and Kenna raised their weapons, but Kenna, bold and fierce, stepped forward and swung at the creature in front of her. Her blade missed and hit the ground.

The great bird lunged at the two and raised its claw, grabbing Kenna with its scaly foot. The fox dropped her dagger and screamed in rage, not fear. Jolted into action, Tegan slashed violently at the creature's beak as it bobbed back and forth, jabbing at the sombel and slicing her wrist. The beastly bird leaned closer, opening its beak. Tegan swung again and made contact this time, causing the bird to jerk back. Her sword blade glowed white and quickly returned to its normal color.

Beckett crawled over to Prince Callum and sat next to him. He held up his sword to protect the prince against this prehistoric beast. The bird stepped closer with its beak open and raised its claw. As it opened its wing to attack, Beckett noticed movement in the sky above them. He raised his sword and the prince held up his dagger, but the beast's wing knocked the two across the forest opening, both losing their weapons in the attack.

The prince sat up again but Beckett groaned. His right shoulder damaged from a hard hit against a large rock, and pain shooting down his arm. Beckett held his arm close to his chest and tried to stand. Prince Callum helped him steady his feet, the two leaning on each other for support.

Suddenly, a loud screech pierced through the sky. The travelers looked up and witnessed a host of owls circling the area above them. Their wings spread impressively over the tree tops and their feathers glowed in the heavy sunlight. Each time the lead owl screeched, the others screeched in return, causing the creatures below to freeze, disabling their attacks.

"It's Lenah!" the prince shouted.

The noisy group of owls flew closer to the wooded area, just out of reach of the black birds. They screeched over and over again until the sound became a deafening resonance. Stunned, the attacking beasts froze, unable to move their legs, their wings, or their heads.

Kenna pushed against her captor's grip and wiggled free from the claw, dropping to the ground. Tegan helped her stand and both ran over to check on Beckett and Prince Callum. The group was dumbfounded. Not one of them had ever seen creatures like these stand motionless, paralyzed from a distinct sound. Seizing the moment, the group scattered to gather their lost weapons and ran deeper into the forest.

As they ran, fluttering in the leaves above them caused the travelers to slow down and turn around. A large white owl descended from the highest branch and landed gracefully on the forest floor.

It was Lenah. She flapped her wings and then tucked them behind her, shaking her feathers and twisting her head to speak to the prince.

"I see you are safe," she said.

"Oh Lenah, thank you for coming to help us!" Prince Callum replied.

Tegan was relieved to see the beautiful owl. "How did you know we were in trouble?" she asked.

The majestic bird replied, "I watched the prince from the mountain top and flew near for a closer look. The Hedfan raptors," she waved her feathery wing, "they were tracking you and your friends, so I asked my clan to help."

"What happened back there?" Beckett asked incredulously. "Why did those creatures freeze like that?"

"The owls can vocalize in a way that immobilizes the raptors," Prince Callum responded.

"Seriously?" Beckett responded.

"Yes," the prince laughed a bit. "It is a special screech, I guess you could say."

Lenah bowed her head in agreement and continued, "I trust you will continue your mission?"

"We are not far from the river. We'll stay under the forest's protection until we arrive at my friend's house for the night," the prince said.

"I am pleased," Lenah's gold eyes flashed at the prince. "Now, I will report to your father and let him know you are safe."

"Thank you again, for your loyalty and protection," Tegan and Kenna bowed their heads in gratitude to the owl. The bird opened her wings and launched into the air, flying through the tree tops and out of their sight.

Kenna leaned over to Tegan and said softly, "Your sword...I saw it light up."

"Yes, it was a gift. I am learning to use it, but the power is difficult to control." Tegan was shaken up and didn't feel like talking at the moment. She pulled her hood up and covered her head.

The travelers could still hear the screeching owls, but the noise gradually grew faint as they made their way under the protection of the trees and brushes, hiking parallel to the creek.

"We can still make it to my friend's place by nightfall. Agh," the prince winced. His wing was torn and he limped on his left leg.

"Are you able to walk?" Tegan asked.

"Yes, I believe I still have strength left," he replied. "And we need to keep moving."

Tegan felt warmth on her paw and looked down to see blood pooled near her wound. It wasn't a long gash, but a deep cut instead. She wrapped it with a section of her cloak and squeezed it gently to stop the bleeding, even though it felt so sore.

Beckett held his arm close to his chest and lumbered behind Tegan and Kenna. A cool wind blew along the path indicating the sun had almost set.

Near a large tree trunk blanketed in moss, Prince Callum paused, then pushed through the bramble to a clearing on the other side. He disappeared off the trail but quickly returned with weary excitement. Visibly in pain, he motioned for the others to follow him. Each one forced themselves through the opening in the vines and brush where the prince had gone before them.

And there it was, in the clearing, the river they were searching for.

CHAPTER 19

Littleton had been all but destroyed. The town on the south river bank (near Old Padley) lay in rubble and ash. A rogue group of rats had recently raided the village and destroyed huts from the inside out, removed cellar doors to get to stored food, and trampled fields of vegetables ready for harvest. The roads were blocked with wagon wheels, timber, kitchen items, bedding, small bits of clothes, and other debris from rats rummaging through household items. And even though smoke billowed from fires throughout the town, Milo believed that this was the best place for his regiment to set up camp. The rats were gone and wouldn't be back.

There were still a few stone buildings in Littleton that survived the attack and remained intact. Much of the army could sleep there. The officers had a harder time piecing together fabric for temporary roofing over smaller stone huts and smoldering clay ovens. But the remaining beds and kitchen pottery were more than enough for the officers in charge to survive the next week or two. Milo had seen much worse.

The evening sun put an odd light on the new military settlement. Soldiers hammered and sawed, setting up their barracks, an assigned cook heated the stew, and several blacksmiths sharpened the weapons they had on hand. This business made Milo feel at home.

Just across the river and up a few miles lay Old Padley. Milo, captain of the sombel army, decided on the Littleton proximity to keep tabs on the rats while waiting for the terms of surrender to be delivered to Greygor. In the meantime, they were far enough away from the rat camp to make a little noise without being heard or seen. Milo dispatched a different scouting party each day to spy on the enemy until the full army caught up to the new soldier camp. So far, there was little to report.

The rats spent a considerable amount of time arguing. Other than that, their soldiers managed to erect a sizeable throne for their rat leader out of loose stone and river rocks. The leader could be seen ordering his dwindling subjects around to find food or drink for his majesty. Milo laughed when he thought about that.

Under a particularly large canopy strapped between two trees sat a sombel shining and buffing a few daggers. That sombel was Arthur. He held a dingy cloth in his paw and rubbed the blades over and over until they were quite polished and smooth.

Arthur joined Milo and his camp because he refused to stay in Haven. He made the trek with Milo over the past few days to offer his help to the coalition in some way. With a son in the army and his daughter on a quest to deliver a contract, Arthur wanted to keep an eye on as much as he could from this distance.

"Here my old friend, drink this," Milo said as he ducked under the tarp and put a warm mug on a makeshift table.

"Thanks Milo, I needed this," Arthur smiled a little.

Milo sat down and inspected the polished daggers one by one. The two sombels had a long history together, so long in fact, that periods of silence were not awkward. Once childhood friends, then military companions in the same unit, Arthur and Milo had been through a lot together. But not every event had been dismal. One of Milo's daughters had married a son of Arthur's some time ago, a celebration that lasted three days! So, they were not only friends, but family as well.

"What can you tell me? Is there anything new?" Arthur asked as he laid down his work and sipped the cup of tea.

"Not really," Milo replied and stoked the embers on the fire. "The rats are still squabbling, but that will soon come to a halt."

"Why is that?"

"One of our scouts has seen the group of rats following Greygor from Homish. They are about a day's march from Old Padley."

"Are they armed?" Arthur asked.

"Very much so," Milo answered gravely.

"Then this will get a lot worse before it gets better," Arthur speculated.

Milo sighed. "I imagine the impending conflict between the rat group holding Lewis and Greygor's troops will be considerable. Major losses on both sides if they do not resolve the power struggle within the ranks."

"This struggle for control will lead to their downfall, you can count on it," Arthur said and tapped the table for emphasis.

A soldier peeked under the canopy and whispered to Milo, "Captain?"

Milo looked up and saw the sombel soldier in his dark tunic and belt.

"Captain," he said again. "We are ready."

"Good, go to the arms tent and I will meet you there," Milo instructed.

The captain dismissed himself from Arthur's shelter and met a small group of soldiers near the arms tent. He handed each one a dagger or a sword, and then instructed the sombels to camp near Old Padley.

"You are to get as close as you can without leaving the tree line. Stay in the forest, but keep a watchful eye out for any aggressive activity," said Milo. "Report to me first thing in the morning."

"Yes sir!" The group said in unison and headed north along a foot path. It only took moments before the soldiers disappeared among the shrubbery.

The sound of the river flowing rapidly over giant rocks soothed the travelers' minds. The gurgling and rushing of the water currents were a sure sign that they were at the right place to locate Prince Callum's friend. The group walked along the river bank, seeking any indication of forest inhabitants.

As they continued wandering around the low-lying trees and tall grasses, the travelers reached a clearing near the bank. Several huts had been noticeably pillaged; the roofs caved in and timber lying around on the ground. Tegan picked up a strip of wood, inspected it indifferently, and threw it back on the ground. Kenna kicked at the rocks on the shore.

Across the river, another two-story shack stood intact, but the front door was wide open. A thin trail of smoke emanated from a stone fire pit near the river's edge. Next door, a wooden shed revealed a completely empty storage space, as there were no goods or supplies stockpiled there. Tegan thought all of this odd.

At that moment, Kenna noticed movement inside the two-story building and told the prince.

"Look over there," she whispered to him.

Prince Callum squinted to observe signs of life inside the home. To him, the hut looked like the right place. But with all the property's destruction, he couldn't be sure. He whistled a short but high pitched, bird-like tune, and waited. As the whistle echoed across the river, a quiet, tranquil ambience surrounded the group as they listened for a response. It only took a minute or two before they heard a similar call in return. Someone was home, and Prince Callum had reached his destination.

A sombel cautiously looked out of the hut's open door and spotted the group across the river. With a brisk wave of his paw, the sombel motioned for the others to join him.

"We made it," the prince said. "That is our resting spot for the night."

A sigh of relief rippled throughout the circle of friends. Not only did they need the rest, but several needed their wounds bandaged. Plus, a good wash and a full belly would indeed benefit them all at this point.

Beckett perked up, "Then let's find a way across this river."

Each of the travelers searched for a shallow place in the river, or a series of huge rocks that could serve as a bridge to help them across. Beckett trotted back to the forest and found a small branch. He sized it up and then broke off the smaller twigs to make a smooth balancing stick for himself.

"Bring me that bit of wood," he said to the prince. "I have an idea."

Prince Callum looked around and spotted a flat piece of timber that had been slightly hollowed out and burned with embers to form a small flotation device. Beckett picked up the wood piece and placed it on the river bank. Tegan and Kenna scavenged the area for supplies, harvesting a long vine and a small V-shaped nail. The prince took the nail and used the handle of his sword to hammer the nail into the wood, jiggling it to make sure the nail would stay. Beckett threaded the vine through the opening of the nail and tied it securely in a knot. Tegan watched as the prince and Beckett moved the wooden float into position. It was small, but practical.

First, Prince Callum stepped onto a large boulder positioned on the edge of the river. He held the vine firmly in his hand and tugged lightly on it, causing the wooden float to wobble some. As the prince jumped from one large rock to another, near the middle of the river, the little raft followed behind him in the water.

To cross the last bit of open water, the prince used his balancing stick to measure the depth of the water. Fortunately, the water was not as deep as he thought, possibly up to his neck. But he didn't want to swim through it; the cold was setting in. So he stepped cautiously in the center of the float and used the balancing stick to push his way to the other side of the river, much like a paddleboard.

As the prince neared the shore, he leaped out onto the ground, turned around, and smiled in victory. The other three praised his success and immediately jumped on the first rock, then the second. The prince placed his balancing stick in the middle of the float and wrapped the vine around his hand in a loop. He leaned back and flung the vine like a lasso to the others.

Tegan caught the vine and reeled in the float like a true fisherman. With the stick in one paw and the vine in the other, she got on the float and gingerly pushed her way out into the river. But each time she put weight on her wounded paw, she cringed in pain. Tegan had to make it to the other side of the river though. She dug the stick into the river bottom and forged ahead.

Suddenly, the stick became wedged in something under the water. It simply would not budge. Tegan worked it back and forth, trying to free it from the stronghold. Back and forth, up and around, she furiously yanked the skinny branch. Tegan bent down to maneuver the stick, when it finally moved and knocked the sombel completely off balance. She toppled over the float and into the frigid water.

Bobbing up and down, she squealed in the icy water and paddled wildly. Kenna and Beckett gasped and shouted Tegan's name. Witnessing her fall, Prince Callum ran up and down his side of the river bank yelling to the sombel.

"Tegan!" the prince cried out.

"Swim! Swim!" Kenna yelled to her.

The cold water soaked Tegan to the core. She swam to the bank and crawled up on the shore. The balancing stick was long lost in the river now.

Shaking the moisture from her fur, Tegan noticed that the vine was still wrapped around her paw. In her frigid state, she managed to pull the float to shore and hand it off to the prince. Shivering from the cold, she dropped her wet messenger bag and soggy cloak and ran to the smoking fire pit for warmth. The prince threw the vine back to the two waiting on the rock.

"You're next," Beckett said to Kenna.

"But the stick....it is lost!" she replied.

Beckett helped the fox onto the float and secured the vine around her ankle. He shrugged and said, "Paddle."

Beckett shoved her out into the river as hard as he could. Kenna dipped her paws into the cold water on either side of the float and paddled as best as she could. The wooden raft wobbled with each stroke. Kenna, determined to make it to shore, kept moving her arms until she almost tipped over.

"Slow down!" Prince Callum shouted.

"Long strokes, Kenna!" Beckett instructed.

Kenna stopped abruptly and hesitated on the water. Her heart pounded wildly and she paused to catch her breath. Focusing on the river bank, the fox pushed her paws back into the icy water and followed Beckett's instructions, slow and steady, slow and steady.

The raft finally leveled out and she reached the shoreline without flipping over.

Kenna tossed the vine to the prince and removed her cloak. She caught up with Tegan at the fire pit and wrapped her dry garment around the shivering sombel. They huddled together for warmth as the prince threw the vine back to Beckett.

It was not long before the wooden float reached the shore with Beckett on top. He took a few steps and collapsed in pain. His arm buckled under him, supported by the other one. Prince Callum helped Beckett to his feet and wrapped the sombel's good arm around his shoulder for support.

As the prince and Beckett hobbled toward the hut, the sombel friend came out of the door and dashed over to help them. Tegan watched the meeting and sensed something familiar about the prince's friend. The three shuffled into the home as Tegan and Kenna followed close behind them.

The humming of voices resonated around the room. As Tegan and Kenna stepped into the doorway, Tegan felt the heat of a blazing fire burning in the back of the house. Beckett sat in a chair next to the fire pit with the prince tending to his arm. Both the prince and his friend turned around when the two approached the fire.

"Tegan?" the friend asked.

She recognized the prince's companion.

It was Pish; Arthur's councilman and fishing friend.

CHAPTER 20

"This is my old friend—"

"Pish?" Tegan finished the prince's sentence. The sombel nodded.

Pish explained to the prince. "I met with Arthur a few days ago; a council meeting in their home." He walked over and shook her paw. "I recognized Beckett as soon as I helped him inside."

Tegan couldn't help but feel relief. Finally, someone familiar after so much time on the road. Her eyes teared up and a lump formed in her throat. *"Why am I so emotional?"* She thought. Tegan cleared her throat and wiped the tears from her eyes. It had been a long day and she hadn't had time for feelings.

Prince Callum motioned for Kenna and Tegan to sit with them near the fire. His arm shook as he grimaced in pain.

Pish walked over to the sink and filled a large bowl with warm water. Then he carried it over to his friends and sat down.

Pish was a scrawny sombel; his long, blonde fur highlighted from long hours in the sun. His raft- building skills kept him outside most of the spring and the summer, except when seasonal rain storms forced him inside. Pish was also fond of fishing and made ends meet by selling his catch at a market in Haven.

Wearing blue overalls with wide pockets, Pish sported a straw hat with holes cut out for his ears. The red kerchief he normally wore around his neck had been dipped in water and placed on Beckett's arm.

"Will you put the kettle on?" the prince asked.

Pish nodded and filled a kettle with water. He placed the kettle handle on a rod and swung it over the fire burning in the fireplace. He opened a small hutch and rummaged around for a few cups.

Kenna approached Pish and introduced herself, "My name is Kenna." She offered her paw.

Pish wiped his paws off on his overalls and greeted her, "Pish." He looked at her suspiciously and thought, *A fox? Why was she with the prince? Didn't they know that a fox can never be trusted?*

"What is that smell?" Tegan asked crinkling her nose.

The prince soaked a cloth in the bowl's water and held it onto Tegan's wound. She winced as the pain singed deep into her wrist and paw.

"It's a touch of melaleuca oil. Pish added it to the water to clean your wound."

The prince wrapped her paw in a clean cloth and tied it securely.

"What about you, Prince Callum?" Tegan asked. "I know you are in pain too." She looked closely at his wing and saw it hanging, split nearly in half.

"I'm working on it," he replied. The prince had been so focused on helping his friends that he managed to keep the pain at bay. Now, as the night unfolded, the throbbing in his wing reached an unbearable level. It took every ounce of his strength to hold on without fainting.

The prince handed the bowl of water to Kenna. She held a clean cloth and examined Beckett's arm.

"Pish thinks it's a torn shoulder muscle," Beckett said.

"Oh no! Let's get it bandaged quickly then," Kenna replied.

She soaked the cloth in the medicated water, squeezed it out, and wrapped it around Beckett's shoulder and arm. Patting it in place, she put a warm blanket over him and turned to check on the kettle.

On the table against the side wall, Pish chopped up carrots and potatoes, and prepared the day's catch for his guests. He put all the food in a clay pot, added some milk, and placed it in the embers to cook slowly. While that simmered, Pish pulled out the tea leaves and handed them to Kenna. He thought, *What is a fox doing here? What is she* really *up to?* He couldn't help but be suspicious. Living on the river banks, Pish had seen the Redlan clan negotiate and then pillage and plunder; using the river as an escape route many times.

Kenna filled each cup with hot water and added the leaves, allowing them to steep for a few minutes before handing out the warm drinks.

"Kenna, bring my bag, please," Prince Callum requested in a weak voice.

The fox found the bag near the entrance where the prince had dropped it earlier. She handed it to him. The prince dug around and pulled out a small, gray pouch.

"What is that?" Tegan asked.

"It's for the pain," he replied. The prince appeared sluggish, burdened by the throbbing in his wing.

Tegan scowled at the prince's answer, so he clarified, "Saol mushrooms." The prince dropped the dried black fungi into his cup and stirred it. As he sipped the concoction, Tegan noticed his muscles relaxing and the tension in his face beginning to ease. The prince wrapped himself in a blanket and settled back into a chair, allowing the medicine to fully work through his weary body.

"Here," he handed the pouch to Kenna. "For Beckett and Tegan."

Kenna offered the sombels a pinch of the herbal remedy to add to their tea. Tegan stirred her drink and inhaled the medicinal aroma.

"Smells a bit like licorice," she mumbled out loud.

"Wait 'til you taste it," Prince Callum smiled feebly.

Tegan sipped her drink and immediately felt the warmth go down her throat and into her stomach. She smacked her lips a few times and scrunched her nose, "Yes, tastes like saffron and licorice."

"You get used to it after a while," he replied.

Beckett spoke up, "I don't care what it tastes like." He leaned forward and gulped down his tea, sighing, "as long as it numbs this pain..." He rubbed his shoulder and covered it again with the blanket.

"What are Saol mushrooms anyway?" Tegan asked, already feeling a bit of relief.

"They are a staple in every pixie's diet. We use them to maintain our health," Prince Callum offered. "However, I'm not sure if they will work on sombels though."

Tegan stretched out her paw and wiggled her fingers. Inspecting her wound under the bandage, she said, "It doesn't hurt as much, so it must be helping." She poured another cup of licorice-smelling tea for herself and drank it slowly.

Beckett felt the fire's heat on his shoulder and removed the blanket. Gently moving his arm, he lifted the cup towards Tegan for a refill.

"The tingling in my shoulder is easing," he added. "These mushrooms are amazing!"

"What else do you have in that bag of yours, Prince Callum?" Kenna asked suspiciously.

The prince seemed to be in his own world. He picked up one of the black mushrooms and rubbed it between his fingers. "Funny how one fungus can change the course of history."

"Why do you say that?" Tegan asked. Her mind had cleared and she could finally think about something other than of the pain in her paw.

The prince, suddenly aware of his surroundings, cleared his throat and asked, "Remember our conversation back in Chipping Farms? About the victory at Braddock Hall?"

Tegan forced her thoughts back to the ordeal she just came from. The pub, the dinner, the escape...so much had happened in Chipping Farms that she forgot about the history of the battle.

The small room felt intoxicatingly warm from the modest fire still burning in the fireplace. Each of the visitors wrapped themselves in colorful wool blankets and the smell of licorice and steaming vegetables wafted in the air. The group rested mostly on pillows and one on a chair; they were weary, but in surprisingly good spirits.

"I remember the pixies sided with the rats of Voldire," Beckett said flatly. "You said that."

"We sided with the rats because of a trade agreement," Prince Callum clarified.

"But what does that have to do with the Saol mushroom?" asked Tegan playing with her bandage.

"That agreement was over *this* mushroom, right here." The prince dropped the fungus into his cup and straightened his blanket.

"What do the rats have to do with the fungi?" asked Beckett.

The prince sipped his tea and continued, "The rats originally lived in Voldire, which is a volcanic plain, and the Saol mushrooms grew wild and plentiful there. We pixies, on the other hand, had only a few fungi forested from a quest there a long time ago. The pixie clan managed to cultivate those spores in various greenhouses along the river and grew a modest crop. Once the summer came and the plants had matured, gardeners harvested the mushrooms and spent the next few weeks preserving them.

But one year, in the fall, the soldiers went to war... across the ocean in the Land of Orga Plum. As the battle wore on, the supplies began to dwindle. They ended up exhausting their entire mushroom crop...just in the first half of the war! Well, there was simply no time to replenish the harvest in time to save our soldiers still fighting on the battlefield.

So the leaders did what they thought was best. When the pixies realized that the rats lived on the same land as the Saol mushrooms, they struck a trade agreement with the rats for the medicinal fungus."

"For how much?" Tegan asked.

"I don't know," Prince Callum answered. "But it was enough to pique the interest of the Redlan clan."

"Why did the fox clan pick a fight?" Tegan asked, glancing at Kenna.

"The supply chain stretched through the Redlan's territory and those foxes noticed our interactions with the rats. Word got out that there was a lot of money exchanging hands, and the foxes wanted a piece of the business. However, we needed the mushrooms to aid our soldiers in war. We just didn't realize the repercussions of our actions."

"And now?" Kenna asked curtly. She had been listening intently.

"And now, we have our own mushroom gardens with plenty preserved in storage," the prince replied.

"No, I mean...."

"I know what you mean," Prince Callum said in a more serious tone. "The rats? Well, we consider the rats of Voldire a despicable tribe. And their callous disregard for the Compromise Treaty is proof that they can never be trusted."

"And the Redlan foxes?" Kenna asked solemnly.

"My father knows more about them than I do," he replied. "But when I was younger, I remember visiting the clan once while my father was on a business quest. The councilman of the Redlan clan hosted us in his home with his family. He was very agreeable. Not what we expected from the fox clan."

"Why is that?" Tegan asked.

"Foxes are....well...," the prince glanced at Kenna, "Foxes have the reputation of being sneaky and compromising...and simply underhanded...."

"Do you remember anything else about the family?" Kenna asked quickly.

The prince paused for a moment. "I only remember the family we stayed with because I played ball with the son, who was about my age. His mother made a delicious meal and spoiled us afterwards with huckleberry ice cream."

The prince remained inside those memories momentarily. "We stayed up late because my father and the councilman talked politics all night. We were just kids...we made tent forts in the kitchen and slept in blankets on the floor at night."

He stopped for a while to finish his tea. "Funny how certain memories just stay with you. The smell of the kitchen, the feel of the blanket, the mother's pink dress...oh!" He stopped and sat up in the chair. "The mother was expecting! I remember her singing about a baby under her breath."

Kenna smiled.

Tegan noticed.

"Kenna, what do you know about this?" Tegan asked.

"That family you speak of is mine," Kenna said confidently. The room suddenly got quiet as everyone turned their attention to the small fox in front of them. "My father was the council member. I remember him talking about the king of the pixies visiting him from time to time," she paused. "And I am the baby," Kenna's face turned somber. "Father was the leader's accountant at the time. He kept up with Edwin's accounts, including all overseas trading. I remember him talking about his business dealings at the dinner table some nights."

"Edwin! *That* was the leader's name!" Prince Callum blurted out.

"My father served him most of his life, he was that dedicated. And Edwin was a strong leader. He had many followers because of his political and military intellect," Kenna stated.

"So what happened then?" Beckett asked. "Why is Reginald in charge now?"

"There was a coup," Pish interjected.

"Yes, you are correct," Kenna looked over at Pish and replied. "The old saying, 'you can't please everyone,' is true. Reginald was originally Edwin's lead advisor. He had a few politically powerful followers that wanted total control over some land on the east side of the river."

"Basically, they disagreed with how it was being used," Pish said. "Reginald had family connections there and didn't like what was going on."

"What *was* going on?" Tegan was intrigued.

"Edwin was cultivating the land so the clan could relocate. They were too close to the rats of Voldire and wanted to move," Kenna said. "And Reginald already had family there conducting business."

"And by 'business,' she means pillaging other tribes," Pish said. "The land was their home base for their operations. Pillage, plunder, then sell what they stole."

"Sounds like what we saw at Chipping Farms," Tegan mumbled. She observed Beckett itching to ask another question.

"How do you know so much about this, Pish?" Beckett asked. "I heard about it from one of the scouts Milo sent out awhile back. He just returned from a mission and spoke freely in the pub after a few drinks...all about the pillaging going on in the east corridor."

"It is true," Kenna said. "For a while, after the uprising, we sought refuge in Old Padley, which is why I know the area so well. My family only moved back to Chipping Farms after some time had passed. But the fallout from Edwin's regime has never returned to normal."

"Why do you still live there? I mean, you returned to a village run by a...by a megalomaniac!" Beckett exclaimed.

"Work, that's why," Kenna said grimly. "We need the jobs there."

"But your cousin is a bodyguard for Reginald!" Beckett said incredulously. "How can he protect a lunatic like that?!"

"It is not as it seems," Kenna replied coarsely.

"Oh, it looks like protection all right!" Beckett muttered.

"It's complicated," she looked around the room. All eyes were fixed on her. "My cousin is planning something."

"Another coup?" Pish asked flippantly.

"No—" Kenna responded.

"It's revenge, isn't it?" the prince asked.

Kenna was speechless. Before judging if her new associates were trustworthy or not, she blurted out, "Yes, revenge."

CHAPTER 21

Tegan needed to think things through, clear her head. She walked over to the fireplace and pulled out the clay pot to inspect the meal inside. Sticking a fork into the soft potatoes, she felt that dinner was finally ready, and needed something in her stomach immediately. Tegan motioned to Pish and filled several bowls with the steaming vegetables and fish. She found two large rolls of bread on the table and sliced them up for her friends. As she prepared the bread, her eyes wandered to the window over the sink where something caught her attention. Just out back, remnants of a shed barely stood upright. Tegan noticed planks of wood missing from the side and the roof of the little shed, the lawn littered with various wooden debris and pieces of rope.

"Did something happen outside?" Tegan asked Pish. "It looks like a strong wind came through and damaged your shed. Have there been any storms recently?"

"No, my dear. No storms," he said quietly. "I was overrun, robbed actually."

"Robbed?!" Tegan gasped.

All the others turned around to hear the conversation.

"Who was robbed?" Beckett asked from across the room.

Pish sighed, "Earlier this morning, I was sitting outside by that firepit." He pointed through the window but it was too dark for the others to see. "I cooked fish on the firepit, like I always do, when I heard rustling in the hedges." Pish handed out the bowls and bread to his guests. "Turns out it was a couple of rats."

"Rats?!" Beckett exclaimed. "The rats that captured Uncle Lewis?!" Tegan asked incredulously.

"The same," Pish responded. "I was waiting for the right time to tell you."

"Is my uncle safe? How did he look?" Tegan heard panic in her voice for the first time in days.

"Don't worry, child. He was safe. The rats had him secured in a cage. He appeared healthy but obviously fatigued," Pish paused. "Then more rats rushed in and tied me to a tree near the river bank. I couldn't do anything to help Lewis. I just looked at him...looked into his eyes. He seemed to know though, that I was helpless....but that somehow, I would get free and send word that he crossed through this area."

Tegan couldn't believe that she had just missed her uncle. She didn't want to consider all the circumstances he had endured, so she reeled in her imagination. Uncle Lewis was in danger, that was for sure. But now was not the time to dwell on the possible brutalities by the black rats. She had to shift her focus.

"So, uh, what happened to the shed then?" Tegan asked.

"Soldiers ran inside and grabbed a couple of the rafts I made. That's why there's damage to the side of the shed and the section of the roof that hangs over the door," said Pish.

"Did they take anything else?" asked Beckett.

"Not that I know of," Pish replied. "They were in such a hurry. One raft and then another, and then off into the river. It took me over an hour to free myself from the ropes. Luckily, a sombel who lives nearby came over to buy fish and cut the ropes for me."

"It sounds like we're only a day's journey behind them," Prince Callum thought out loud.

Tegan had so many questions. Her uncle just passed through here and she was only hours away. What were they waiting for? What should they do next? Before she could ask those questions, Pish spoke up.

"Do you have a plan?" Pish asked the prince.

"Honestly?" the prince asked and shook his head. "No."

Tegan's eyes widened. *There's no plan? So I am to deliver the terms of surrender to a band of bloodthirsty rats armed only with a mysterious sword and some green gems?! They will capture me for sure...I might even be killed!!!* Her heart pounded wildly. Her thoughts scattered. Then, her uncle's face crept into her mind along with her father's words about the prophecy. Her only solace lay with a new sense of duty and the fulfillment of the prophecy. To rescue her uncle meant that the quest had to be completed. She was afraid of the future, but willing to perform the task given to her.

Prince Callum noticed Tegan's anxiety. "Tegan, we will come up with a solid plan. That is why we hired Kenna...to sneak us in and deliver those terms as safely as possible."

"You hired a <u>fox</u> to get you into the encampment without being seen?" Pish asked the prince. "Do you expect her to keep her end of the deal?"

"Sir," Kenna spoke up before the prince had a chance to say anything. "I realize that you do not trust our fox clan. I get it. We are sneaky, cunning, and untrustworthy, right?"

Pish remained quiet.

"I am the daughter of a councilman to the previous king. I don't care if you trust me or not. But I speak the truth now. The money promised to me for this quest will be used for a special mission back home. A mission that will remove Reginald from office and thrust Edwin back to his leadership role. My father has promised it."

Silence ensued.

"Where is your father now?" the prince asked.

"He is in hiding," she answered.

"Where?" Prince Callum pushed.

"It is not your concern," she replied sharply.

"It is now," the prince said flatly. "You said your family moved back to Chipping Farms after Reginald's power stabilized. So where is he hiding?"

Kenna looked from face to face, all staring at her. She was resolute in her standing; it was not their concern. This job provided the finances needed to operate a proper rebellion. She weighed her options. *If I lie about father's hiding place, I risk losing this job and the silver,* she thought.

"He's at the Boar's Nest, in the back room," she relented, deciding truth over lies would secure this employment further. Who knows? Maybe there will be follow up chances to make extra money? "There's only one entrance to that area, and it is hidden behind a cupboard."

The prince ruminated on that information for some time. As the others finished their meals and stacked their dirty bowls, Prince Callum pictured Reginald in his blue robe again, prancing around the stage, shouting orders to his minions. That robed fox was clearly delusional. And why would his father send him to Chipping Farms knowing this? Maybe the pixie king was unaware of the transition of power?

"Kenna," the prince said, "what happened immediately after the coup? Was Reginald always this crazy?"

"No, Reginald began as a runner and scout for King Edwin. He learned very early on how to get invaluable information from his contacts and deliver those reports to the king. He was charming, cunning, and charismatic. So, after a few years, he earned the king's trust and eventually climbed the ranks to become the crown's main council," Kenna stated.

"He was legitimate?" the prince asked.

"For a while," Kenna replied. "But then something happened...I'm not sure what...that pushed Reginald over the edge, mentally, that is. He spent more and more time with the other council members crafting schemes for the Redlan clan...plans to explore and to plunder. And when Edwin found out, he banned Reginald from the council and from Chipping Farms altogether.'

'But it didn't matter at that point. Reginald had convinced a group of foxes that his plans would put money in their pockets, and so they backed him. They marched, swords in paw, and overran Edwin's bodyguards and a handful of soldiers. Reginald's forces caught Edwin off guard and removed the king from his throne.'

'From that moment on, Reginald banned Edwin's followers from the village. We lost our homes...our livelihoods. At one point, those that remained in the village were seized by Reginald's soldiers and compelled to participate in raids on other towns. So, we moved to Old Padley with a few other families. We needed the time to put our minds together and figure out what to do next." Kenna said.

The group sat quietly.

Prince Callum was in his own world. He knew that it had been a few years since a representative from the Redland clan attended any of the national conferences. Those meetings were crucial to conduct peace negotiations and maintain proper business dealings. Now the prince understood why the Redlans had been absent for so long. Surely his father must have known Reginald before the takeover, as a rational councilman, not a power-hungry tyrant, and that's why he suggested his son meet with him. With all this new information, the prince decided to get word back to his father about this uprising. But he had more questions.

"When did this insurgence take place?" the prince asked.

"About nine months ago," Kenna replied and pulled on her tunic. Talking about this event made Kenna angry and distressed, all at the same time. Reginald turned into the biggest traitor in the history of the Redlan clan, and destroyed so many families in the process of securing his top position. And then, she had a thought. *Maybe this job, right now, was bigger than just a scouting mission...*

"When did you move back to Chipping Farms?" Tegan asked.

Kenna returned her attention to those in the room around her. "My family and I have been back for about two months now," she said. "The rest of the families stayed in Old Padley."

"I gather you've figured out a way to overthrow Reginald then?" Prince Callum asked.

"The silver you promised will go a long way in securing protection for Edwin and his clan," Kenna said stoically. "But as far as tangible plans go, I'm waiting on word from my contacts in Old Padley."

"That sounds complicated....why the loyalty?" asked Tegan.

"By our standards, Edwin is a sensible leader—one with good judgment. While he does have his vices, Edwin does not believe in taking advantage of others......no pillaging, no plundering. My family supports him because of this and because of the generous way he treats his followers," Kenna stated. She took a deep breath and let it out slowly. "And my father WILL return to his position when Edwin is back on the throne."

"Do the families in Old Padley know about the rats setting up camp there? On the river bank?" asked the prince.

"They are aware, yes," Kenna said. "When it first happened, several foxes heard loud noises on the bank and sent scouts to investigate."

"And?" Tegan asked.

"And they watched the rats scurry around while the leader shouted orders at them," Kenna laughed. "From what I know, the rats stayed and built a temporary shelter and a ridiculous throne for their leader. My contact called it 'utter chaos'."

"How do you know all this?" asked Beckett. "You have been with us the whole time."

Kenna yawned and rubbed her face. The fatigue had set in and she was ready for bed. "Remember the banquet with Reginald? The group of soldiers who came back with carts of supplies?" Kenna asked sleepily. "Well, my cousin, the bodyguard, was on that raid with Reginald. They snuck into a town just south of Old Padley and raided it. But as they rode back with the stolen goods, my cousin secretly met with an informant near the edge of the village. When he returned to Chipping Farms, my cousin shared what he learned with my father and me."

Kenna was spent. She crawled closer to the fire, curled up with a blanket and a few pillows, and fell deep asleep. The other travelers with heavy eyes rooted around until they got comfortable, falling asleep quickly under the snug roof and warm atmosphere of the tiny dwelling.

The only one still awake was Prince Callum. He sat for a while contemplating the uprising and overthrow of Edwin's throne. Then his thoughts centered on the quest, the journey to deliver the terms of surrender to the rats. It wouldn't be long now, and he hoped Tegan was ready.

CHAPTER 22

Tegan tossed and turned during the night. She could hear faint drops of rain as her body restlessly struggled to sleep. Her mind drifted to Haven and her family there, the green meadows, the firelights at night. Then she pictured King Fallon and her father, haloed by a greenish glow. As she dreamed, Tegan questioned herself. *Where was she? Why was she thinking about the pixie king and her father?*

The dream sequence quickly changed to a heavy fog. An object in the sky flew closer and closer. A silvery gray dragon with glowing green eyes swooped down and landed in front of her. It puffed smoke from his nose and folded his wings behind his arms. Tegan squinted her eyes to focus on the beast before her. *Tanwyn? Is that you?* The dragon opened its mouth and Tegan instinctively ducked, preparing for a deadly breath of fire. Instead, the dragon spoke as spirals of smoke trailed from his nose, "the green moonstone. You must learn to use the moonstone."

Tegan woke to the sounds of sawing outside. The methodic rhythm of metal slicing through wood brought back memories for the sombel. She rubbed her eyes and looked out the window. It had rained during the night and everything was wet from a seasonal shower.

The sun peeked through the trees so she could see the extent of the rats' destruction outside. The ground was littered with scraps of wood, tree branches and leaves, ropes, and muddy footprints by the river bank. The firepit had been dismantled with blackened firewood and stones moved about. Thick ropes lay at the base of a birch tree near the pit, just as Pish had described.

Tegan added a few logs to the fire inside and stoked it until the embers burned hot. Then she placed a kettle of water over the embers to brew morning tea. She watched as the others continued sleeping under their blankets in the shadows of the dawn. In the moment, Tegan sat with her thoughts, quietly meditating on the dream she had. She needed to learn more about the gem stone....its strengths, its weaknesses...and how to wield its power.

As steam rose from the kettle, Tegan removed the pot from the fire and poured two cups of tea. She quietly opened the door and stepped outside to find the source of the cutting noises.

Pish stood near the riverbank with several planks of wood and a pile of dried-up vines nearby. He continued sawing through wood pieces until he shaped one end of a floating structure and tied the pieces together with a vine. He stood up, placed his paws on his hips, and stretched his back.

"Morning, sir," Tegan said softly so as not to startle him. "I brought you some tea."

Pish turned around and smiled, "Good morning, dear." He took the mug and cupped it in both paws, smelling the contents within. "Thank you for this. I've been up for a while, but didn't want to wake anyone by puttering around the room for tea." He chuckled gently.

Tegan waited a few minutes before asking Pish about his construction, "What are you building?"

"A raft," he said. "You will need to travel quickly down the river to reach Old Padley." Pish stopped to wipe his face with a kerchief. "I started working on this raft before the rats tore everything up.

It wasn't completed, so they didn't take it. I had to borrow wood from the shed over there to secure the float. It might be a rough ride."

"Why is that?" she asked.

"It rained last night and the river is high," he said. "See the bank over there?" He pointed to a spot where the group crossed last night. "The largest stone is now partially covered by the river. It will take some time for the river's swelling to wane."

"Will it be safe for travel?" Tegan asked. The thought of raging water, and who knows what else that might live in the river, seized her attention.

"Time will tell," Pish replied. "Let's see how it looks in a few hours." He handed her his empty cup and continued working on the raft.

Greygor grabbed his war vest, the one with thorns adorning both the front and the back of the garment, and put it on. This was it; he would subdue this mutiny once and for all. Lewis was *his* prisoner and *his* informant to find that tunnel entrance. He would get that green moonstone one way or another.

He pointed to the trebuchet and the wagon with swords in it. "Fill that wagon with all your weapons and bring it. The trebuchet too. We are going to war!"

The rats scurried around, jumping over each other in a frenzy. They gathered around the trebuchet and flung ropes over the structure so it could be pulled, while other rats pushed. They heaved over and over again until the heavy structure moved a bit on its primitive wheels. More rats joined the others to push the trebuchet in the direction of their next military move...to squash the resistance.

"Sir," a high officer approached Greygor. "Why are we moving the trebuchet??" He pointed to the slowly moving structure propelled by foot soldiers. "This is a simple matter of suppressing a small group of miscreants. Shouldn't we preserve our weapons...our soldiers...for a bigger conflict?"

"Ha!" Greygor shouted. "You have no idea what I am up against." He turned around with his arms in the air, like he was showing off his war vest. "I am not only relocating our camp; I am preparing for the procurement of green moonstone."

"But—"

"Load the weapons!" Greygor interrupted. "And you..." he pointed to the officer. "*You* are responsible for the wagon." The officer stood motionless, processing the command.

"Now, go!" the rat king ordered.

The rat officer raced off, looking over his shoulder at the king. He gathered the rats and directed them to load all the daggers and swords into the wagon. Watching as they deposited their forged weapons, the officer rounded up soldiers to both push and pull the vehicle as Greygor ordered.

All night, the rats worked furiously to gather their encampment belongings: cooking utensils, forging items, plates and cups, clothing, and other materials. Indeed, this was a major relocation strategy and Greygor miscalculated how much they had to transport.

The rat king jumped up on the lead cart and settled back into his seat. He held a long walking stick that he directed with and shouted orders to his troops. Several rats pushed the cart from behind to get it started. Once the cart started rolling, they picked up the ropes in front and pulled the wagon slowly across the sticky mud of the wetlands.

"North!" Greygor shouted and pointed his stick in the precise direction.

The soldiers pulled and shoved the structures across a flat swamp of mud and short grasses. The rain had passed through hours ago, but the humidity and morning dew captured the moisture and kept it from drying out in the morning sun.

The carts pressed through a hazy fog and barely dodged one of the tallest trees in the swamp. But as the trebuchet passed underneath, the tip of the arm with the rope became entangled in the branch of that tree. The rats continued pushing the machine until it started to tip over.

"Stop!" A rat soldier shouted.

The trebuchet rocked back and forth until it finally came to a standstill. The rats waited for a direct command. Taking matters into his own paws, the rat soldier scrambled up the machine and pulled on the ropes connecting the arm to the pulley. The snag did not budge.

"You there!" the soldier pointed down to another. "Up the tree!"

The rat hastily climbed the tree and tiptoed across the branch. He inspected the jumbled rope twisted up in the leaves and small offshoots of the branch. He tugged on the twigs and offshoots before deciding to gnaw through them with his ghastly yellow teeth. Once the underbrush of the branch was cleared, the rope finally pulled free. The trebuchet could move unrestricted again.

Hundreds of rats made their way over the wetlands, heading toward Old Padley...the mid-morning fog slowly burning off and giving way to a brighter and warmer sky. As the rat soldiers marched, they grumbled amongst themselves. Their thirst for battle and for blood seemingly insatiable.

One of the soldiers near the back of the troop nudged a second rat with the end of his blade, "Oi! You ready for this?"

"Aye," the second rat responded and pushed the soldier back with his shoulder.

"You think 'ol Greygor will squeeze the right information from the prisoner?"

"He'd better! Or I will do it for him..."

"With the end of this here, blade? Ha!!" The two laughed boisterously as they clinked their swords together in mock battle.

"I WANT TO FIGHT!!!" the first one roared and beat his chest.

"Yes!! When can we fight?!!"

"Captain says we need the green moonstone for power."

"Then let's go get it!"

In their excitement, the two soldiers held up their blades and rushed forward through the throngs of other rats, and closed in on the trebuchet. They jumped on the backs of the rats pushing the structure and leapt onto the machine in a frenzy. The troops shouted and cheered the two on as they grasped the ropes and the arm, and waved their blades around in the air like they were in a parade.

The noise caught Greygor's attention and he swung around to see the commotion. Halting his cart, the king jumped down and walked solemnly toward the trebuchet. As he approached the machine and its troublemaking riders, the other soldiers parted and made a path for the king to walk through.

"What are you two vermin doing?" the rat king called out.

"We are ready to FIGHT!" one rider bellowed.

"Yes, well, you will have your chance to do that," Greygor responded. "Now get down before I come up there and make you regret this." He stared down the riders until they relented.

Greygor marched back to the front of the troop and hoisted himself back into his cart. The two rats climbed down from their high loft on the trebuchet and assembled behind the machine.

Once the troop resumed their march, the first rat soldier said to the other, "I don't think he knows what's coming."

"Who? The prisoner?"

"No." There was a long pause. "Greygor."

CHAPTER 23

Tegan held the tea cups closely and made her way back to the house, stepping cautiously over stones and debris. She could hear voices inside the home as she neared the door. Instead of walking in, she hesitated outside. She had questions, and today, she needed answers.

Inside, Prince Callum and Beckett stood near the fireplace warming themselves. The prince stretched and fluttered his wings. The torn wing had completely healed with no sign of trauma.

"Your wing!" Tegan blurted out. "It has healed!"

The prince smiled and replied, "Yes, as good as new."

Beckett bounded over to her, "And look." He lifted his arms and flapped them around. "My shoulder muscle is normal again...even better!" He flapped off to the fireplace where a cooking pot had been placed back in the orange embers.

"Tegan, how is your paw?" the prince asked.

She paused and opened her paw, having forgotten about her injury since she felt no pain. "Completely restored," Tegan replied in amazement, moving her fingers and wrist about to show her friends.

The sombel looked around the room and asked, "Where's Kenna?"

A muffled sound rose from underneath a blanket near the fireplace, "I'm awake." Kenna's ears popped out from a red blanket nearest to the wall. "I *really* don't like mornings." She sat up and rubbed her face. "What did I miss?"

"We're watching Beckett flap around like a bird," Prince Callum said and the others laughed.

"Yes, my shoulder feels new again!" He flapped his arms once more for Kenna.

As the room quieted down, Tegan announced, "Pish is outside."

The group could hear sawing noises from the open window. Beckett hopped over a floor cushion and leaned out the opening, "What is he doing out there?" he asked.

"Building a raft," Tegan responded. "We're heading down the river soon."

Beckett searched Prince Callum's face for answers.

"It's the fastest way to get to Old Padley...and we need to get there quickly," the prince responded.

"But the river is dangerous," Kenna said. "I've heard stories of sea monsters and—"

"Sea monsters?!" Beckett asked astounded.

Tegan's mind fluttered with thoughts of sea beasts and rough waters. She gripped her sword in fear of what might be ahead. *The stone....what about the green moonstone?* Tegan remembered her dream, the vision that unmistakably spoke to her. She had a purpose, and that gem would serve a very important role. But how?

"Prince Callum," Tegan spoke up. "I must talk with you about the moonstone."

The prince poured hot water over tea leaves in his cup. "What do you want to know?"

"You described the gem before and some of its abilities, but I...well, I've experienced something new," Tegan pulled out her sword and showed the prince where she placed the gem. "Look at the design."

The prince leaned over and analyzed the symbol on the handle. It clearly matched the design on the stone. He smiled. More and more, the elements of the prophecy were falling into place.

"Beckett and I were training when the blade began to glow," Tegan said. "Then, when he swung hard and I defended with my blade, a translucent force field of sorts covered me. I didn't feel a thing. What does that mean?"

"As I mentioned before, the moonstone augments what is already in your heart," the prince responded. "The stone understands your true intentions, a pure motive, and joins forces with your blade's motions." He sipped his tea. "This particular stone was given to you; therefore, you must concentrate and learn to use the power properly."

"Why do the rats want the stone so badly?" Tegan asked.

"The rats of Voldire simply have black hearts," he responded. "They want the bigger stones to power machines so they can destroy and take over the world. It is as basic as that. Our only hope at this point is to serve them the terms of surrender and pressure them into signing it to buy us more time."

"More time?" Tegan asked.

"Time before what?" Kenna asked.

"War," the prince responded. "Unfortunately, it is inevitable. But we need time to recruit other clans into our plan of defense. My father has been negotiating with the other villages in hopes of support. Our country depends on this."

Tegan stood up despite the emotional weight on her shoulders. She had the prophecy and the stone, nothing else mattered at this moment. It was time to prepare for the journey down the river.

"I need to check on the raft," she said.

"I will come too," the prince said and motioned to the other two, "Pack our supplies. We will leave soon."

Tegan and Prince Callum left the house and walked out to the river bank where Pish was finishing up the raft. He pulled at vines woven tightly throughout the structure to keep the timber together during its voyage. The moisture from last night's rainfall felt heavy in the air and the sombel felt it hard to breathe.

"The water is high," Pish said to the prince. "It might be a rough ride."

"But is it doable?" the prince asked.

"Yes, but mind the banks as the water recedes," he hesitated. "And watch for sea creatures."

"I believe we are prepared. Those beasts….well, we might avoid them if we stop half way down the river at the stone arch," said the prince.

"What's at the stone arch?" Tegan asked.

"There's a village of dwarfs that live among the trees there," Pish responded. "You can barter for weapons and some food to continue your quest. Unfortunately, I don't have much to offer you here."

Pish looked down but the prince patted his back. "You have done more than enough, my friend," Prince Callum offered. "We are in your debt."

"It has been my pleasure," Pish responded.

Kenna and Beckett came out of the house with their supplies tucked under their arms; a couple of blankets, a little food, and their weapons all in tow.

"We are traveling on this?" Kenna asked looking fearfully at the structure before her.

"It's not pretty, but it will get you down the river," Pish smiled a little and stepped onto the raft. "Allow me." He stretched out his paw to Tegan and helped her step up onto the craft. Next, he assisted Beckett as he secured the supplies on the back of the float. The prince and Kenna boarded last; the prince took the helm while Kenna settled at the back of the float.

Pish stepped off onto the shore and shoved the raft as hard as he could. It took a few tries before it finally dipped into the river and freed itself from the bank. The structure, with its four passengers, slowly inched into the current flowing down the middle of the river. Pish waved, and the group waved back.

A gentle breeze tickled the whiskers on Tegan's face as the raft wandered down the river. The sun's rays peeked through the haze, and the trees and grasses lining the banks of the river swayed with the wind and dabbled their leaves into the water. A blue butterfly zipped past, and on the other side of the river, a short wall with loose stones divided the water from the land. Some of the rocks had fallen from their perch and a few left askew, but the wall stretched as far as the sombel could see.

Prince Callum stepped closer to Tegan, who sat at the front of the structure. He held a basic oar in one hand and a long pole in the other; both needed to propel the float and dodge obstructions in the river. The prince sat down next to Tegan, placing the tools beside him.

"What is that stone wall all about?" Tegan asked.

"Well, from the looks of the stone structure, I'd say a tribe of dwarfs built it," the prince responded. "And quite a long time ago."

Dwarfs....she knew they were a fickle bunch. While the creatures could be helpful, they were often known for their petty pilfering and sneaky pranks. On the other hand, dwarfs were master forgers of metalwork and swords; they even held knowledge of enchanted secrets in the forest.

Her father, Arthur, visited a tribe of dwarfs once before. When he became mayor of Haven years ago, Arthur set out to request a specific sword for his new position. One that only a dwarf could forge, one that could impart wisdom as he prepared to govern his home village. And as payment, her father took several baskets of her mother's fig and pear oat cakes. Oh, how her ma had baked for hours in that tiny kitchen of hers, so proud and yet a bit fearful of her husband's new position and responsibilities. Tegan was little, but she still remembered the smell of the cakes baking in the oven. And the dwarfs, it turns out, fancied those fruity oat cakes!

Prince Callum handed the oar to Beckett and said, "Keep us moving, my friend."

Beckett slowly paddled the float along with the current. The prince cradled the wooden pole in his arm, ready to push the craft away from any large boulders in the water.

"We'll follow this stone wall until we reach an archway," the prince said. "Be on the lookout for that."

"Will we stop there?" Tegan asked.

"Yes. Pish suggested we get supplies from this particular tribe," the prince said. "Hopefully, they're a welcoming group."

"What happens if they're not?" Beckett asked.

Prince Callum lowered his head, "Then we'll have to make some difficult decisions."

No one asked what those decisions would be. They didn't need to.

CHAPTER 24

A few feet from the shore lay a path of large gray stones, many of which had been arranged and wedged into a stair case design. An organized pile of rocks, shaped into a magnificent, cold throne. A grimacing, black creature...the rat leader...scaled the steps, one by one, dragging his bent sword behind him. The sound of metal on rock penetrated his ears and dulled his senses.

Holding a roll of parchment paper under one arm and a cup in the other, the leader reached the top of the stairs and collapsed in his formidable chair. He grumbled and grunted, shoving the papers around in front of him.

The air sat heavily on the shore, thick from the smoke of forging metals in makeshift stone pits. Amid the haze, rat soldiers hustled around the base of the throne preparing food and carrying supplies foraged from the woods.

The rat leader spotted the second in command sitting under the shadow of the structure and shouted to him, "Bring me the prisoner!"

The commander nodded to the leader and walked around behind the throne toward a large birch tree in the forest. There stood Lewis behind a makeshift wooden gate attached to the trunk of the tree. His holding cell consisted of a hollowed-out cavity in the trunk of the ancient tree, complete with a door made of gnarly, withered branches. A small opening allowed for a little light and the ability for Lewis to see outside.

The commander approached the opening and said, "The leader wishes to see you." He fiddled with the branches and pulled the door slightly open---just enough for Lewis to slide through.

"Stand here," the commander stated.

Lewis slid out of the entrance sideways and blinked into the sunlight. Even though the morning light was mostly filtered by the fog, Lewis still had to adjust his vision under the bombardment of the sunlight. He noted his surroundings as the commander tied his paws together with a scrap of vine.

"This way," the commander pulled on the vines and marched toward the leader's throne.

Lewis followed behind the rat, dreading the interrogation before him. His duty to protect the tunnel entrance was the sole reason he kept the secret; the gem stones, the community that lived there...those lives depended on him. Instead of sleeping, he spent most of night devising a plan to distract the leader from this tunnel destination, or at least, lure him on a fabricated trail. Negotiations with his captor would be futile at this point. It was better to buy some time until he was rescued. And he had faith that his brother, Arthur, had a plan to free him from these miserable rodents.

When the two reached the foot of the structure, the commander pushed Lewis up the stones toward the throne. The leader shoved his papers aside and growled, "Ah, Lewis, protector of the tunnels." He settled back in his chair and glared at the sombel. "I need information from you."

Lewis stood silent in front of the leader.

"Well, don't you want to know the question I have for you?" the leader asked.

The commander pushed on Lewis to answer. The sombel reluctantly replied, "I believe I already know your question."

The leader laughed and commented to the commander, "Smart sombel, isn't he? Already knows, this one does."

The commander chuckled as well. Lewis felt uneasy as he looked into the eyes of the menacing leader. Those glaring eyes devoid of emotion.

The leader stiffened and asked his prisoner slowly, "Where is the tunnel entrance?"

Lewis remained silent, which infuriated the leader. He then yelled, "Answer me!!"

The sombel refused to answer, so the commander hit him on the shoulder with the handle of his spear. Lewis fell to his knees. With a deep breath, he replied, "I cannot tell you the location. It is a sacred place for many."

"Sacred? Ha!" the leader scoffed. "Listen to me, Lewis, you <u>will</u> tell me where the entrance is, or you will wish that you had when the king gets here. He is not nearly as.....as diplomatic as I am!" He grinned eerily and played with his greasy whiskers.

The commander pressed his spear into Lewis's back and the sombel cringed. Lewis remained silent although the pain seared through his spine and radiated to his right shoulder. He crumpled to the ground without a response.

"I see," the leader said and turned to the commander. "Take him back," he waved his puny rat arms. "Give him some time and he'll talk."

The commander pulled the sombel up to his feet and led him back down the stairs.

"Commander!" the rat leader shouted and motioned from his seat. "Come here, I need to speak with you privately."

The commander nodded and handed off the prisoner to another soldier marching by.

"Take this prisoner back to his cell. The leader wants to talk," ordered the commander.

The soldier grabbed the vine tethered to the prisoner's paws and walked off toward the forest with Lewis in tow.

Scaling the stairs for a second time, the commander climbed back to the throne. "What is it, sir?"

"Sit," the leader motioned for the rat to stay awhile. The commander sat near the throne and waited for the rat leader to continue. "We don't have much time, commander," he said in a low, gravelly voice. "Make the prisoner talk."

"Sir, I thought we were waiting for Greygor to interrogate Lewis?" the commander responded.

"Greygor?!" the leader laughed boisterously and punched the commander on the arm. "I have the prisoner, so I will get the treasure. I just need Lewis to talk."

The commander rubbed his arm and said, "But the king will be here any day now—"

"I don't care!" he interrupted. "Look, you and I have had our differences. But this is my chance to rise up and overthrow that old rat."

"But you are talking mutiny!"

"Call it what you want," the leader said coolly. "I am tired of serving Greygor."

"So, you want to be king?" the commander asked.

"Yes!" he hissed. "I like the sound of that."

"Greygor has many supporters. It will be difficult to depose him."

"I will handle the king <u>and</u> his followers," the leader said. "I need you to make the prisoner talk."

"What if he won't?" the commander asked.

"Then use any means necessary to make him. You understand?"

The commander nodded in return.

The stone wall curved in and out along the shoreline. Tegan wondered how many years had passed since the structure had been created. She watched as the sun lifted its lazy head to rest high above the trees. As the raft drifted along the river, the sombel grew drowsy with the soft motions of the bobbing craft.

Water passed underneath their wooden float as Prince Callum hummed a tune under his breath. It was peaceful and serene with only a warm breeze pushing the little craft along.

Beckett broke the silence. "What's over there?"

He pointed to a spot in front of them, a bubbling pool, near a sizable boulder. The others squinted to see what he was pointing to. Suddenly, the bubbling pool moved in their direction.

"What is it?" Tegan asked nervously.

"I'm not sure," the prince responded hesitantly.

Closer and closer, the bubbles made their way near enough to the raft that the travelers instinctively gathered in the center of the wooden craft, away from the edges and away from the unknown. Waiting, watching, their nerves tingling.

Then, a rush of water parted ways as a slimy, black head breached the surface. It opened its giant mouth and showed its gnarly teeth. Tegan and Beckett both gasped out loud while Kenna shrieked in terror. The meripeto sea beasts were hungry, and unforgiving.

Prince Callum readied his sword, "Get your weapons out!" he shouted.

Beckett and Tegan pulled out their swords while Kenna held on to the raft and the supplies. She hunkered down and closed her eyes in fear. For once, she stayed behind, afraid of the danger in the waves.

The black beast plunged into the water, its long slick body and short fins dove down and circled underneath the raft. The anxious travelers watched for any signs of disturbance. To their right, the beast raised its scaly head and thrusted itself forward, barely missing the raft. Tegan fell to the planked floor as the structure rocked with the attack.

The prince helped her up and she readied herself again. The beast raised its head and let out a dreadful howl, a hideous warning of impending carnage. It circled the raft again and again, forcing the structure to change direction and spin slowly counter clockwise. Beckett jabbed at the creature's head, seeing its cold, gold eyes and catfish-like whiskers. He crashed down on the scales of its elongated neck with a high-pitched clinking sound.

"This side!" the prince yelled.

Beckett and Prince Callum attacked the beast's tail as it flipped over and disappeared before them. In the distance, Tegan noticed several more pools of bubbles emerge. She froze as panic washed over her and down her spine.

"More! More!" Tegan yelled, pointing at the other bubbles heading their way.

The beast bumped the raft with its massive, muscular body and sent it flying to the left. Parts of the structure flooded in the movement and Tegan rolled with the sudden motion, ultimately falling into the river. She screamed in fright.

Beckett and the prince reached over and grabbed her paws, pulling as hard as they could to retrieve her from the water. But the sea beast rolled and popped his head up while the other creatures swam close to the raft. The entire structure was surrounded with the ghastly meripeto monsters.

Tegan kicked her feet and scrambled as best she could. With one final heave, Beckett hoisted her onto the raft, just as one of the beasts lunged and chomped on the side of the structure where she had just escaped. Tegan crawled frantically to the back of the raft where Kenna was still crouched and mumbling in fear. The sombel was soaked. She patted her sides, the bag and sword were still thankfully there.

The prince stood back up and held his sword out, watching the water around them. He slashed at another beast as the creature attacked the corner of the raft. As his sword connected with its head, the beast let out a fierce growl and struck at the prince.

Both the prince and Beckett fought with their swords, but the beast outmaneuvered them. Its hideous teeth chomped down on their weapons, ripping them away from their grip. Back under water, the monster swam with the swords. Beckett laid back and breathed heavily, his chest heaving up and down in noticeable movements. Another bump from the beast and water washed over the entire raft.

The prince continued to fend off the sea beasts from destroying the raft, but it wouldn't be long before there wasn't much left of it. If they could just get to the shore....he looked over and noticed that the stone wall was missing. Side to side he turned, searching desperately for a land mark.

Where was he?

One of the beasts called to the others in a raspy, guttural howl. Prince Callum, the only one standing, looked at the others with fatigue in his eyes.

Just beyond where Tegan and Kenna sat, he noticed the stone arch, the landmark he missed. With renewed hope, he called out to Beckett, "Get the pole!"

Beckett grabbed the piece of wood as the prince shuffled around for the makeshift oar.

"Paddle to the shore as hard as you can!" the prince ordered.

Both the prince and the sombel struggled against the waves caused by the massive creatures circling their raft. The structure rolled and the wood creaked beneath them as the supplies shifted around. They were still too far from the shore to jump off the raft, so it had to stay intact a little longer.

Then the structure tilted too far to the right, tossing all the supplies into the river. Little by little, the food drifted out of the sacks that they were packed in; the veggies, the bread, the fruit....all lost. Tegan watched helplessly as the last of their blackberries emptied into the river.

"Berries!" Tegan shouted. Seeing the blackberries triggered a thought, and immediately she recalled the athru berries...weren't they mood changers? She dug around in her bag and pulled out the package given to her by the tinker in the woods.

"Prince Callum!" she called out and presented the berries to him. "Throw them into the river!"

The prince seemed confused. His sweaty, fearful face revealed that he was resigned to an ominous fate on the river. But the berries intrigued him. "Berries," he repeated.

A beast swam by and readied its jaws to take another bite of the craft. But the prince threw the berries into the river and shouted, "Taste these you filthy monsters!"

The berries floated on top of the water, bobbing up and down as the waves raged from side to side. The beasts impulsively gobbled up the disturbance on the surface of the water without investigating it.

The travelers waited for what seemed like forever.

There was nothing, not a sound. Then the waves in the river calmed a bit. The meripeto creatures continued to swim around the craft, but didn't attack the structure. Rolling and flipping, the beasts seemed to play with each other as they floated on their backs and smacked their tails on the surface of the water.

Seeing this, Tegan breathed an audible sigh of relief, and Kenna ceased whimpering. What was left of the raft floated quietly along a gentle current.

The beasts swam near the structure again. Calm from the effects of the berries, the monsters sensed the need to dock the raft on the shore. They dove under the wooden float and carried it on their backs to the river bank. Sliding up on the sandy shore line, the travelers frantically jumped off the structure and dug their feet into the dry land.

The meripeto beasts swam off and dove under the water, their bubbles disappearing in the distance. The travelers stood mesmerized in disbelief. The river took everything they had, but they were finally safe.

"We lost our supplies," Tegan said sadly. She walked over to Kenna and Beckett, double checking that they were safe from the ride.

"The dwarfs can help us," the prince responded.

Before speaking again, he hesitated, using the time to gather his senses. "Hopefully, we're not too far from our landmark." Prince Callum surveyed the river, searching for the stone arch. "We will need to back track a bit to find their village."

Tegan squeezed the water from her cloak and sighed, "Then let's go."

CHAPTER 25

A loud commotion arose from the shrubbery. Milo stood up from his chair and put his cup of coffee down on the table beside him. From the forest emerged a somber soldier with his crew, straight from their scouting mission to the rat leader's camp. As they got closer, Milo noticed an additional member of the group...a scruffy rat, his paws tied together securely with ropes.

"What is this?" Milo asked the first soldier.

"Captain, we captured this scout en route to the rat leader's camp," the soldier responded. "And he was spying on us."

Milo walked around the prisoner, observing him from top to bottom. The small rat twitched and hissed at his captor, his black fur covered in leaves and a few loose thorns.

"State your name, rat," Milo commanded.

The rodent hissed and growled, struggling with the ropes.

"Captain asked your name!" the soldier shouted and pulled on the ropes.

The prisoner grimaced, "Pel, the name is Pel."

Milo was intrigued. "What is your business here?" he demanded.

The prisoner twisted and yanked on his tethered vines. "Greygor," he hissed. "I serve the rat king!"

Milo looked at his soldiers. He had seen this behavior before. In past battles, he witnessed rodents running messages back and forth between camps, exchanging information, until they were finally apprehended. Then the prisoners twitched and hissed like this one, but never gave up their secrets.

"He's running messages to and from the camps....Greygor and the rat leader," Milo said. "I am sure of it."

Pel's eyes squinted and scowled.

"Yes, the rat is intel," Milo confirmed. The prisoner might be useful for his knowledge, especially in regards to Lewis.

"Where is the prisoner? The sombel captured by the rat leader?" Milo demanded from the rat. "I know you have information about him!"

Pel laughed fiercely, "That sombel is doomed!" He laughed again, with a menacing howl.

The soldiers threw Pel on the ground and held a dagger to his throat. "Tell us what you know!" they yelled at him.

Pel grimaced and hissed, wiggling around until he bit the paw gripping the blade held against him. The soldier pinning him down jumped back. "Filthy animal!" he seethed.

"Get him out of here!" Milo shouted in disgust. His heart sank as he knew time was ticking and Lewis's safety and usefulness to the king would soon be limited at best.

"What should we do with him, Captain?"

"Take him to the edge of camp and secure him in one of the old structures. We'll need his intelligence later," Milo replied.

The soldier jerked hard on the ropes, forcing the rat to follow him. Milo motioned for the other soldiers to stay, hoping they witnessed Lewis at the rat camp.

"Anything else to report, soldiers?" Milo asked.

"Sir, the rats are forging weapons and preparing for something big," one soldier responded.

"Hmm," Milo muttered to himself. "Any signs of the prisoner?"

"We didn't see a prisoner, sir," the soldier replied.

Milo sighed with disappointment. He needed a plan.

"Thank you soldier, you may return to your camp," the captain responded.

Where are they keeping Lewis? he wondered. *I have to know.... I must know how he's being treated.*

Milo walked in a circle, thinking about his options. He should send someone to check on Lewis, or at least to locate him within the camp. A soldier that could perform this task in confidence. Or maybe he should handle it himself? He went over the scenario in his head; a quick, half day mission to secure the prisoner's location. He could even take supplies to Lewis, assuming he could get close enough to deliver them without being seen.

I can hike there and back before anyone knows I am gone. Yes, I will run this quest by myself.

Near the old stone wall resided a tribe of dwarfs called the Corrach. These ancient peoples had occupied this part of the country for thousands of years. However, the dwellers were rarely seen because most of their activity took place in a nearby valley or in quarries underground. But over the years, the Corrach mined stone from the mountains to build small homes under the trees close to the river. They also constructed a stone wall around the little village to unify their residence. They called their home, Dun Glen, for they made sure the walls stood tall and strong.

Aside from the mining and blacksmith duties, men of the Corrach tribe lived similarly to others in the forest. Each had their duties...fish, farm, build, and defend. The women gathered and cooked, sewed, cared for children, and cleaned their homes of stone. The Corrach men and women both grew long hair, braided down their backs. However, the men had shaggy beards and donned pointed, velvet hats.

Aside from their appearance, the Corrach tribe possessed a unique trait. Because of their small stature, these particular dwarfs befriended a group of pine martens that lived in the trees above the village. These creatures resembled ferrets but were chestnut brown in color with small, sharp teeth. Their long, sleek bodies and slight paws were perfect for sneaking around the forest unnoticed.

Pine martens could scramble up tree trunks and crawl out onto branches, flattening their furry bellies onto the bark for camouflage. They have particularly keen eyesight in the darkness, unlike the dwarfs, and can be as silent as the night. The pine martens often served as watch guards for their diminutive neighbors.

In the past, the pine martens alerted the dwarfs to invaders from the river so the villagers could defend themselves and save their homes. In return, the dwarfs supplied berries and nuts to the creatures during the winter months when forest supplies were scarce.

Legends say that the mighty Corrach were always warriors. You can still read about these stories in traditional manuscripts; the most notorious example originates from the earliest document in King Fallon's library. The narrative describes beastly toads that invaded from the river banks and attacked the dwarf tribe many years ago. The toads, nearly the same size as the dwarfs, penetrated the stone gate and ravished the homes and storehouses of Dun Glen village. The toads desired to know the secret of how dwarfs gave power to their forged metals, and destroyed everything in sight looking for it.

For several days, the battle raged on and off...the dwarfs defended their homes and their secret. Until a handful of mercenaries climbed the famed Overlook oak tree and proposed a strategy that the others had disregarded. The pine martens.

Although the details are unclear, the author states in the ancient document that the pine martens were sent forth to hunt and then devour the toads. One by one, the mutant amphibians were exterminated by the martens and removed from the glen. While the pine martens supplied relief, the dwarfs reassembled their troops and defended their wall successfully, driving out what was left of the perpetrators (back into the water), with minimal bloodshed on the dwarfs' side.

But the truth is that the village developed their reputation from those stone formations that serve as a defense, a stalwart against invaders. The dwarfs spent years building the impressive stone wall positioned along the river, a wall that expanded many kilometers and stood nearly triple their height!

And that is not all. Though mystery surrounds the dwarfs of Dun Glen, these clever creatures were also known for their impressive weaponry; and the formidable armor they forged. Only a few outsiders were privileged enough to procure a sword, shield, or even a battle helmet from these blacksmiths; for the villagers stashed these items away for themselves...in case of war.

Why would anyone seek weapons or armor from the Corrach tribe? Because the dwarfs hold the secret for infusing elements into their pieces of metal, a craft called impartation or Sparradh. These elements can range from wisdom to shape shifting to prophecy. To this day, no one knows how this power is transferred into the metal; no one but the dwarfs. And the secret has never been revealed.

In an attempt to explain this impartation, the creatures of Fellnore speculate that the dwarfs are simply magical beings. Others say that their leader is a wizard and uses some sort of crystal ball to enhance the armor. In any case, the dwarfs have been practicing Sparradh for generations and are frighteningly protective of their craft.

The truth is, there is a science behind this craft. This science includes the alignment of certain stars in the sky, along with the moon and its particular phase. And once all these celestial bodies line up, an elite dwarf can impart an element into a special metal. But this alignment only happens once in three hundred years, so the timing is both essential and critical for this "magic" to occur.

It was into this setting that Tegan and her travelers found themselves. Weary from their journey down the river, these hikers made their way through the tall grasses until they reached the stone arch—the opening to the once impressive wall.

The area before them looked like it had been abandoned for some time. Tall grass and random rocks as far as they could see. But there was a small footpath between two large trees that the prince pointed to; and with that, the travelers set forward in search of Dun Glen.

Both Beckett and Tegan questioned the stopover in the Glen. Sure, they needed to replace their food and weapon supply...thanks to those river beasts, but couldn't they do that once they reached Old Padley? Kenna assured them that the fox families north of the village would care for them while Tegan completed her quest. They would support her. They would protect her.

But why the Glen? Why now? Especially since they were actually walking in the opposite direction of Old Padley. Tegan needed to know.

"Why are we stopping in Dun Glen?" she asked the prince.

"To replenish our supplies, of course," he responded.

"Yes, but why *specifically* the Glen? Can't we wait until we reach Old Padley?" Tegan asked. "Kenna, how far are we from the outskirts of the village?"

"We are only a few hours from Old Padley," the little fox replied.

"I say we skip the Glen and those pesky dwarfs and head straight to our safe haven," Beckett said and yawned. "Besides, I am already tired...I could use a nap."

The prince stopped and addressed the group. "There is a particular reason for stopping in Dun Glen," he said. "I am searching for a distinct weapon. A weapon that only the Corragh tribe owns."

Beckett was intrigued, "What kind of weapon is it?"

"The Corragh tribe possesses an extraordinary cloak that helps camouflage the one who wears it at night," the prince said. "It is my strategy for Tegan to use this cloak as her means of delivering the terms of surrender to the rat king."

"Protection under the darkness of night," Tegan mumbled.

"I do have a plan, Tegan," Prince Callum said gently.

She nodded timidly.

"How does the cloak work?" Beckett asked.

"My father once told me about the cloak of Fis. His ancestors passed the story down among our elders about a legendary cloak. This mythical cloak can disguise you under the cover of night; to help you blend in to your surroundings. Supposedly, it was used in the battle of Duncan's Hill, and became a turning point in that war."

"What happened?"

"One night, a brave soldier wore the cloak and slipped in behind enemy lines at Harlingotn Castle. Once inside, he ran up and down the palace's corridors in search of the holding cells. He finally made it to the basement and wrangled with the door until it opened just enough for the prisoner to slip out. The two escaped before the guards realized the prisoner was gone," the prince said. "By morning, the battle was over."

"What? How??" Beckett was astonished.

The prince laughed a little and said, "Apparently, the prisoner was actually a dragon master. As soon as he made it back to camp, he summoned his fiercest dragon to destroy the enemy's base.'""A dragon??" now Tegan was amazed.

"Yes, that dragon blasted the castle with fire and burned it to the ground," the prince replied. "The ruins of the castle walls are still visible today. But you have to walk farther east to see them."

"How did the dwarfs get the cloak then?" Beckett asked.

"They actually made the cloak," the prince replied. "It's a simple garment, but the important part is the impartation of an element. For this particular cloak, they imparted the element of camouflage."

"Dwarfs can do that?" Tegan asked. She remembered her father's sword. He always referred to it as the sword of wisdom; Eagna was its name. Now she understood the meaning of its moniker on a whole new level.

"Yes, that is their gift. It's called Sparradh, or the process of imparting elements into pieces of metal that they forge themselves," the prince replied.

"But you said the cloak was a simple garment," Tegan observed. "How did they impart the camouflage element to it?"

"I believe the cloth is lined with very thin strands of metallic threading. Though not as strong as a full metal blade, the threading would certainly be enough to hold the imparted element needed to disguise oneself at night," he replied.

Suddenly, a commotion occurred in the trees above their head. Two chestnut brown pine martens dropped to the path below them and stood in front of Prince Callum, the leader of the expedition.

"Stop there!" they hissed, showing small, sharp teeth. They stood up on their back legs and extended their claws, revealing very pointed nails.

The group of travelers froze in their tracks.

"Who are you?" asked one of the pine martens.

"What is your business here?" asked the other.

"I....I am Prince Callum," he replied. "I am heir to the pixie clan in Fellnore." He looked at the pine martens holding daggers before him. "My father is King Fallon." He took a step back. "We come seeking only refuge and supplies."

Tegan looked over the prince's shoulder at the animals, "Sirs, we crashed landed here after escaping the sea monsters—"

"You survived the meripeto?" One pine marten asked.

"Yes, yes, they did!" the other chattered.

The pine martens lowered their daggers and inspected the weary visitors. They searched deep into the prince's eyes and observed Tegan's wet cloak. Both Beckett and Kenna remained silent.

"You may speak to Gar," said one of the martens. "He will know what to do."

"Will this...Gar...help us?" Tegan asked timidly.

"Come with me," the other marten answered.

And with that, the visitors followed the tree creatures through the grasses and around large, mossy rocks. Soon, a few small, clunky stone houses came into view. Flickering lights glowed from stone hearths through their window openings, and dwarfs bustled around within.

The dwellings stood fairly high, tall enough for a sombel to stand in. The doors appeared to be cloth or fabric that hung from the lentil, opening and closing much like a curtain. Though the walls appeared cold and hard, the dwarfs used flowers and thistles to decorate their windows with color and fragrance. The floors and roofs consisted of river reeds used to soften the surfaces and thatch the coverings overhead.

To her left, several dwarfs used hammers and saws, working on a wooden box for a tiny garden. When the pine martens arrived with their visitors, the dwarfs stopped operating their tools.

"Where is Gar?" one of the martens asked.

The worker with the hammer wiped his brow and replied, "In the storehouse, I think."

"Fine," the marten said and pointed to the travelers. "You stay here and I will fetch the leader." He leaned over and whispered something into the other marten's ear. Both of the creatures nodded their heads.

The first pine marten announced to the group, "Neti, here, will keep an eye on you while I'm gone." Then he hopped off behind the garden and towards a few stone buildings to search for Gar.

Would these dwarfs be friendly? Even helpful? Or would they have to flee into the forest for shelter again? Tegan felt anxiety settle in her chest. She had come so far and dealt with so many challenges already. The sombel never guessed that this journey would take so much out of her. But nevertheless, here she was, and she had to prepare herself for whatever happened next.

CHAPTER 26

Lewis could barely see out of the little opening in his makeshift cell. He thought if he could just reach the dagger hidden inside his vest, he might be able to cut the ropes tying his paws together. Wiggling his fingers and twisting his wrists, Lewis strained to wrestle free of the vine tethering his paws.

From outside, the little window suddenly darkened. Someone was there.

"Hello?" Lewis called out.

"Why do you refuse to talk, prisoner?" It was the rat commander.

Lewis sighed.

How long could he put off these rats before he ended up seriously wounded? Or worse....dead? Lewis had protected the tunnels for ages, sitting on the front row as wars waged for those precious gemstones.

For a moment, he remembered the day he was assigned the title of Protector. His brother, Arthur, had just been elected Haven's mayor. And under those circumstances, Arthur needed to reestablish good will with the neighboring clans. He spent days talking with other leaders in hopes of planning a successful strategy for peace and economic enrichment. And it paid off greatly.

While Arthur was a planner and optimistically outspoken, Lewis was a quiet, methodical sombel. In fact, Lewis spent most of his adult life in the military and as a liaison to other clans. Because of this vital experience, his brother knew that Lewis was the perfect candidate to conceal the tunnels' location and protect the residents inside.

The day Lewis accepted this position marked a turn in events for the pixie clan. With the sombels of Haven an official guardian, rival clans began testing the waters. The foxes of Branwell and the dwarfs of Calham Run were the first. But Lewis used his savvy to negotiate with their leaders for a peaceful resolution.

But the brown rats of Lower Karras, cousins to the rats of Voldire, fought aggressively for the rights to the tunnel. In fact, after three days, Lewis was forced to bring in the army to squelch the uprising. And for the first time, the skirmish left him shaken. He quickly understood just how important his role was.

Now the black rats of Voldire wanted their turn. And Lewis had to change tactics.

"I am their protector," replied Lewis. "Just like you are second in command. You see to all the leader's requests, right?"

"Yes, but I follow a leader who will overturn Greygor and be the next king!" the commander hissed excitedly. "And do you know what will happen then?"

"What?" Lewis played along.

"I will be next in line to the new KING!"

Lewis hesitated for a moment. "So, you do everything the leader asks of you?"

"Yes."

"EVERY thing?"

"What are you getting at?"

"Oh nothing," Lewis replied indifferently. "Just that I never considered you to be his lapdog." He looked up to watch the rat's response.

"I am NOT his lapdog!"

"But you said—""I know what I said, but I am NOT his servant!"

"It seems to me that you have your differences with the leader. I watched you on the raft, and then on the shore. You are testing his boundaries."

"The leader is weak. He is blindsided by power!" said the commander. "The only way he will overturn the king is if we do it for him."

"And you are stronger than he is? Perhaps smarter?"

"I am," the commander grinned eerily.

"Then why is he in charge here instead of you?"

The rat stomped his feet and pointed his bony finger at Lewis, "I know what you are doing!" He shrieked. "And I—"

Unexpectedly, a thunderous boom blasted through the forest. The stunned rat fell on his back as the ground shook beneath him. Several rat soldiers rushed toward him shouting, "Commander! Commander! We need you at the camp, now!"

Speechless, the commander stood up and looked at Lewis with confusion in his eyes. He turned around just as another loud noise echoed through the trees, along with a thud. The commander staggered, trying to stabilize his legs so he could walk. He reached out for a tree branch, fumbled around and steadied himself against the trunk. He then pushed his body off the trunk and ran with the other soldiers toward the throne.

Lewis could hear shouting and turmoil in the distance. *What just happened? Where were they going??*

The second in command ran to the camp and quickly stopped in his tracks. Before him, a few yards away, stood a tremendous machine...a trebuchet. He had never seen anything so large in his life!

A group of soldiers on each side of the mechanism pushed and pulled it, while others prepped the basket with stones and flammable debris. Frozen in place, the commander watched as the arm swung overhead, flinging fireballs and rocks into the camp.

Several makeshift structures were already destroyed, the kitchen and two clay ovens serving as blacksmith workshops. Debris littered the camp and ash clouded the sky. Lines and lines of rat soldiers followed the machines and filled the area closest to the throne.

Then the commander saw him...the rat king, Greygor. The king sat high on a platform held by eight soldiers. As they walked into camp, the platform swayed a bit but Greygor held on like a champ. His arms waved and he shouted directions to his soldiers.

At his command, the rats lowered the platform to the ground so Greygor could step off. He stood with his sword in royal fashion, surrounded by his most loyal soldiers. As he surveyed the site, he called out, "Where is the leader of your camp?"

Greygor strolled through the crowd of soldiers. Then the king shouted to the rats on his left, "Go find him!" and motioned with his sword.

The commander searched the camp, hoping to spot the leader. *Where did he go? Is he in hiding??* He pushed his way through the crowd of soldiers and on to the stone throne. A quick motion caught his attention and he ducked behind the structure to investigate.

There he saw the rat leader scurrying down the path leading to the prisoner. Two soldiers followed quickly behind him. The commander knew what he was up to and hid among the trees lining the path. He watched as the leader reached the prisoner's cell and started untying the gate holding Lewis hostage.

"There you are!" the commander shouted, startling the leader.

"What are you doing here?" the leader seethed. The soldiers held their spears out toward the commander. But realizing they were in the same camp, they lowered their weapons.

"Are you hiding from your king?!" the commander asked sarcastically, knowing this indeed was the leader's motive.

"I am not hiding!" he screamed incredulously.

"Then why are you here?" the commander looked over the leader's shoulder. "Are you stealing our prisoner?"

The rat leader faced the commander head on. He squinted his eyes and pointed his bony finger, "You have a choice to make." He stepped closer to the commander. "Are you with me? Or are you Greygor's pawn to use as he sees fit?"

The commander paused to weigh his options. He desired power, and desired it greatly.

The rat king already had soldiers entrusted with important tasks. How long would it take to rise in those ranks, to become the closest to the king? Too long.

With the rat leader, he was already in the highest position possible. But if they were captured, the king would surely kill them both for being traitors.

The rat leader observed the commander's hesitance and took advantage of it.

"The way I see it," the leader continued, "If we get the prisoner out now, we can use him to find the tunnels ourselves. We won't need the king to tell us what to do. And we won't have to share any of the plunder!" He smiled an evil, toothy grin.

"What if Greygor finds us?" the commander asked. "He's looking for you right now."

"That's why we need to hurry," he responded. "Come here," he motioned. "Unlock this door."

"How do I know you won't make me your lackey? Your pawn to move about at your will?" The commander asked. "You know, I could go to Greygor right now and tell him where you are."

Enraged, the leader roared and lunged at the commander with his sword. The commander jumped back and the blade barely missed his head. He readied his sword and swung back at the leader with all his might. He would not be anyone's minion anymore.

After a few exchanges of blades and combatting back and forth, the commander had had enough. He backed up and ran toward the leader with his blade up, shouting as he did so. The leader's eyes widened and the commander jumped on top of him, pinning the leader against the prisoner's cell door with his sword.

"I will NOT be your servant," the rat said. "I am the commander! Say it!"

The leader struggled under the weight of the commander and his blade. The other soldiers backed away, avoiding any involvement in this brawl. The commander pressed harder until the two rats locked eyes.

"You are commander," the leader begrudgingly squeaked.

The commander recognized this as an agreement between the two. The leader would lead, and the commander would enforce.

How long the agreement would last, he didn't know. But right now, they had to focus on getting Lewis out, and fast.

CHAPTER 27

Neti paused in front of the travelers with his dagger tucked neatly in his belt. The pine marten stood nearly as tall as the sombels with sleek, brown fur and black paws. He paced back and forth like a patrolman on duty. Seeing him, Kenna settled impatiently next to Prince Callum, and Tegan and Beckett buddied together beside them.

In the distance, a pine marten emerged with a dwarf behind him, both heading toward the visitors. When they arrived, Tegan studied the dwarf's face closely. He was obviously aged with silvery hair and a long gray beard. Wrinkles peaked out from under that green felt hat, and his skin was rosy due to either the sun or the mountain wind...maybe both.

And when Gar spoke, gaps showed where a few teeth were missing, which made him whistle as he talked. "Who are you?" the dwarf asked.

The prince introduced himself and the travelers. He presented his hand for a friendly shake, but Gar just looked at him blankly, and the pine marten growled.

"What do you want from us?" Gar demanded.

"Sir, we simply request a few supplies and we will leave straight away," the prince replied humbly. "Some food, a rest, and a couple of weapons."

"We do not like visitors here," the old dwarf grumbled. "Leave us!"

The pine martens raised their daggers and moved forward. Tegan and Beckett stepped back, but Kenna jumped up. "You can't turn us away! We're hungry and—"

Beckett grabbed her arm and pulled her back with him, shushing her in the process.

But the prince held up his hands in submission and tried his request again; this time, he meant business, "Sir, I come seeking a unique weapon in your possession. The cloak of Fis."

The dwarf narrowed his eyes.

"Do you have this secrecy cloak?" the prince asked.

"I might," Gar said. "But I might not. What is it to you?"

"We need this protection for a special mission we have been tasked with," frustrated, the prince stared at the old dwarf. "We are to cross enemy lines and deliver a document to a despised leader."

"The cloak of Fis has been in our family since the ancient days. You are not worthy of its power," Gar said dryly. "It is not for sale."

"Then teach us how to use it responsibly," the prince replied. "We are here to request its use for our quest, to borrow it. You have my word that it will be returned immediately after the completion of the mission."

Now Gar was curious. "Why this desire for our cloak?" He looked at Tegan's sword peeking out of her own cloak and pointed to it. "Don't you have swords and daggers of your own? Use those in your pursuit for power!"

The prince paced a fine line between negotiating and completely losing his temper. Not only were the dwarfs disagreeable, they were also unwilling to compromise.

"The cloak of Fis is the only weapon that can guarantee our safety!"

"So it is safety you want, I see," the old dwarf said. "What's in it for us?"

"I have payment—"

"We don't need your money!" Gar interrupted.

The prince held his pale hand up and then dug into his bag, "Would you be interested in a green moonstone?" He held out the stone for the dwarf to see.

Gar walked closer to the prince to have a look. The green gem glowed warmly in Prince Callum's hand. It was so beautiful that it captured Gar's full attention. He leaned in to grab the stone, but the prince quickly closed his hand.

"Do we have an arrangement then?" the prince asked.

Gar seemingly woke up from a trance, "Who did you say you were?"

"I am Prince Callum, son of King Fallon, of the pixie clan in Fellnore."

Gar looked at another dwarf who walked up to hear what was going on. "I have heard rumors of the green moonstone, but I have never seen one first hand. Where did you get it from?"

"The stone is protected," the prince replied as he returned the gemstone to his bag. "But I have permission to barter a few small pieces as needed for our quest."

Gar motioned for the travelers to follow him into a small stone dwelling, away from other curious eyes. Inside, a few logs burned in the corner fire pit. Tegan stretched out her paws and warmed them near the blaze.

Around the room, several shelves filled with colorful plates and cups made the space feel cheerful, in contrast to the home's dull gray, stone façade. Curtains printed with tiny flowers covered the window, and a wooden table and chairs completed the main room. To the side of the fireplace, a small, wobbly staircase disappeared up to a second floor, leading to what was most likely the bedroom.

Once inside, the travelers gathered together and sat on the floor, which was covered in river grass. Gar collected himself and asked in a hushed voice, "You said 'a quest' earlier. What do you mean by that?"

"We are en route to Old Padley to deliver a message to the rat king," the prince said flatly.

"And here we sit, talking to you, instead of saving our nation from warmongering rats!" Kenna stated boldly. Weary of setbacks, Kenna had an agenda of her own. Once this scouting mission was complete and she earned her money, the fox could gather her own crew and plan an end to Reginald's power trip back home.

"Sir, if I may?" Tegan asked confidently. This quest now consumed her. For days, she endured dangerous landscapes, terrifying sea monsters, and being held against her will. How much longer would this mission take? How much more could she bear? Tegan sorely missed home...her ma's cooking, her papa's voice. Just to watch the sun set on her little front porch made her sigh.

But she pressed on, determined to see this journey through so she could return to Haven. The dwarfs *had* to agree to help, there was no other way. Tegan searched the prince's face and he nodded in agreement.

She addressed Gar directly, "We are in a hurry to deliver the terms of surrender to the rats of Voldire. They have taken my uncle hostage and set up camp in Old Padley. King Fallon has ordered the rats to cease and desist, as they are raiding towns again and breaking the contract they signed many years ago. It is my duty to deliver that parchment to try and prevent impending war." Satisfied, she sat back down.

Gar looked at Prince Callum, "She speaks the truth," the prince said.

"We cannot afford another war. Our stone walls have yet to be repaired and fortified," the dwarf responded and walked to the small window to look out over the glen. The rats would demolish everything they had worked for.

The workshops would suffer greatly and that was a big deal. The midseason celestial alignment would be here soon, and that only happened once in every three hundred years! If they missed this event, then there would be no sparradh, or impartation, into their new weapon...the sword of Neart. Plus, the chosen dwarf for the event was already selected; they just needed to finish forging the blade within a week's time.

And...the gemstone might help speed the forging process along. It was said to accelerate a machine's power, so why not a black-smith's job? Gar knew what his decision would be. He picked up his smoking pipe laying on the table and emptied the contents in a bowl. Refilling the pipe, he lit it with a match stick and puffed a few times.

"We will help you," he said. The pipe smoke billowed in a circle over his head like a filthy halo.

"Good," said the prince. "But there is one more thing." He spoke candidly. "In the case of war, do I have your word that the Corrach dwarfs support the pixie clan of Fellnore?"

"What does that mean for us?" the dwarf asked skeptically.

"It means that if war breaks out, your dwarf armies fight along-side us against the rats. In return, you have the protection of both the pixie clan and the sombel army...a mighty force that will fortify your village and secure it from destruction," the prince said.

What more could he say to convince this curmudgeon?

Then he had an idea. "We will also provide workers to help repair your walls and safeguard the village."

The old dwarf puffed on his wooden pipe as the group waited tensely for an answer.

"You have my word then," Gar replied and stuck out his hand.

The prince shook it and smiled in relief.

Though the sun was high, Milo scurried in the shade provided by the magnificent birch trees overhead. His mission? To locate Lewis in the rat encampment and see for himself how the prisoner was being treated. He focused on the path ahead of him, an old logging trail from settlers long gone. Weaving in and out of the tall grasses, Milo could smell the river nearby. His senses told him that he was on the right track.

The captain scaled a few rocks and stepped up onto a boulder. In the clearing, Milo caught a glimpse of the river. It snaked around the countryside and disappeared behind the massive willow trees. He remembered fishing trips to the river with his family, farther north, near the mountains. All his brothers would pack a lunch and get up early enough to walk to the riverbank by dawn. Each tried their paws at catching a fish with old bamboo fishing poles. And whatever they caught that day would be a delicious dinner that night.

That evening, while his ma cooked the fish, the brothers told stories of how "the big one" got away. His oldest brother was a master storyteller and could talk well until bedtime! Milo remembered steam billowing from freshly cooked fish on the dinner table, and could still taste that spicy flavor in his mouth.

As he descended the other side of the boulder, the captain noticed a few mice sitting under the shade of a parasol mushroom. He instinctively pulled out his small binoculars from a messenger bag and looked through them for a closer view.

The mice were enjoying a picnic. The mother sat on a pink blanket drinking from her tiny cup, her straw hat shaded her eyes and delicate face from the bright sun. A picnic basket and small, white plates were sprinkled across the checkered fabric. Around her, three small mice frolicked and played. One had a ball that he tossed to another, and the baby played with its bottle.

Milo was entranced. In the middle of all the destruction in Littleton, and the rat encampment in Old Padley, here was a heart-warming scene....a welcomed relief for this sombel to continue his mission. He watched the children as they squealed and ran after their little, brown ball. He had been that same little boy years and years ago...

Milo remained on the path toward Old Padley; he could sense that he was almost there. The breeze picked up and he heard the leaves rustling in the birch trees overhead. Once he noticed more and more of the wild privet shrubs native to Old Padley, Milo decided to scale a tall evergreen tree and catch a glimpse of the rat encampment there.

As he surveyed the forest for the best vantage point, a noise grabbed his attention from the bush beside him. Out peeked a ladybug in perfect red and black uniform. But this was no ordinary ladybug, as Milo realized, this insect served in the military, just like himself.

"Sir," it said and saluted. The bug wore a vest embroidered with a symbol and a few letters. Its hat was slightly crooked but indicated his ranking as sergeant. It motioned with a dagger and three more ladybugs walked out from underneath the shrubbery. They stood at attention while their leader conducted business, their thin twig-like arms resting by their sides.

Milo saluted in return. "Good day to you, sir," he responded.

"What is your business here?" the sergeant ladybug asked.

"I am on a mission...maybe you can help me?" Milo leaned closer to the bug and continued. "Have you seen anything unusual around here?"

"You mean aside from the rat encampment on the shore?" the bug shook his head. "No."

"Have you seen the site for yourself?"

"Yes, we patrol every day around the outskirts of the settlement, and most nights too," the ladybug sighed. "It's nasty in there. Rats destroy everything you know? Houses are in a pile of rubble, vegetation has been flattened, the smoke chokes out all living things but the rodents...the southside of Old Padley is a mess."

"I am looking for a prisoner captured by those rats. Any sign of a holding cell or a sombel tied up with ropes, perhaps?"

The sergeant paused as he thought, "I believe there is a prisoner, yes. Well, you should check the large birch tree behind the camp at least. We patrolled the area last evening and spotted a rat soldier talking into a hole in the tree. Must be something or someone in there!"

"A birch tree?" Milo asked. "Thank you, sergeant." He saluted and began to walk away.

"Oi!" the ladybug called out; Milo turned around.

"Were any of your soldiers out near the camp last night?"

"Yes, they returned earlier this morning. Did you see them?"

"Aye, sir. They marched along this same path. While we were patrolling the east side of the camp, we nearly ran into them. My boys hid under a brambleberry hedge and watched the sombels climb that tree over there," he pointed with his dagger to an ancient yew tree behind him. "The sombels sat up there for hours taking notes. I guess they had a much better view of the camp than we have down here."

"Thank you for your help," Milo replied.

And with that, the sombel captain left the sergeant and his soldiers, and approached the yew tree. He scrambled up the trunk and onto the branches until he was more than halfway up the tree. Completely hidden by the leaves, Milo peered out toward the rat camp. The sergeant was right; the ground had been blackened by ash from the blacksmith pits and stone rubble littered the entire area. Black rats scurried here and there and....

Milo climbed up a few more branches to get a better view. *What is that?!* He marveled at the giant machine with the long arm. *Is it really a trebuchet? Had the rats actually obtained this technology?* It appeared that, undeniably, the rats of Voldire were fighting amongst themselves. His intuition had been correct.

He analyzed the camp, now in shambles, away from the river shore. Farther out, he recognized a stone structure that looked like a massive throne. Cups, papers, bones, and other debris were scattered amongst the ceremonial stones.

And behind the monument, Milo spotted the birch tree. Its magnificent branches overflowing with leaves, a truly ancient birch indeed. He struggled to see anything that would hold a prisoner. He pulled out his binoculars and observed again.

Then he witnessed two rats fighting one another; one pinning the other down. Behind them, a rudely crafted door barely hung to the trunk of the tree. Milo noticed a set of paws, tied with rope, showing through the opening of the door.

Lewis!

He got so excited that he almost dropped his binoculars. Milo watched as the rats settled down from their fight...a resolution perhaps? One of them pulled aggressively on the prisoner's door and yanked it open. Another rat grabbed Lewis by the rope tethered to his paws and dragged him out of the makeshift cell.

As they began walking, Milo realized he needed to get back to his own soldiers. If the rats were moving the prisoner, then he must change his strategy. The sombel scrambled down the tree and back onto the path.

As he ran back to his camp, Milo could not help but think about the terms of surrender and how far the rats had violated the Compromise Treaty. There was no doubt the rodents wanted war. The fact that Tegan had the document to deliver to the rat king was really just a formality. But it needed to be done to satisfy the terms under which the treaty had been constructed.

And Arthur told him about the prophecy. Tegan is the deliverer...or so the prophecy says. But how could she thwart an upcoming battle, much less deliver the enemies to judgment? After all, she is only one sombel. Shouldn't an army be in charge of serving those papers? An army like his own??

Milo shook his head. He needed to consult with the scouting soldiers back at camp and immediately devise a secondary plan.

CHAPTER 28

Gar nodded to Prince Callum, requesting him to follow the dwarf leader and his pine marten guard. They climbed a step stone incline that twisted around a hill...a hill covered with scraggly brush and sizeable boulders. Prince Callum paused to look out over the land below, swimming with green foliage.

The hikers approached a faded wooden door near a rock precipice. The door stood a little crooked with gashes, dents, and other weapon marks embossed on the front of it. Gar pulled at a rusty metal lock attached to the side of the door and moved the obstruction to the side. Behind this wooden door was a second one. This entryway, composed of metal, resembled a gate. Large gaps in between the iron bars allowed the hikers to see a light glowing from the darkness.

The dwarf leader pulled out a small hammer and pounded loudly on the metal frame to summon the guard. The three waited for several minutes before there was an answer. Another dwarf with a scruffy beard and red hat popped up through the opening. The smell of fire and wood burning radiated from the little creature's tattered clothing.

"Oi!" he said, with soot smeared across his nose and face. He tilted his head back and squinted his eyes in the sunlight. "Oh, hallo, Sir!" he acknowledged his leader. "I didn't recognize you at first!"

The greeter dwarf banged on a metal piece attached to the inside of the gate until they heard a *ping* sound. The mine-like gate swung open, and the prince felt a puff of cool air wash across his face.

The dwarf at the gate motioned for the others to step into the metal cage with him. One by one, the guests entered the enclosure as it swayed a bit from side to side. The prince stepped in last as he had to crouch down, just to fit in.

Once inside, the dwarf closed the metal door with a loud *bang!* He pushed a lever to maneuver a chain connected to the elevator box, and descended into the cavern below. Clackety clackety, the chains lumbered around a series of large rollers, enabling the inhabitants to ride down to the main floor ...slowly, unsteadily.

Once the cage came to a complete stop, a busy scene unfolded before them. Dwarfs, as far as they could see, worked almost in solidarity as they chopped and hammered at the walls of the cave, and collected rubble from the cavern floor. They mined and gathered rocks and gems into their box carts, and pushed those carts along small rails to other stations. The clinking of metal against rock echoed in the prince's ears.

As the dwarfs toiled deep in the cave, their primary source of light came from blazing torches and lanterns attached to the cavern walls. These light sources provided a warm glow and faint smell of ash.

As the laboring dwarfs realized their leader entered the cave, they paused their work and waved their tools around their heads, shouting out to him. "Sir!" "Hallo, sir!!" They grunted excitedly in their low, gruff voices. Gar nodded to them and saluted; the dwarfs cheered, delighted by the distraction, and settled back into their work again...chopping, hammering, collecting.

The dwarf leader turned to Prince Callum, in the midst of the noise, and said, "Wait here and I'll fetch the cloak."

While Gar hobbled off into another area of the cavern, the prince watched the activity around him. Determined and steady, the workers hacked and chopped at the walls. Laborers beside him sang a melody as they swung their hammers.

"Lo, hey, ho
I swing my hammer oh,
Today I work and drink my beer,
'Cause the prophecy
May be near to 'ere,
Lo, hey, ho"

Gar appeared behind the prince with a bundle wrapped in brown fabric. The dwarf leader hesitated as he presented the bundle to the prince. Then he unwrapped the package and pulled out a beautiful, silvery cloak.

"I present to you, the Cloak of Fis," Gar stated with a firmness in his throaty voice.

The brown fabric fell to the floor as the majestic cloak unfolded. The reflection of the torches inside the cave mirrored their warm light against the cloak's fabric. The prince held the magical garment in both of his hands, marveling at the intricacy of the woven threads. The cloak appeared to shimmer as the prince moved it around to examine its handmade artistry.

"Remember," Gar warned. "This cloak must be worn at night for its power to activate." He took the garment from the prince and wrapped it back into the fabric. As he handed the bundle to Prince Callum, the dwarf leader added, "You're in luck, you know?"

"How so?" Prince Callum asked.

"The moon is full these next few days," he looked up and waved his pipe around. "The cloak of Fis is most powerful when the moon is full, the invisibility reaches its peak potential during this time."

"Thank you, Gar," the prince replied.

The dwarf leader grunted and said, "Now, it is your turn. Where is the moonstone?"

The prince produced the gem from his bag and gradually handed it to the dwarf. Spellbound, Gar grabbed the stone and scurried back to the metal elevator. The vital exchange concluded. Prince Callum breathed a sigh of relief as he clutched the garment with both hands. The prince and the guard turned and followed Gar into the elevator, securing themselves inside the contraption. The chains rattled and the box creaked as they lifted...up, up, up, to the surface of the mining shaft.

Once they reached the wooden door, the prince stepped out first with the bundle in his hands. The sun felt warm on his face, and judging by its position, it would soon be late afternoon. The travelers needed food, and now, so they could set out for Old Padley.

As the prince rejoined Tegan, Beckett, and Kenna, the sombels and fox sat on several toadstools around a small camp fire. A little wooden tray held a tea pot and some sort of mini sweet cakes. Tegan and Kenna drank from tiny tea cups and Beckett continued eating what looked like carrot cake bites.

"Prince Callum," Beckett said with food in his mouth. "You have to try these cakes! They're so delicious!" He swallowed with a huge gulp and grabbed another delectable from the tray.

Tegan placed her cup on the tray and said, "Agnes fed us." She reached for another cake. "She is the wife of one of these guards. She makes the most delicious tea and sweets! Here, have some."

The prince sat down with his bundle and ate the little cake. So much cinnamon, anise, and hints of clove! The cake nearly melted in his mouth. The combination of flavors sent him back in time to the midlands celebrations in Haven. It had been a few years since he last attended the festival, but now he promised himself he would go again...this year.

Prince Callum sighed as he remembered the cheerfulness of these celebrations; the dancing, the singing, and the story telling. He missed the simplicity of village life. And he never thought this particular mission would drain him so much mentally. But here he was, assisting in the biggest quest Fellnore had seen in hundreds of years. The prince hoped he'd look back on this experience one day and admire his own accomplishments. Until then, he picked up his little cup and drank his tea.

"She also gave us a few cakes for the journey," Tegan patted her bag.

"Did you get the cloak?" Beckett asked.

"Yes, we have everything we need," the prince replied. He opened the fabric for the group so they could see the impressive threading of the silvery cloak.

Tegan gasped at the reflection, "Oh, it is magnificent!"

"It really is," the prince replied. He rubbed his pale fingers over the smooth fabric.

"Can I try it on?" she asked.

Prince Callum thought back to Gar's warning. "Gar told me to wear it only at night. But I think it's fine to try on quickly."

He handed the cloak to Tegan, who marveled at how light the garment felt. She turned it around and around, inspecting it in the sunlight. Never had she held anything so stunning in her life! The threads swirled around, in and out of each other, creating a perplexing pattern that mesmerized her.

Tegan removed her well-worn green cloak and shook the dust from it. Beckett stepped over and held the shimmering garment so she could put it around her neck and over her shoulders. Tegan felt the fabric hug her closely, and she twirled around in it laughing.

"Can you see me? Am I invisible yet?" she asked and pulled the hood over her head.

Beckett and Kenna clapped, just as she pretended to be royalty.

"Oh, it suits you, Tegan," Kenna commented.

"You said it, Kenna!" Beckett echoed.

"Prince Callum, how does the cloak of Fis hide those that wear it?" Tegan asked.

"Well," the prince stood up and wiped the crumbs from his face. "Gar told me that it camouflages you at night. And works particularly well during a full moon event," he said. "Which just happens to be this week."

Tegan smiled, "Perfect."

She took one last look at the magical cloak and then removed it, wrapping it up again in the brown fabric and placing it in her bag. Tegan picked up her green cloak and put it back on.

Sensing the mood had changed, the group lazily gathered their things and stashed the leftover cakes in their bags. They needed to move out before sunset, which meant leaving now. Prince Callum, Tegan, Beckett, and Kenna said their goodbyes to the dwarf leader and his guards. Next stop was Old Padley, and this time, Kenna led the way.

CHAPTER 29

As Tegan, Beckett, Kenna, and Prince Callum hiked south, the travelers were unusually quiet. Each needed time to sort through their thoughts. This mission would reach its pinnacle soon...the delivery of the terms. But no one believed Greygor would surrender. And why should he? The rat king was simply that...a rat; and that meant war was in his blood.

Kenna hummed as she walked and Tegan fell in line behind her. Brambly hedges and flowering plants flanked each side of the footpath. And there was a faint smell of clover and berries that hung over their heads. Tegan heard Beckett (behind her) swatting at thorns with his sword as he walked. Prince Callum brought up the rear, serving as both protector and lookout for the group.

The little fox stopped humming and said softly, "It's been a while since I've been back here. I remember these trees though, and the hedges." She touched the leaves on one of the bushes as she passed by.

"Kenna," Tegan said. "Tell me about the families that live in Old Padley now."

The fox smiled, "Several of the families that served in Edwin's army still live there...the military head with his wife and three kids, the lieutenant—who was falsely accused, I might add—brought his wife and baby, and then there's little Daisy. She and her parents relocated because she overheard Reginald's plans to overthrow Edwin."

"She did?" asked Tegan.

"Yes," Kenna replied. "She told one of the soldiers guarding the leader's house, but that soldier turned traitor and ended up serving as one of Reginald's soldiers."

"So how did Daisy hear about this plan?" Tegan asked.

Kenna laughed, "She was a cook in the pub where the conspirators met."

"Wait, Reginald met his fellow conspirators in a *pub* to discuss mutiny?!" Tegan scoffed. "How unexciting. I expected something more flamboyant to match his outrageous personality!"

"What? Like a golden chariot surrounded by singing birds?" Kenna asked playfully.

"A *flying* golden chariot ablaze with flames!" Tegan played along.

"...and singing birds!" The two snickered together.

Kenna continued, "There are still others in Old Padley. A few business owners decided to make the village their new home, refusing to move back to Chipping Farms. For them, it was better to start all over rather than risk their lives under Reginald's regime." She stopped in her tracks and turned around to announce, "Ah, here we are."

An immense, ancient tree stood before them. The trunk, massive and gnarly, towered above the travelers. Its long leaves hung from willowy branches like flimsy curtains. On closer inspection, the tree contained several holes in the lower part of the trunk, where candle lights flickered through soft, muslin drapes.

Creatures lived here.

Puffs of smoke curled out of small chimneys near the roots, and umbrella-like mushrooms flourished around the ground in front of the tree.

Kenna barked little fox chirps, and then waited. The woods remained quiet, hushed even. Puzzled, Tegan watched the little fox as she used her paws to cup her mouth and chirp again. Beckett stood next to her in his own world. He stared at the scene in front of him, not sure of what to make of it. This appeared to be a small commune residing in an ancient tree. But it seemed the residents were away for lunch or something...or possibly hiding?

At that moment, a throaty barking sound echoed back, from high up in the tree branches. The travelers looked up to see where the noise came from, and saw a furry head pop out of a nest made of twigs and straw.

"Hello?" Kenna called out.

"Kenna?" the furry head asked. "Is that really you?" The head disappeared and rustled through the leaves on the branch. "Ma!" it continued, "do you know who's here? It's Kenna!"

Another head emerged. This time, a female fox appeared holding a smaller one in her arms. "I say!" the fox exclaimed. "It *has* been a while!" The baby giggled in her arms. "Wait there and I will send down the ladder."

"We're going up?" Beckett asked.

"Looks like it," Tegan replied with a bit of confusion.

A long rope unrolled from the branch to almost the bottom of the tree. It contained small planks of wood for footholds tied together with vines. Kenna tugged on the rope....it felt strong enough, but also seemed hastily assembled.

Kenna stepped onto the first plank and hoisted herself up. Carefully, she climbed the creaky vine and wood ladder as it flopped against the trunk of the ancient tree. Higher and higher she ascended until she could touch the rim of the nest with her paw. Kenna raised her head to look over the nest wall and saw the baby's face right in front of hers...the baby squealed and startled Kenna, causing her foot to slip off the top plank.

Witnessing this from the ground, Tegan gasped and clutched her paws together.

"I'm fine!" Kenna called down to her friends. The little fox swung her legs over the twiggy wall of the nest and rolled into the middle of the structure. Warm, fluffy down feathers padded the bottom of the nest, along with a few woolen blankets. Kenna leaned over the wall and motioned for Tegan to climb up next.

The baby fox crawled over to Kenna as she waited for the sombel to scale the ladder.

"Pip!" Kenna picked up the furry little fox and kissed him on the top of his head. She turned to the baby's mother and hugged her saying, "So good to see you again, Mella."

"Aye, you too! How are your parents doing?" Mella asked as she handed Pip a warm bottle.

"They are still the same....in hiding, but making plans."

"Tell them to come back, we've plenty of room, you know," Mella said and then added. "We miss them."

"It's been hard for them to adjust. But Ma and Pa will visit again, and be thrilled to meet your little ones!" Kenna laughed. "Where are your other kids?"

"Ah, well, you already saw Tessie when she called out to you from up here. And Dermot has Amon inside trying to give him a bath. Pip, here, just needed some fresh air," Mella said as she cradled the baby again. "Dinner is almost ready. Bring your friends inside and we will eat together."

Kenna looked over her shoulder and saw Tegan pull herself up and over the nest wall. Right behind her was Beckett. They both rolled into the center of the nest and sat up. Kenna pulled the rope ladder back up and asked, "Where's Prince Callum?"

At that moment, a gust of air announced the prince's arrival. He flew up to the nest like a nimble butterfly with long, rapidly flapping wings. The pixie flew over the wall of the nest and landed ever so gently next to Tegan.

"Look!" Tessie pointed to the prince and shouted. "It's a giant bug!"

"Tessie!" Kenna half laughed and half scolded.

"It's alright," the prince responded gently and chuckled. He approached the little fox and kneeled in front of her. "I am a pixie. We have wings too. My name is Prince Callum." He presented his hand for a friendly handshake, and she accepted.

"My ma said you are eating dinner with us," Tessie said to the prince. "You can sit next to me."

Kenna, Tegan, and Beckett smiled.

"Guess we know who Tessie's new best friend is!" Kenna said to the sombels.

They laughed. It was good to make light conversation, as well as meet new faces. It felt so refreshing.

The group ducked their heads and huddled into an opening in the tree trunk covered with heavy blue fabric. Inside the room, each one took a seat at a long table (consisting of two short tables pulled together). The walls were covered with shelves holding little white bowls, plates, cups, and a funny little tea pot. A short curtain hid what must be the pantry...a small broom lay against a sack of flour in the corner. In the back of the room sat a black pot on a pile of hot embers in the fireplace; steam rolling out of the lid that rested crookedly on top.

Another room or two splintered off into the hallway. A male fox carrying a baby entered the dining area and sat down at the head of the table. He placed the baby in a high chair next to him.

"Hello, Kenna," he said. "Mella told me you were here. Welcome."

"Mr. Dermot, hi!" Kenna reached over to shake his paw. "And this must be, Amon?" She nodded to the baby and ruffled the fur on top of his head.

"Yes, he gave me quite the workout in the bath tub today," Dermot replied shaking his head.

Amon bounced up and down in his chair babbling.

Kenna turned to her friends, "This is Dermot. He is the head of the military, or was, when Edwin was king. This is his wife, Mella, and their kids, Amon, Tessie, and Pip. Dermot served under Edwin for years until..."

"Until Reginald's mutiny happened," Dermot said.

The atmosphere fell into a bit of awkwardness. But Kenna introduced Tegan, Beckett, and Prince Callum in a delicate but amiable tone.

"Prince Callum," Dermot started. "Are you related to King Fallon?"

"He is my father," the prince replied.

"I met him many years ago," said Dermot. "Give him my regards."

Mella walked around with bowls of stew and handed them to each of the visitors, along with chunks of barley bread. The bread, itself, was still too hot to touch but the stew's temperature was perfect. Beckett dove in like he hadn't eaten in a week. Tegan elbowed him to slow down.

"Kenna, my wife says your parents are doing well," Dermot stated. He sipped the stew from his spoon and continued, "Why do you visit without them?"

"Sir, I have been asked to help these travelers sneak into Old Padley," Kenna replied.

Dermot put his utensil down and asked, "But why? You do know that the rats of Voldire landed near the shore not far from here?" He didn't wait for an answer. "They set up camp and won't leave until they've destroyed everything in their path."

"Old Padley is not the only village that the rats have invaded," Prince Callum said. "The truth is, those black rats have been breaking the rules of the Compromise Treaty for months now. Something needs to be done before war breaks out again. Even this community here is in urgent danger. My father has drawn up a document that we are to deliver to the rat king...which is why we need all the help we can get."

"Sir, I am to take the document to the rat king," Tegan added.

"You?" Dermot asked incredulously. "To Greygor?!" The military fox laughed dryly. "But you are just a sombel. You will need an army to back you up!" He shook his head.

"I have been mocked and doubted since I started this journey. And to the point where I began doubting myself," Tegan replied. "But with all due respect, sir, I intend to fulfill the destiny that's been given to me so I can return home...to my family." She lowered her eyes and continued eating with the others.

Prince Callum stepped in to explain, "We believe Tegan is the one that's been prophesied about. Have you heard this prophesy?"

"Of course, but can you be sure she is *the* one? I mean, it's been foretold many times, but never fulfilled," replied Dermot.

Tegan stood up and turned around, showing off her red tail. Dermot's eyes widened.

"So you see, we are very serious about this mission and its completion," Tegan said and sat back down.

"Do you actually think Greygor will stop?" Dermot smirked and continued to eat.

"In my opinion? No," the prince responded. "However, our mission is to deliver the terms and that is all. Whatever happens after that is for the military to respond to," the prince used his spoon to illustrate his words. "Right now, an army of sombels are waiting in a village to the north of us; watching, waiting, preparing for any war-like movements from Greygor's group."

Dermot and his wife ate in silence for a few minutes with the rest of the travelers. Each had their own thoughts swirling around in their heads.

"What do you need from us then?" asked Dermot.

"Just a place to rest," the prince replied. "And protection while we plan our strategy."

Dermot sat up straight and nodded, "Then you shall have it." He motioned to Mella, "Ask Castor and Moss to join us." Mella wiped her paws on her apron and disappeared down the hall and the staircase. Dermot turned back to the group and said, "Castor is my lieutenant, and Moss is second in command. Both have specific knowledge that might be useful for this mission."

"We are in your debt," Prince Callum replied.

Mella's steps echoed in the hallway; she rounded the corner and announced to the guests in the dining area, "Come! Let's go out on the back terrace where our friends are playing music. We could use a little amusement, and they want to meet you all," she said cheerfully.

Tegan and Beckett stood up and placed their dishes in the sink, following Mella out of the room. Prince Callum paced around nervously. He watched as the sombels disappeared up a staircase and through a door to the deck outside. As he hesitated near the sink, Kenna asked Dermot, "Why do you live so far up in the tree branches? The last time I was here, all the families dwelled in fox holes or rooms in the lower part of the trunk."

"Since the rats showed up, we've had to move our homes farther up the tree for protection," Dermot replied and shifted in his chair. "There are a couple of families still conducting business at the bottom, but most of us with wee ones live up here now. Besides, the old owl nest is comfortable and warm for the kids to play in. Sometimes we sleep out there when the stars are particularly bright." He sighed, "It's not ideal, I know. But we're hoping this will soon pass and the rats will move on. We have a guard here already monitoring their movements."

"You can see the camp from here?" the prince asked intrigued.

"Yes," Dermot replied. "There's a branch near the top of this tree that houses an old squirrel nest. We call it 'the landing.' It's the best hiding place since we can watch the camp easily without being seen."

"Fascinating..." Prince Callum mused. "Will you show it to me?"

"Of course," Dermot said and stood up. "Let's go."

Suddenly, another fox, dressed in a camouflaged tunic, bolted into the dining room, holding his chest and panting. He addressed Dermot and exclaimed, "Sir, come with me to the landing. You need to see this!"

CHAPTER 30

The rat commander pointed his weapon away and pulled the rat leader off the cell door.

"Move!" he waved his sword. The leader slinked to the side, away from the prisoner's holding cell.

The commander dropped his weapon and produced a dagger, picking the knot that held the door closed. To the commander's side, the rat leader stepped farther and farther away from the action, very slowly, so as not to attract any attention. The leader leaned over to his nearest soldier and whispered something into the rat's ear. The soldier nodded and then slipped away.

It was only a few moments before the commander sensed something was off and turned around. "Wasn't there another soldier here a minute ago?" he asked suspiciously.

"Oh, I sent him back to the frontlines," the leader said hesitantly.

"You're not going back on our little agreement, are you?" the commander asked waving his dagger in the leader's face.

"No, no, you're the commander," the leader snarled.

The commander locked eyes with the leader and held his stare. Eventually, the commander released his glare and turned his attention back to the cell door.

"It's a shame that the two of you cannot get along," Lewis piped up. "That doesn't bode well for your leader."

The commander stopped picking at the knot and asked, "What do you mean?"

"Suppose your leader *does* succeed in overthrowing Greygor and takes over his reign, how do you know you can trust him? I mean, do you think this leader will keep his word and allow you to maintain your commander status? Or will he turn you out and take over everything...and everyone, including you?" Lewis mused out loud.

The commander returned to his knot, "Just like last time," he muttered.

"Pardon?" Lewis asked.

The rat commander cleared his throat and commented loud enough for the leader to hear, "That won't be a problem, will it my leader?"

The rat leader turned his attention to the commander and coolly replied, "That all depends."

"On what?!" the commander shouted at him.

The leader strutted forward and placed one paw on his hip, the other paw extended a finger that pointed at the commander's nose, "Your place depends on your loyalty."

The rat commander threw his dagger at the leader's head but missed. Then he swung his fists in fury. The first strike missed its target, as the leader ducked and stood up again. Leaning back with paws on each hip, the leader guffawed at the commander who stayed there huffing and puffing.

The commander rushed again and landed a thrusted fist into the gut of the laughing leader, causing the wounded rat to double over and gasp for air. The commander jumped on top of the leader and put his paws around his neck, his yellow teeth bared, hatred dripping from his mouth. Stunned from the solid punch, the leader struggled to lessen the commander's grip, rocking from side to side in an effort to shake off his perpetrator.

Watching the commotion, Lewis reflected, "And so the pendulum swings." As the ruckus continued between the leader and the commander, Lewis jiggled the door frame hoping to loosen the knot that held him captive. Seeing it start to unwind, he pulled his own dagger out, which was shrewdly hidden in his vest, and sawed back and forth on the frayed area of the vines. The sombel pushed down on the tethers one more time and they finally snapped. He was free!

Lewis opened the door quietly, peeked out, and waited for the right moment. As soon as the commander wrestled the leader back to the ground, Lewis jumpstarted out of the prison cell door. He leapt over the fighting rats and stumbled along the path leading back to the shore. Every step he took, his heart raced even more. Where should he go? Which direction is safe?

Lewis heard a howling shriek from behind him and guessed the rats discovered his escape. He ran parallel to the footpath to cover his tracks. If he could reach the river, the sombel could escape downstream...somehow.

Over some brambly hedges and under saggy tree limbs, Lewis fled. Panicked and weary, his only source of energy was adrenaline. What little food he had eaten over the past few days was nothing less than disgusting, even rotten. He managed to secure a few berries through the openings of his cage, and even scored a handful of peas as they wheeled through the last settlement. Though the rats did offer their slop to the sombel, he refused to eat it. Lewis swore after the first meal that his vision had been somehow impaired by the little he had eaten...and for sure, his digestion.

Rounding a huge boulder, Lewis scampered between two smaller rocks and suddenly came face to face with a rat soldier. He skidded to a stop as the soldier swung a large strip of wood and smacked him across his head. Lewis fell face down in the grass and blacked out.

"Fool!" Greygor shouted and threw his helmet at the soldier, hitting him in the chest.

The rat soldier dropped the piece of wood and struggled to remain on his feet. He then slumped down to check on the prisoner and said, "He's still alive."

"It's a good thing he is, for your sake," Greygor replied. "Get him up and into the wagon."

The wounded shoulder grabbed both of Lewis' feet while the other soldiers lifted his arms and head. They hoisted his body into the bed of a poorly built wagon. The structure itself was not so shoddy in construction, but the pieces of wood didn't seem to quite fit together. So any weight put on it made the boards creak and sometimes sag. Lewis' weight, unfortunately, made the wagon squeal.

"Did you see any others?" the rat king asked a soldier tying up the back of the wagon.

"No, sir," he replied and stood up. "No one."

"Fine, it doesn't matter much anyway," Greygor replied. "I'll have the gemstones in no time now." He gestured toward the camp, "Take the prisoner away. As soon as he wakes up, we roll!"

Prince Callum followed Dermot and the fox guard into the landing box perched high up on a tree limb. The box offered complete secrecy to its inhabitants thanks to the leaves that covered it from top to bottom. Inside, the tiny thatched roof sheltered a wooden floor, a small table, two chairs, and a storage chest made of bark. A little lantern hung from the roof that gave the room a warm, orange glow.

The fox guard stepped inside first and handed a small pair of binoculars to Dermot. As he viewed the scene below, Dermot shook his head and handed the binoculars to the prince. And what the prince saw below them, made him hold his breath.

A wagon carrying a sombel rolled under the trees. A couple of rat soldiers pulled the cart in the front while one soldier pushed from behind. Slowly, it made its way along a skinny footpath towards the rat's campsite.

"Is he...?" the prince tried to ask.

"No, I don't think he's dead." Dermot replied. "They need information from him. He is too valuable to the king."

Prince Callum sat motionless, scrutinizing the scene below him. No one said anything; all they could hear was each other's breathing. The prince continued watching the wagon as it crept close to the campsite. And then it stopped; the soldiers dropped the ropes and turned their backs to the wagon to guard it.

While the king waited for Lewis to regain consciousness, he ordered his minions to gather supplies and dump them into the same wagon as the sombel. Rats scurried from the clay ovens to the cook's firepit, and back to the wagon, while Greygor sat on the throne above and watched.

Lowering the binoculars, the prince said to Dermot, "Let's meet with the others now!"

Dermot shot toward the door and raced off to gather a few of the foxes he knew would be helpful for the mission. Not only were Castor and Moss rounded up, but Dermot found Daisy as well.

The group entered Mella's home again and sat around the table, with Dermot and the prince sitting side by side.

Castor pulled out a hand-drawn map of the campsite and shoreline. He handed it to Dermot so he could show the prince, and the two discussed the best entry into the enemy's territory. As the foxes and pixie asked questions and strategized, the sun began to set. Shadows presented themselves throughout the little home, and Mella walked around lighting candles and lanterns to keep the room as bright as possible.

She watched as the planners listened to one another, turning the map around and around, pointing to various entryways, and noting landmarks with color ink. The voices hummed and droned as the group finally agreed on the safest course of action.

"There, this is her entry, and Kenna knows it perfectly," Castor stated.

"Mella?" Dermot called, "Mella, will you find our guests and bring them here?"

"Yes, of course," Mella replied and zipped out of the room.

Mella followed the sound of stringed music down the stairs and around to the terrace. The little lights hanging from the balcony twinkled and bounced as the dancers hopped around on the floor. The band consisted of three foxes, each playing a different instrument: a fiddle, a mandolin, and a flute. The jolly tunes lightened the mood and eased the tension mounting amidst the rat campsite.

Tegan and Beckett took to the dance floor and tried their best at dancing, laughing as they swung each other around. Kenna joined them, even though she claimed she couldn't dance. But the merriment got the best of her and soon the rest of the fox families, including the wee ones, were frolicking to various country folk dances.

To the side of the folk band, a table decorated with fresh purple petals hosted a clay pitcher full of fresh ale. With so many parched dancers, this ale stood ready to offer the best refreshment on the dance floor. Tegan reached for a small clay mug and poured the ale into her cup. As she drank the ale, the taste reminded her of the first days of autumn. A hint of apple and spices tingled on her tongue. She offered a cup to Beckett when Mella showed up.

"Tegan, Beckett, are you enjoying yourselves?" Mella asked.

"Very much so," Tegan smiled. "The band is *fantastic!*"

"And so is the ale," Beckett replied and poured another drink.

"Friends, Dermot and the prince are ready to see you now," Mella said. She motioned to Kenna to follow her, "Kenna, you too."

The three visitors wound their way back down the stairs and into the snug room where Dermot, Castor, Moss, Daisy, and the prince waited at the table. Tegan and Beckett sat down on fancy cushions next to the table and Kenna stood on the opposite side, staring intensely at the map before her.

"We discussed delivering the terms of surrender during the day, as well as at night," Prince Callum started. "But we couldn't decide on the safest method of delivery. As for the time of delivery, Castor suggested dawn. And I believe we all agree on that?"

The foxes at the table nodded in agreement and mumbled 'yes' under their breath. Tegan felt a sense of foreboding in her chest. The end of her quest drew near. And after travelling so far with her friends, she knew this mission was something she had to do alone.

Or did she?

"Will anyone else accompany me?" Tegan asked.

Moss spoke up, "Kenna will be there to lead the way. She'll get you close enough to hand off the document—"

"Wearing the cloak of Fis, of course," the prince interrupted.

"Yes, I will speak with Kenna about the exact path to take," Moss said. "In the meantime, we have agreed as a group to watch from the landing box."

"I'll watch from the ground," Beckett stated. He felt nervous now that the end was in sight. "I want to be as close as possible in case...."

"She will be fine," Daisy assured the sombel. This was the first time Daisy spoke up and the visitors were intrigued. "Maybe it's best to have someone on the ground level anyway." She nodded to Beckett and smiled.

"Of course," Dermot responded. "Daisy has been keeping an eye on the camp since the rats landed here."

"For a while, the rats built a throne and forged weapons in their fire ovens," Daisy said solemnly. "But over the last 24 hours, the atmosphere has changed. Machines have rolled in....the rats are scrambling, scurrying, packing their belongings...." She took a deep breath. "From what the guards have seen from the landing, it looks like the rats are moving soon."

"And taking their prisoner with them," Castor said.

Tegan looked at the prince. She was visibly shaken.

"This is your destiny, Tegan," the prince reassured her. "I've watched you throughout this journey; you are not the same sombel I first met in the tunnels. You've struggled, you've fought, but you're more confident in yourself now than ever before.

The prophecy claims that you are the deliverer. We also believe that you are the deliverer. But for the prophecy to come to fruition, you must fulfill the quest. You've learned defensive skills with your sword, and will be protected by the cloak of Fis. Besides, we will be watching over you." Even the prince felt fear deep in his pixie heart, but he calmed his voice before speaking again. "It will be over soon. Keep a cool head, my friend, just think about going home."

"And Uncle Lewis?" Tegan asked distraught.

"The rats will not harm him," the prince said. "He holds the information they need. Remember that the sombel army will be here soon, and they will rescue him, somehow. I'm sure of it."

Mella slipped in and opened the heated oven, releasing the fragrance of fresh barley bread. The delicious aroma filled the air and overturned the somber atmosphere.

"Our clan has a tradition," Mella said as she placed the warm bread on the table. "Before a momentous occasion," she spoke slow and intentionally, "we gather for barley bread and wine. It's a symbolic moment for us to come together as a group and offer our loyalty and faith to those about to go into battle....whether it be an actual war or a momentous quest."

Mella sliced the fragrant bread with a knife and handed a slice to each one in the room. Dermot stood up and collected cups for the wine. As Dermot poured the wine into the mugs and handed each one out, he raised his cup and spoke, "To those of us chosen for this quest, I speak blessings and favor."

The foxes raised their cups in unison and agreed, "Aye!"

The sombels and the prince copied their actions. Everyone drank their wine together.

Then Dermot held his slice of bread and spoke, "To those setting out on this particular mission, we speak safety and completion of the quest!"

Again, the group raised their slices and shouted, "Aye!" Then they ate their bread.

"More wine, dear?" Mella asked Tegan.

"Yes, please," she replied. Tegan felt empowered. As simple as the ceremony was, it had bolstered her confidence and even managed to make her smile. It was comforting to know so many believed in her and supported her mission.

"Fill your cups, my friends," Dermot announced. "We have a prophesy to fulfill at dawn!"

The warm room and the flickering candles made Tegan sleepy. She finished her wine and found a cozy spot near the fireplace. In the midst of the noise, she curled up, covering her head with her warm cloak. She felt overwhelmed with information and decided to leave the details to those still awake. The last thing she overheard was Kenna and Castor discussing the entry point for the morning's run. But it was late and she needed sleep.

"Poor thing," Mella whispered to her husband. "Tegan is worn out." She picked up a wool blanket and covered the sombel with it, tucking the sides in around her. "She has the world on her shoulders," she muttered.

"Let her sleep, she needs it," Dermot whispered and turned to the prince, "the dawn will reveal what the future holds...for all of us."

CHAPTER 31

"Where have you been?!" Arthur screeched as he ran to meet the captain.

"I'm back from the campsite," Milo said out of breath. The sombel captain spent the past few hours scurrying back to the army site to inform his unit about a new plan.

"Well, while you were gone, the reinforcements showed up. We have the full army now at your command," Arthur said.

"Good, we're going to need them," responded Milo. He caught one of the soldiers by the tunic and asked him to round up the other officers. "Tell them to meet me immediately in the planning tent. I want to change up a few things."

"Change? Change what??" Arthur raced behind Milo as the captain headed toward the tent.

"Strategy...change strategy," Milo replied.

"You don't mean—" Arthur was interrupted by a rush of soldiers flooding past them and into the tent. They gathered around a makeshift table, waiting for their leader to begin.

"Soldiers, I have returned from a visit to the rat campsite," Milo began. "It is clear to me that we must strike immediately, in order to get Lewis back safely. There's no time to waste, so we're not holding out for pixie soldiers or other clans to join us," he said gravely. "I have a map and a possible entry point that I think our troops can overtake---"

"But won't that put Tegan's mission in jeopardy?" Arthur asked softly as to keep his dissension hidden from the soldiers.

Milo grunted. "Tegan's quest is a fantasy. How can she deliver the terms without getting captured or hurt," Milo said. "Those terms of surrender should be delivered by a strong army. An army like ours!" He then softened his voice to address Arthur, "I'm afraid Tegan will get hurt, Arthur."

"But it is the *prophecy*; don't you believe in that?" Arthur asked.

"I believe in what I can see," Milo said. "Besides, the rats are restless and Lewis must be rescued tonight. We must act now! I saw it with my own eyes! We march in an hour."

"In that case, I cannot stop you, Milo," Arthur said. "But I do want to ask a favor, my friend. Suppose the prophecy is really true...Tegan believes in it and so do I. If you engage those rats before she has a chance to deliver the document, then she will walk into a lion's den, and we gamble with her life...and the lives of Beckett and Prince Callum. Please, for the families involved in this mission, will you please consider waiting until morning? We'll have a better view then."

"What about Lewis?" Milo asked.

"Lewis is a retired military soldier, he can take care of himself for a little longer...at least until we can figure this out," Arthur said.

Milo looked long and hard at Arthur. The sombel had a point, Lewis was tough. But Milo didn't want to give these rats any more leeway. He turned to observe his soldiers and rubbed his forehead, groaning while he considered these thoughts over and over in his head.

"Fine," Milo sighed, "we will wait until dawn." He then addressed the soldiers, "Get your weapons and a few supplies together. We leave at daybreak."

"Thank you," Arthur said. "I do expect news on Tegan's whereabouts by then."

Milo nodded in return. "Now let's hope she gets to the campsite before we do."

"Tegan, dear, it's time to leave," Mella said as she gently woke the sombel.

Tegan opened her eyes and realized it was still dark outside. From where she slept, she could see the moon high in the sky....a curious shade of red. Never had she witnessed a blood moon before, and it didn't sit well within her. She quietly searched Beckett's bag for the terms of surrender document and placed it in her own bag, next to the cloak of Fis. Dressed in her wool cloak and her short sword, Tegan was now ready to go. She met Kenna near her room.

Kenna wore her gear too: a bag, a belt with a small dagger, and a brown hood to cover her head and eyes. She met Tegan in the stairwell and said, "Tegan, come this way. The others are waiting for us."

"Did you see the moon?" Tegan asked.

"Yes," Kenna replied, "a blood moon it seems."

The two climbed down the stairs until they made it to the large nest. Mella handed Tegan a bit of bread and some water while Prince Callum and Beckett circled around her.

"Follow Kenna," the prince advised, "and I'll watch you from the landing."

"I'll go on foot with you two for awhile, and then hang back for support," Beckett said.

Tegan looked over the prince's shoulders and caught a glimpse of a few foxes bundled in scarves; Castor, Moss, and Daisy. Then Dermot walked up behind them and signaled to Tegan, "Godspeed! The best to you on your mission!" The other foxes lifted their paws in support.

"Go now, before the sun breaks on the horizon," the prince said and hesitated, noting the odd, reddish color of the moon.

Tegan, Beckett, and Kenna scaled down the rope ladder and jumped to the ground. The grass felt wet from dew and a little chilly to the touch. The red moon peeked out from behind a few scattered clouds, providing an eerie tinted light along the footpath they walked on.

Tegan kept her eyes on Kenna as they hiked, not allowing herself any thoughts...good or bad. She needed to get through this mission with a clear head. After a stretch on the trail, Kenna motioned to the others to follow her off the path and under a tangled arch of vines. Each one stepped through the small opening, unsure of what was next.

Little splashes of light illuminated the walkway as tiny fluorescent mushrooms offered the travelers a way to see in front of them. Through the protection of the vines, the group heard rushing water. Mist, cooler temperatures, and damp air signaled that they were near a fast-moving water source.

"Quick, this way!" Kenna whispered, but somehow it echoed loudly.

The group approached a sizeable waterfall and quickly realized they were positioned *behind* the falls. The rush of the water crashing down on the rocks in front of them created a natural veil as well as noise cancellation. The hikers squeezed around the side of the thunderous waterfall and out onto grass again.

"If we get separated or in trouble, meet back here," Kenna said quietly. "Do you see that giant birch tree in the distance?" She pointed to a massive tree behind her. Tegan nodded. "That is your target. It's a safe haven. The rats are encamped near it and the river is not far from there." Kenna paused for a moment, "Tegan, be very careful." Then she hugged the sombel.

Beckett said, "I'll track you from the bushes here. I don't have a magic cloak, so I have to stay hidden." He hugged his friend, "Good luck and stay safe."

Tegan took a deep breath and pulled out the cloak of Fis from her bag. Leaving her old cloak on a rock near the waterfall, she slipped into the magical cloak and tied it closely to her. Her body from the neck down suddenly disappeared into the night. She looked at her paws and then turned around in the moonlight to see the invisibility for herself.

Beckett chuckled, "I am so jealous! The cloak is splendid!"

Tegan smiled and rummaged through her bag. "Can't forget this," she held up the terms of surrender in her paw. And with that, Tegan grabbed the edges of the magical hood and pulled it over her head and eyes. As her head disappeared with the rest of her body, Tegan stepped out on her own. Kenna and Beckett retreated to their designated "meet up" spot. The little fox gathered Tegan's old wool cloak and stuffed it into her bag.

It was as though the night became a silvery veil in and of itself. As Tegan hiked toward the ancient birch tree, she practically floated over the rocks and stones below her feet. The small, nocturnal animals that foraged under the protection of darkness showed no reaction as the sombel passed by. They could not see her.

Around a large boulder and over a fallen tree trunk she climbed. The closer Tegan got to the camp, the faster her heart raced. She took a few deep breaths to calm her nerves. She needed to stay focused.

The sombel finally reached a clearing of stones and timber, debris spread across the land as if destruction had just passed through. Tegan got close enough to see a clump of rats sleeping near a dwindling fire; kicking, pushing, wrestling for a position, even in their sleep. Tiptoeing around the edge of the dreaming rodents, Tegan noticed huge machines...machines that she had never seen before, even in her school books! They were massive, with levers and ropes and large wheels. She stood there, silent, in awe, allowing the severity of the moment to settle in. It suddenly dawned on Tegan that this mission was not about her. It was, in fact, about whether war could be prevented.

Around the machines she tiptoed lightly, fearing the very sight of them as she paced. She reached an area where a stone path appeared to lead up to a giant structure of some kind. Tegan tried to get closer, but could not see well, even with her cat-like night vision.

Curiosity compelled her to climb those stairs, one by one, slowly...steadily, until at last, she stood face to face with the rat king himself, Greygor!

Terrified, Tegan froze in full panic as she watched the rat king mumble and come in and out of sleep, snoring, drooling from that toothy mouth. The sight of the ghastly rodent frightened her so much that she instinctively backed up....and lost her footing. Tegan toppled over the stony edge, hitting her knee first on a rock and then her arm, and landed square on the ground, flat on her back. With the wind knocked out of her, she gasped for air. The sombel rolled over and sat up, groaning under her breath and stretching her limbs. Nothing broken, but she was sure her body would be hurting later in the day.

The noise roused a sleeping rat entangled in the rodent pile near the fire. His ears twitched and his eyes opened. Without seeing anything, the rat scratched its belly and repositioned itself, pushing on the rat next to him with his back legs. A chain reaction occurred where each of the rats felt a push or nudge by the one next to it, and woke the slumbering rodents to a groggy awareness.

Tegan rapidly checked for the moon...still there, still red; and it wasn't dawn yet. She felt for her bag and patted her side. Something was off. *Where is my sword?* Tegan frantically searched the dark landscape for her weapon. Even with her night vision, she had trouble spotting—*oh, there it is!*

Right in the middle of that pile of rats, laid the beautiful blade gifted to her from the pixie king. It must have come loose when she fell. She crept closer to the drowsy group hoping the rats would drift off to sleep again. Knowing her invisibility was tied to the darkness and the moonlight, Tegan calculated the odds in her head. The odds of climbing over a few ghastly rodents to rescue her beloved sword. Time was running out; she didn't have a choice.

After evaluating the best way in, Tegan took a tiny step forward and balanced herself between two snoring beasts. She felt the heat from the burning embers and smelled decay and death all around her. Holding her breath, she steadied herself by placing each paw on the shoulders of the rats beside her. She waited to see if they moved. Then she stepped up and placed her foot on the belly of one of the rodents, and then the head of another. If this situation wasn't so horrendous, she would laugh at the absurdity of it all.

High enough now to see the tip of the sword, she reached her arm out but still couldn't grab it. Another step onto matted black fur, another, and another. Easy and steady, the sombel balanced on the limbs and backs of the dreaded rats to reach her sword. Tegan stretched as far as she could and finally grasped the handle. As she pulled the weapon out of the pile, it sliced a rodent's ear and the rat jerked his head up, causing the others to move around. Tegan lost her balance. She rolled over and down the mound onto the ground, clasping the sword with all her strength.

Tegan held her sword in front of her, ready for attack. But the rats squirmed and stretched, confused as to the commotion. She checked her hood and the cloak. *Where was the rat king?* She looked quickly to the right and saw a shadow pass under the moon's light above. Frantic, she clasped the sword and scampered back to the stone stairs, dreading the climb back up; but eager to relinquish the document that she held on to.

Stepping onto the stones, Tegan felt the cold under her feet. One by one she scaled the stairs until she reached the top. This time, she would be even more cautious. As she approached the stone throne, Tegan noticed the sun breaking through the early morning clouds. Over the horizon, pink and orange clouds manifested the day break. The blood red moon became overshadowed by the clouds. And with that, the cloak of Fis shimmered a translucent shine. Tegan looked down and could now scarcely make out her arms and chest through the cloak. The invisibility power was fading!

She grabbed the terms from her bag and reached out to place the document on the throne. But the king was not in the chair!

"Well, what do we have here?" Greygor snarled from behind the sombel.

Tegan froze.

CHAPTER 32

From the bushes, Beckett watched his friend as she struggled to stay hidden in the predawn hours. He realized Tegan needed help and ran back to the meeting spot near the waterfall. Surely Kenna would be there and they could summon the others to rescue her.

Beckett searched for Kenna and finally spied her waiting behind the rushing waters of the falls. Stepping out, Kenna spotted Beckett and read the worried look on his face. "Is Tegan in danger?" she asked.

"Yes!" Beckett managed to speak in between breaths. "We need backup! Go get the prince and the others!" The sombel dashed off again and disappeared in the bushes, determined to infiltrate the campsite despite only having a sword to defend himself. He refused to wait for backup.

Kenna's heart sank and she had difficulty swallowing. She retraced her steps all the way back to the ancient tree where they had spent the night. Much of the journey was a complete blur as the fox relied purely on instinct and adrenaline to get her there. As Kenna neared the tree, she saw the prince, Dermot, and Moss already descending the rope ladder. A few more foxes gathered around them on the ground; all circling, angry, and preparing for war.

"Tegan's in trouble!" Kenna squeaked out frantically.

"We saw it," the prince responded as he slipped on his bow and quiver of arrows. Dermot and Moss geared up as well, their bows positioned on their backs.

"Show us the way, Kenna," Dermot said. "The rest of the soldiers will catch up with us."

Kenna heard rustling in the tree branches above her. She could see shadows of the foxes' heads and the points of the bows as they carried the weapons on their backs. As the others jumped from the ladder to the ground, Kenna asked the prince, "Ready?" He nodded in return.

The prince and the foxes filed behind Kenna waiting for direction. She quickly scampered down the path as the morning light began to break. It was officially dawn. As she ran, all the fox could think about were those hideous yellow teeth and greasy black fur. The stench...oh the stench of those beasts! And poor Tegan was right in the middle of it.

Kenna looked back to make sure Prince Callum and the others were following her. She could barely see them in between the light. Gusts of wind howled from above and shadows passed over the ground. The little fox hoped there would be no storms today. The morning had proved to be difficult already.

Through the small opening in the brambly bushes and onto the mushroom fields, the group finally neared the backside of the waterfall. Kenna motioned for the followers to duck around the falls and step out to the side. From there, the little fox pointed out the birch tree...the landmark among decay and doom. The growth in the middle of destruction...that was their destination.

Dermot assumed the lead and headed in the direction of the tree. His plan? It was two-fold. The first was to take his group out on the branches and lead an assault with bows and arrows. The other was to approach the rat camp from the north side of that birch tree. If they had to plan a rescue mission, for two this time, then the tree would be the best place from which to launch their campaign, and to hide in.

Tegan shrieked and turned around, looking the rat beast in his beady red eyes. She backed up as far as she could without tipping over the edge again, but Greygor blocked the steps. The sombel gripped the handle of her sword with all her might as the rat king examined the curious creature in front of him.

"What is this?" Greygor asked intrigued.

"It's a visitor!" the rat commander, who had been sleeping and woke to the king's voice, replied sarcastically.

The rat king growled at the commander. What was this little creature doing here?

Tegan shivered in the coldness of the rat's stare and quickly presented the terms of surrender to the rat king. He snatched the paper from her paws. There, her part was done. Now she wanted out! She turned to slip away under the curtain of dawn, but the commander stopped her.

"Where are you going, sombel?" the commander asked. "Stay awhile," he ordered and held onto her cloak.

Tegan stood before Greygor, shaking and speechless, watching the black, filthy beast unroll and read the document she just handed to him. "I see," the king muttered as he scanned the writing.

"Yes....no,no,no.....ha!....oh this is all wrong......" he looked up from the document and laughed. A high-pitched laugh that rang in Tegan's ears. She looked over her shoulder and noticed the piles of sleeping rats waking to the noise of their fiendish king. They stretched and reached for their weapons as they realized another creature had infiltrated their camp.

Greygor witnessed the movement and put his paws in the air, waving the document above him. "Easy soldiers," the rat king said. "This sombel is not a threat. She brings us a document!" He glared at Tegan and continued, "a useless—" Greygor ripped the terms in two, "worthless...." He tore it again, "hopeless piece of paper!" He wadded up what was left and threw it out into the audience of rat soldiers, who ravished the paper clumps at sight.

"Sir," Tegan found her voice, even though it was squeaky. "Sir, if you would please reconsider the terms and agree to stop fighting.... to go back to the wetlands...to quit destroying—"

"As if you have the power to stop me....you and your army of sombels," Greygor turned around and looked out over the horizon. "I am sure you're out there!!" He hollered out to the tree tops and the low side of the mountain in the distance. His growly voice caused Tegan's fur to stand on end. It echoed in the early morning hours, a grotesque disturbance among the otherwise peaceful atmosphere.

"Tegan?!" a voice called out, shrill and desperate. It was Lewis.

Startled, Tegan whipped her head around to behold her uncle seated in a poorly made wagon, paws tied together with some kind of rope. He appeared weak, tired maybe, with torn clothes and matted fur. But he managed a toothy smile. Finally, someone found him!

"Uncle Lewis," Tegan breathed out heavily as the weight of the situation dawned on her. Lewis was in inescapable danger. The rats would get what they wanted from him, or die trying.

"So, I see you two know each other?" Greygor mused out loud. Both sombels remained silent. "Of course, you do," the rat king sighed. "How charming."

Tegan pulled away from the rat commander holding her arm, and stood with her paw gripping her sword. *How would she ever get out of here? And take her uncle with her?*

"Go on, go see your friend," Greygor said slowly and emphatically. He encouraged the sombel to walk over to Lewis.

She tentatively stepped down the stairs, one by one, and scampered over to the wagon that held her uncle. The wagon tilted with his weight, but he sat up and shrieked, "Tegan?? It *is* you!"

Tegan jumped into the wagon with Lewis and hugged him tightly. She could feel his ribs through his vest and hear his heart beating wildly. It had been awhile since Tegan had seen him, and she truly savored this moment....Lewis was alive...but now, they needed an escape plan.

"Exactly where we want you," the commander scolded.

"Precisely," added Greygor. The rat king followed Tegan to the wagon. Several high-ranking rat soldiers formed a circle around the structure, entrapping the sombels on the cart. Greygor commanded, "Tie her up too. We'll take both of them to the tunnels to get my gemstones."

But before the rats could grab her paws, Tegan stood up and presented her sword.

"Back away," she shouted, "or I'll use it!" That was the only thing she could think to say. Some of the soldiers instinctively pulled away when they saw the shiny sword. But Greygor laughed. He laughed with a hateful, spiteful laugh, and then shouted angrily, "Enough of this nonsense!!"

Tegan interrupted him, "You, sir, are unreasonable!" His haughty and selfish attitude angered her to the point of no return. Boldness boiled within her and she pointed her sword at the grizzly looking beast, "did you even read the terms of surrender? Did you see the list of infractions on your account? Littleton, Winters Landing, Callding Creek, the list goes on and on. You and your goons have been breaching the Compromise Treaty for months, looting and stealing..." she waved her sword around, "and this stops now!"

Lewis leaned in and whispered to his niece, "Please, Tegan. I'll do what they want so you can be free." Her heart sank. She would not leave her uncle there.

"You have no army to stop us!" the rat king replied. "And I will get my paws on those moonstones!" He motioned to the commander next to him. "Restrain those two. We leave now! Soldiers, get to the machines and lead us away from here."

Tegan pointed her sword directly at the rat commander, "We will not comply," she stated under her breath.

"You will take the rat king to the entrance of that tunnel or I will make sure you never see your family again," the rat commander breathed back.

The fire in Tegan's heart rose to her head, and she grasped her sword with both paws. "No!" she shouted.

As the rat commander jumped forward to subdue the sombel, Tegan pointed her sword upwards and the green moonstone in the hilt began to glow. A slow glimmer at first, then a jolt of pure green radiance that transformed into a translucent dome to cover the two sombels, protecting them from the wrath of the commander. Smacking face first into the dome, the rat commander backed up to see what just happened to him. Confused, he pounded on the protective dome as Tegan struggled to hold the magnificent defense in place.

Lewis was completely dumbfounded. He scrambled for his dagger and pulled Tegan close to protect her. She might have the magic, but it was his duty to watch out for her!

As the rat commander and other soldiers stood watching the mystic dome before them, Greygor spied the moonstone in Tegan's sword.

"What is that?!" the rat king hissed. He pushed the soldiers out of the way and stood in front of the sombel. "Give me that gem!" He demanded.

Tegan struggled to keep the dome over herself and her uncle. She observed more rat soldiers scrambling towards the wagon to aid Greygor. Other rat soldiers ran like ants over and under tree limbs and rocks to form an offensive formation. As they lined up, Tegan panicked. Her dome flickered in and out. She was losing her concentration and Greygor knew that. He waited and watched.

Fatigued, Tegan finally broke her focus. The dome disappeared and the rat king seized the opportunity to snatch Tegan's sword. Greygor struggled to get it out of her paw as Lewis held on to it tightly as well. In the struggle, the little green moonstone popped out of the sword's handle and landed on the ground beneath them. Tegan dove for the jewel but the rat commander was faster. He scooped it up and handed it over to Greygor. The rat king now had the power of the moonstone right there in his paw. The tables had turned.

CHAPTER 33

S *woosh!*

The rat commander shrieked.

Swoosh, swoosh! Something zipped by Tegan's head. *What was that?!* A round of arrows rained from the sky, targeting the commander, the rat king, and rat soldiers. One arrow lodged itself in the commander's leg, leaving him unable to stand and fight. Other arrows hit or missed the small group of rats protecting Greygor. As the rodents howled and hissed, Tegan saw Greygor duck and back away from the wagon. Still clutching her gem-less sword, Tegan quickly cut the ropes tying Lewis to the cart and freed his paws.

Lewis held on to Tegan and pulled her to the side, away from the chaos. He spotted Greygor trotting toward a shelter, determined to flee with the moonstone. Lewis pointed in the same direction and both sombels ran. Though Lewis was malnourished and dehydrated, he outran the petite Tegan by a couple of strides. Ducking through the shower of arrows, they dodged injured rat soldiers confused by the overhead assault. As the sombels caught up to Greygor, Lewis took off running and snatched the green moonstone right from the rat king's grip. Greygor never saw it coming!

The rat king furiously twisted around and screamed a horrible, high-pitched sound that reverberated throughout the camp.

"YOU! Come back here with my gemstone!" He yelled to the sombels. But Tegan and Lewis cut through the low-lying bramble towards the ancient tree, north of the rat camp.

Finding an opening in a fallen log, the sombels stopped to catch their breaths. Lewis reached out and handed Tegan the small green moonstone, the precious gem that protected them earlier. She placed it back into the handle of her sword, relieved.

"Where do we go now?" Tegan asked.

Lewis was clearly in pain. He just used his last bit of energy to recover the gemstone and flee. He was done, and his face showed it. The sombel sighed, "I can't go on, Tegan. I need help to stand on my own two feet, and you're not strong enough to steady me." He winced as he straightened his back. "Do you see that giant birch tree to the north? The fox refugees use it as a view point. Go there and bring back help."

"But the rats will find you here," Tegan argued. "I'm not leaving you. We'll find another way." She stuck her head out of the shelter, looking for a solution, then pulled it back in. "If those beasts catch you again—"

"I'll be fine right here," Lewis interrupted with a reassuring tone. He stroked the fur on the top of her head, and she melted into his hug.

As they huddled in the log opening, the sound of voices reached their ears. Another round of arrows flew overhead. A black shadow swiftly cast a short-lived darkness over their hiding spot. Tegan and Lewis looked up, but couldn't figure out what caused the darkening all around them.

"Did you see that?" Tegan asked.

Before Lewis could answer, the shadow passed again.

"I thought I saw—" Lewis was interrupted by something coming towards them. Out of the bushes, Beckett ran to the hollow log and squeezed himself in with Lewis and Tegan.

"I am so glad to see you!" Tegan exclaimed.

"I've been tracking you since dawn," Beckett replied. "But this is the first time I could get close."

Lewis relaxed a bit and said, "If this strong, young sombel can help me stand, maybe we can make it to that ancient tree together after all."

Beckett lifted Lewis' arm and wrapped it around his shoulder. Then he grabbed Lewis' waist and helped hoist him up. The three sombels crept in the direction of the ancient tree, hoping they could find shelter there. Lewis steadied himself against Beckett on one side and a walking stick he picked up along the way on the other.

As the sombels trekked under the cover of the bushes and bramble, the arrows seemed to quiet down. However, there was still a hum in the air.

Just on the other side of the hedgerow, the sound of marching and metal clanking caused Greygor's soldiers to pause what they were doing, and locate the source of the noise. It was the sombel army with Milo in the lead.

Milo marched to the forest's edge, dressed in his military vest and wearing his metal sword. His face contorted as he surveyed the camp. Rocks, debris, lumber, machinery parts, fabric, arrows...the landscape appeared just as chaotic and unkempt as the squatters that stayed there. Milo squinted his eyes to locate Greygor through the smoke of burning logs and garbage piles. And there the rat king stood, near what used to be a stone staircase to his throne.

Greygor maintained his authority even though their site appeared apocalyptic. Most of the rat soldiers formed groups in front of him, in a defensive stance, while Milo's sombel army positioned themselves slightly behind the captain (with a few rogue sombels away on separate missions). From Milo's perspective, the rats were just far enough away that he could shout and still be heard by Greygor. Maybe fifty yards or more. Milo held his soldiers in line, waiting for the right moment to address the rat king in the confusion.

To the north of the rat camp stood the birch tree; and from its branches both Dermot and Moss assigned duties to their small group of fox warriors. Each of the fighters crouched on a particular branch, positioned for optimal range. Bows drawn and eyes on their target, the foxes watched the armies align themselves alongside their leaders. Aside from that, two foxes focused specifically on Tegan and her mission. As she walked, they repositioned themselves around the tree for ideal positioning.

"Reload archers!" Dermot called out to his group.

Each of the foxes lowered their bows and refilled their quivers with arrows. Their paws furiously packed the ammunition to prepare for the next attack. This batch was the last of their supplies, so Dermot hoped the arrows lasted the entire battle. He preferred long range warfare to fighting face to face with swords.

"Hold your fire until my orders," Dermot instructed. "Do you have a location for Tegan?" He asked the second in command.

"Sir, she has Lewis with her. They appear to be navigating through the bushes on the north side of the hedgerow," Moss replied.

"Why the north side I wonder?" Dermot asked.

"From what I see, it looks like Lewis is injured," Moss said. "They may chance the river instead. There's a path along the bank that leads to this tree.....assuming they pass through the Goldcrest slip."

"Ready, sir!" the nearest archer said.

"Good, wait for my command," Dermot replied.

Down in the encampment, Milo stood before the rats, ready to engage the enemy. He took a deep breath and called out to rat king, "Greygor!" Through the smoke and the stench, the rats chattered their teeth and jumped up and down. "GREYGOR!" Milo shouted.

The rat king took his time to respond, "What do you want?!" he commanded.

The sound of his grisly voice shook through the sombel army line. The sombels instinctively readied themselves with swords and bows and arrows, aligning closely with each other in defense.

"You received the terms of surrender, did you not?" Milo asked.

"I did," Greygor scoffed.

"Then you and your rats must cease and desist all invasions and attacks at once, and return to Homish, according to the decree by King Fallon," Milo stated.

"He is no king. I am the KING!" Greygor shouted. All the rats cheered and clinked their weapons together. The dreadful sound sent shivers down Milo's spine. He waited for the rats to settle down again.

"You must respect the orders given to you by the pixie king of Fellnore," Milo answered.

"And what if we don't?" the rat king added.

"Do you really want to lose lives over this?" Milo asked.

Greygor just shrugged his shoulders and mocked the sombel captain.

"Then by your actions, you have shown that you agree to have broken the Compromise Treaty and refused the terms of surrender. Be it known that, upon this day, the rats of Voldire will be no more. You, Greygor, have decided your own destiny and will therefore be delivered unto us for justice," Milo declared.

The sombel army cheered and readied themselves for attack, but an eerie quiet fell on the camp. A bitter, acrid smell burned in Milo's nose and he could literally taste ash on his tongue. As a military captain, Milo had fought many battles over the years, under various circumstances, and in numerous lands. He hated war; but ironically, he was skilled at it.

And then there was Lewis. Twenty years in the army and he had excelled; but battle fatigue overcame him and he requested permission to leave the military—honorable discharge. With all his experience in negotiations in the lands he fought in, Lewis naturally transitioned to a liaison. And Milo was sincerely happy for him. But considering the circumstances they now found themselves in, Milo hoped Lewis remembered the survival skills he learned in the military all those years ago.

With Beckett on his right side, Lewis hobbled behind Tegan. The path laden with thick grasses and briers, and stones tricky to navigate. But with the rats and sombels covering the camp, these three sombels decided to head around the battleground towards the river. From there, they hoped to follow the bank to the north and reach the birch tree quickly; Lewis needed medical attention as soon as possible.

Tegan rounded a large boulder and caught sight of the water. "I see it!" she called out to the others. Lewis sighed with relief. Stepping carefully, the sombels parted through the tall grasses as they trekked toward the bank. Tegan could smell the river, the unique fish-like aroma of the water, and the dirt and soggy plant smell of the bank.

As she neared the footpath along the river bank, Tegan noticed something moving in the bushes. Her heart pounded and she stopped to watch.

"What is it?" Beckett asked.

Tegan pointed her nose in the direction of the commotion and took in a deep breath. She smelled.....death.

Panic seized her and she shouted to the others, "Run!"

Tegan grabbed Lewis' other arm and helped him run as fast as he could manage. If they could just get to the tree......She looked over her shoulder and saw a black rat barreling towards them. Yellow teeth bared, growling, drooling, spear tilted toward them.

Beckett hollered to Tegan, "We can't make it. We need to stop and face them."

The three sombels slowed down and turned around. Immediately, the black rat caught up with them, tackling Beckett and wrapping its paws around his neck to strangle him.

"Get off of him, you fool!" Lewis delivered a solid punch to the rat's side, causing the rat to squeal and roll off the sombel. The rat clutched his side and scrambled for his spear.

Tegan pointed her sword at the black rat as Beckett coughed and stood up. "Back off you filthy rodent!" Tegan demanded.

"There will be others," the rat hissed.

As if on cue, four more rats raced to the scene. They stood with spears ready, breathing heavily, and drooling from their filthy mouths. Now, the sombels were outnumbered when they were so close to safety.

"What do you plan to do?" Beckett asked, putting on an aggressive façade, even though he was terrified underneath.

"You will give us that gem!" the rat shrieked. "Or I will take it from you!!"

The rat jumped forward with his spear and aimed for Tegan. She thrust her sword up, diverting its blade, and struck the rat on the shoulder. He fell and rolled over, clutching his wound with his paw. Growling, he stood up again and moved closer to the sombel, pointing his spear in her face. Tegan backed away, her eyes widened in fear, watching the spear get closer and closer. The rat reared his arm back with the spear and thrust the weapon toward Tegan's body. She grasped the handle of her sword with both paws and raised it. The moonstone glowed a deep green and created a dome of protection around the sombels.

The group huddled together under the gem's magical defensive weapon. Howling in frustration, the rat witnessed his spear bounce off the dome and fall to the ground, useless. The sombels backed up under the protection.

"What do we do now?" Tegan squeaked out.

No one spoke. Silence, with the only sound of blood thumping in their ears. The rats gathered around the dome, waiting for the chance to attack once the protection disappeared. Jumping and growling, the rats encircled the sombels, tapping and hacking at the cloudy layer between the rats themselves and the green moonstone within. If they could get their paws on the gem, they could wield unimaginable power!

Suddenly, a shadow passed over the group and a ghastly wind blew through them. A horrible, dreadful screech echoed in the sky and throughout the camp, causing everyone to cover their ears. More velvety shadows, more hair-raising winds...another frightening screech. All the rats and sombels searched the sky for answers.

What was that?!

And then, Tegan caught sight of the enigma and gasped.

CHAPTER 34

As the sounds of shouting burned in his ears, Prince Callum made his way to a clearing near the river. War was inevitable; he could smell it in the air.

The rats prepared their machines for battle, lined the wheels up, and took a few proactive steps forward. Rat soldiers danced around the bottom of the structure, heaving stones into the baskets, and hoisting the debris over into the other camp. The prince ran toward the clearing, keeping the birch tree in his sight. He stayed under the coverage of native hedges until he could see the showdown in front of him. It was one thing to witness the chaos from above, in the fox tree. But now he needed a closer view, one not obscured with fire and smoke.

The shouting closed in and the prince backed into a rock crevice to hide. He stood there motionless against the cold, flat stone surface under the shadow of the great bushes growing nearby. Several rat troops scurried past him, unaware of the royalty hiding so close to them.

Once the rats left, Prince Callum climbed on top of the large rock to get a better view of his surroundings, and to locate Tegan. He peeked through the branches next to him and witnessed rats positioning their machines, ready to launch into battle. In fact, those rats did not wait. They took turns filling the baskets with flammables and lighting them with an open flame. Rat soldiers pulled on the ropes, holding the blazing trebuchet arms until the tension built up. The rope snapped and the fiery debris flew across the sky. Screams and shouts penetrated the landscape...war had commenced.

The prince crouched down under the threat of blazing debris. As he turned to jump off the rock, he caught a glimpse of a few rats huddled together, backs to him, and flailing wildly. He studied the soldiers and realized they were threatening Tegan and two others. Tegan stood with her arms in the air, holding her sword, with a thin, shaky protective dome covering the sombels. But the weak protection wouldn't last much longer. Prince Callum had to act quickly.

He pulled his bow and arrows, hoping to eliminate the rodents before Tegan's dome diminished. The prince drew back his bow, aimed, and...swoosh! The arrow sailed through the leafy branches in front of him and landed squarely in the back of one of the rats. It fell on top of the protective dome, slid down, and collapsed on the ground. The surrounding rats shrieked and jumped up and down.

Swoosh! Swoosh! Swoosh!! The rapid firing of arrows wiped out the small number of dreadful rats holding Tegan, Beckett, and Lewis hostage. As the rats fell into a lump of black evil, Tegan let go of her sword, fatigued from holding the protection for so long. She dropped to her knees and rubbed her arms and paws vigorously.

"Let's go!" Beckett picked up Tegan's weapon and handed it back to her.

The sombels darted around the mound of dead rats and scurried toward the river. Tegan helped her uncle navigate the rocky landscape until they reached a narrow footpath, barely visible from the layers of shrubbery surrounding it.

"There!" Tegan shouted.

Once they hurried through the opening in the bushes, the landscape unfolded. Only short grasses and small rocks lined the trail.

It appeared that the path headed in the same northern direction as the birch tree—their safety.

As the sound of battle ensued, the sombels heard the shouts of soldiers and clanking of metal in the distance. Then, a loud *thud* as fiery rocks from a trebuchet plummeted to the ground. The force so strong that it shook the very ground beneath them, causing both Lewis and Beckett to stumble and fall.

Even the prince, still crouching on the large rock, felt the impact of the trebuchet's force and lost his balance. He tumbled off the rock and landed face down in the grass. Quickly, he stood up and shook himself off. The prince needed to catch up with the sombels and fast!

In the sky, the clouds swelled and gathered, eventually covering the sun. Instead of a bright midday glow, the landscape was fully shadowed and grim. Flares of burning embers seared the air, causing both rats and sombels to breathe in ash all around.

Milo watched as his unit pushed forward, hand-to-hand combat with swords and daggers, while others shot arrows from the flanks. As rat casualties piled up, the captain was keen to strategically direct his forces on Greygor. Sombel soldiers fiercely fought through the first line of rats and rallied around in small groups to engage in close combat with the rats guarding Greygor. Milo even dispatched sombel soldiers to destroy the two trebuchets that kept devastating the sombel reserves.

Three sombel soldiers crept near the first trebuchet, swords raised. As the rat soldier reloaded the basket on the arm of the machine, the sombels ran toward him and struck him in the chest with their swords. The rat fell, but three others jumped on the sombels, slashing and jabbing, yellow teeth bared, and foaming at the mouth. The sombels fought back. Pushing the rodents backward, then slashing, swiping, and dodging the rat attacks.

One by one, the rat guards fell. The sombel soldiers suffered wounds to their shoulder and chest. The unscathed sombel jumped up on the trebuchet and slashed the ropes holding the basket to the arm. As the basket toppled over with debris inside, he continued hacking at the ropes holding the counterweight. Once those restraints unraveled, the rest of the tethers loosened and fell off. The other wounded sombel soldiers hammered with their swords and dislodged the wheels from the structure. Without the support of its wheels, the trebuchet collapsed, rendering it useless.

The sombel soldiers took note of their victory and darted around a large rock structure to siege the next machine. As they prepared to charge, a ball of fire plummeted to the ground in front of them--*boom*! The sombel troops tumbled and fell from the close impact. Fiery rocks scattered across the ground, burning and consuming all vegetation in sight. The sombel soldiers were forced to reconsider their approach as the land before them lay scorched with a huge hole in the ground.

The sombel troops looked at each other, feeling the heat of the impact.

"Go back and request more scouts," the unharmed soldier said to the injured ones.

The two nodded and rushed toward Milo's camp, unknowingly bypassing a group of rats hiding under the hedgerow along the same path. This cluster of rats hunkered down among the leaves and held their breath, silent, protecting the most important member of their small faction, Greygor.

The rat king, himself, hungered for that gemstone. He NEEDED it. Burning with anger, Greygor pushed with his soldiers toward Tegan. He could smell those fugitive sombels in the air, tracking them with his insanely heightened sense of smell. Not only was his adrenaline at an all-time high, but the rat king's murderous desire for power and domination compelled him to track the sombel down. How dare she escape!! Tegan was only one pathetic sombel...why was she in possession of such a precious moonstone? She would pay for her insolence. And Lewis? Well,

Greygor knew how to force that sombel to show him the secrets of the tunnel entrance. From there, the rat king would have all the moonstone he craved, and then use it to conquer the world!

Tegan hastened along the footpath with Beckett and Lewis right behind her. She checked to see how her uncle was holding up as Beckett lumbered along with him. All around them, the sounds of shouting pierced the sky while another fireball plummeted to the ground behind them. The impact shook their footing so much that the sombels lost their balance and toppled over again.

Dusting themselves off, the group spotted the path diverging into an area covered by twisted vines and green leaves. As they approached the foliage, Tegan drew her sword and chopped at the vegetation to clear the obstruction. Behind it stood a row of large stones, two of which leaned against each other in a way that there was barely an opening to squeeze through. The rocks appeared almost yellow in color, and depicted birds carved into the stone with outstretched wings.

"Goldcrest Slip," Lewis read an inscription above the entry.

"There's no way we can climb over this," Tegan said. The rocks were slick from weathering so there was no foothold to allow for stepping over or around the structure. She stuck her head through the opening in between the rocks and felt the cold stone on her cheeks. Squatting down, Tegan pushed an arm through the opening and wiggled it. There was just enough space for her to squeeze through, but she doubted that Beckett or Lewis could fit.

"We are so close!" Tegan shrieked. She sized up their proximity to the birch tree and motioned for the other two to come closer. "Beckett, see if you can fit through."

Beckett helped Lewis sit down on a tree log before he skipped over to the structure. Beckett surveyed the opening and rested his paws on the side of the entryway, ready to duck under. As he pushed his head through, the sombel wiggled his body around, but couldn't make himself slide through easily.

He stood back up, put his paws on his hips, and sighed.

"Someone's coming!" Lewis called out. He could barely see over the hedges, but noticed something black getting closer.

Tegan and Beckett lifted Lewis to his feet, preparing to flee, when a voice shouted, "You have nowhere to run, sombels!"

Tegan gulped loudly at the sight of Greygor's dripping, drooling, mouth. She had no idea how he approached them so quickly. The rat king breathed heavily as he held a dagger in one paw and a long spear in the other, ready to jab at the sombels with any movement. Accompanying him were two other rats who jumped up and down, chattering their yellow teeth. Their nervous energy caused the sombels to back up until they stood pinned against the stone structure, fearful of what might happen next.

"You have something I want," Greygor stepped closer to Tegan and opened his paw. "Give the gemstone to me, NOW!"

She felt the thunder from his voice resonate down her spine. One step closer and she would feel his hot breath on her face. Tegan pulled her cloak snugly around her, covering her sword sheathed on her waist. "I have nothing of yours," she responded.

"You insolent beast!" the rat king hissed. Greygor lunged forward and seized the sombel by the collar of her cloak. He lifted her off the ground and glared into her eyes at his level. Beckett drew his sword and thrust it at the rat king. But the other rat soldiers pounced on him and knocked him down, snatching his sword with their paws, and laughing obnoxiously.

Petrified, Tegan instinctively pulled up her legs and grasped them around her chest in a ball. She wiggled around and managed to slip out of her cloak, leaving the empty garment in the hands of a seething rat. As she dropped to the ground, Greygor threw the cloak down and leaned over to seize her again. Only this time, Tegan pulled out her sword and sliced his face with the tip of the blade. The rat king howled and stepped back, covering the open wound with his paw.

He was done.

"Get rid of them!" Greygor ordered his soldiers.

As if on cue, the horizon darkened and a multitude of rat soldiers ran frenzied toward their leader. Scurrying over rocks and hedges, nipping with their grotesque teeth, the rabid soldiers inundated the landscape. Thunder clapped and roared in the distance...or was that the sound of battle?

Startled by the noise, Tegan raised her sword in defense. The green moonstone glowed dimly at first, then brighter and stronger. The protective force enveloped the group bravely standing their ground against an evil, vindictive band of wicked rats. Tegan knew she couldn't hold this shield over them forever, and her arms weakened the more she utilized the gem's power. She began to panic and watched as the sky darkened again and thunder clapped.

But resting high in a branch of a nearby beech tree, Prince Callum waited and watched. As only one pixie against hundreds, maybe thousands of rats, he knew the situation was critical. The prince hoped the foxes would provide backup, but so far, he'd only witnessed Milo's army engaging in warfare. And his own clan promised to send forces, but they were a day behind. Something had happened. The foxes had to be out there.... somewhere.

Watching Tegan struggle to protect herself, along with Beckett and Lewis, distressed the prince, and he had finally reached his breaking point. Around his neck, Prince Callum pulled out a threaded necklace hidden under his tunic. A small, pipe-like whistle dangled loosely from the band. He held it firmly between his finger and thumb, and blew it several times; short and chirpy. From the tiny instrument, a sweet and high-pitched sound resonated through the atmosphere, penetrating the battle cries, and floated across the open land.

The prince held his breath and paused for a response. This was it, the final effort to subdue the rats and destroy their dominance, running rampant across the country. His heart pounded in his chest as he waited.

CHAPTER 35

Lewis recognized the helplessness in Tegan's face. She struggled to hold the protection over her uncle and her friend. Slowly, the dome flickered and her strength waned. Beckett stepped in alongside Tegan and helped her hold her sword up...the only shield separating the sombels from the deviant rats.

But the black army kept rolling towards them; teeth gnashing and metal from their spears clanking, like wind chimes caught up in a tornado. The pounding of the grotesque paws on the ground echoed in the sombels' ears. Lewis searched the sky for any sign of redemption. Instead, he saw fire and smoke, burning trees and smashed machinery, along with units of bloodthirsty rodents.

And then Tegan shrieked. Her arms gave out and she dropped her sword on the ground before her. The protection she held over her group completely disappeared. Now dangerously vulnerable, Tegan felt as if time stood still...her eyes widened with terror as she watched Greygor and his goons thrust towards her. The sombel grabbed her sword again, held it up, and screamed wildly and passionately, from deep within her soul. She had nothing left to lose.

Prince Callum paused, speechless, at the sight before him. From his hiding spot, he witnessed Tegan's sword burst into flames, thrusting a single ray of fire straight up and over her head. The prince followed the stream of fire upwards and noticed movement in the tree tops near the slip. The fox soldiers, perched on the branches of the birch tree, pointed wildly to something in the sky. And armed foxes waved their arrows above their heads, shouting to each other.

Before he could get their attention, the prince felt a gush of wind pass over his head, causing his hair to flutter in the breeze. A deep, throaty growl pierced the atmosphere....then another, and another.

Above their heads, an enormous flying beast flapped its wings, swooping down low and then soaring up high, keeping its green eyes on the commotion below. Tegan's flame burst alerted the beast of her location. The dragon growled wildly, drawing in a breath of air, and then pushing it out; scorching the ground with his fiery, heated breath.

The startled sombels huddled together instinctively and watched the gray scaly monster fly back and forth in the sky.

"Is that...?" Tegan whispered.

The rats hesitated, then jumped in a crazed-like state. They didn't know which way to run, and crashed into each other, stumbling to the right and the left. Large rocks and thick hedgerows slowed the armies in their retreat. And from around the corner, Milo's army marched, closing off the only escape route for the rats.

"Tanwyn!" the prince whooped and cheered. "Tanwyn!!! Sios (down)!!!" Excited, Prince Callum walked into a clearing and whistled again to his dragon friend.

Tanwyn rolled and glided toward the prince, keeping watch as spears launched in his direction from delirious and bloodthirsty rats. The sleek, scaly dragon flew over the prince, just low enough for the pixie to touch the beast's belly. Tanwyn roared a sulfuric, smoke-filled cry.

"Tanwyn, dul (go)!" the prince commanded. "Tine (fire)!"

259

The dragon lifted his tail and thrust himself higher in the sky. He then turned around and flew toward the rat army, opened his mouth, and breathed out a stream of flames, incinerating a group of rats climbing onto the remaining trebuchet. Tanwyn then swung his muscular tail at the machine and smashed it into many, splintered pieces.

Milo's army cheered and shouted encouragement to the beast, keeping a healthy distance between the dragon and themselves. Tanwyn circled the camp, watching the rats scatter, and dove again, using his fiery breath to burn up another line of Greygor's army.

Tegan, Beckett, and Lewis let their guard down for the first time that day. They cheered and laughed a little, watching the massive dragon gracefully dance in the sky and obliterate their enemies. Tanwyn swooped in closer to Tegan's group; she felt the heat from his breath as he flew by. The smell of ash trailed behind him as well. She stared into his green glowing eyes as he blew flames down on the rats nearest to them.

The remnants of the rat army scattered like ants, and hid from the devastation. Many of them ran right into the front lines of Milo's army, surrendering their spears, and accepting defeat. As Prince Callum watched the scene, the prophecy infiltrated his mind. He meditated on it as he witnessed the words fulfilled before him.

"And the red-tailed one will deliver those enemies into the hands of judgment."

He mused out loud, "just as the prophecy foretold, the rats of Voldire have been handed over to the sombel army for judgement." *Milo's unit will now decide the fate of those black rats.*

Taking advantage of the chaos, the prince ran toward Tegan's group, dodging piles of burning wood and scorched boulders. As Tanwyn flapped his wings, the gusts of air stirred up fires on the ground, causing them to spread. Now, there was a new danger...fire.

Tegan's group huddled near the slip, waiting for a chance to flee. As smoke engulfed the atmosphere, the sombels wondered if they could see their way out. In addition to the smoke hazard, flames from a fire began encroaching on them. Closer and closer, the flames roared, pressing the sombels against the stone, with no way to escape except for the slip.

Prince Callum could barely make out the three due to the fires. As he neared the group, he called out to them, "Tegan, I'm here! Hold on!" He whistled for Tanwyn and waited for the monstrous beast to appear.

Tanwyn circled the camp again. He lowered his massive head, and flew toward the prince. As the beast landed next to him, the ground shook with the dragon's weight. Through the smoke, Tegan could see the sharp talons at the end of his claws and the long scaly tail, swishing in the smoke. Now that she saw Tanwyn in the daylight, Tegan stood humbled by the size of the mighty dragon. She froze as he positioned himself there with his prominent scales, heaving in and out with each breath he took.

Prince Callum held tight to the dragon's neck and motioned to the sombels, "Come, get on!"

The group stood there, terrified, unable to move.

"Don't worry," said the prince. "He's safe to ride short distances. He will take you to the birch tree where you'll be safe."

Lewis stepped forward and climbed onto Tanwyn's back. He stretched out his paw for Tegan, and she forced herself to step up to her uncle. Beckett followed behind her. Once the sombels sat securely on the dragon's back, the prince shouted, "Hold on tight to Tanwyn! He can be a bit spry!" Prince Callum backed up and hollered, "I will see you there." He motioned to the dragon, "Tanwyn, dul *(go)*!"

With that, the beast lowered his front legs and pushed off the ground with his back legs, soaring high into the sky with its massive wings flapping up and down. The sombels clung to the scales and bits of fur on the dragon's back, struggling to secure themselves as the monster flew towards the tree. From the dragon's back, Tegan observed the devastation below. Scorched lands, burnt structures, rat carcasses; the scene was unbelievable. Grateful to fly over the destruction, she couldn't imagine walking through it.

Prince Callum signaled to Milo with a wave; Tegan's group arrived safely. The sombel captain shouted out to his troops and commanded them to round up the remaining rats for imprisonment. The soldiers squirreled around the fires and amassed what was left of the rat unit, cornering them against a stone façade. As Milo looked over the hundred or so rats, he noticed something alarming...Greygor was not among them.

Where was he? Had the rat king escaped?

Only time would tell. The captain knew it would be several days before the carnage of this battle cleared, and he could make an accurate assessment of what remained. In the meantime, Milo had plans to march the prisoners south, back to the swamp lands of Homish. There, he would receive orders as to how the prisoners would be handled, and most likely, punished.

Milo charged his troops to gather what supplies they had left and fall into formation. Half of the unit mobilized at the front, ahead of the prisoners; and the other half assembled behind them, guarding the rear.

The sombel captain dreaded the journey ahead of them. The wet lands were a two-day march to the south, over a barren, desolate landscape. But Milo believed they could make it before sunset the next day; that is, if they left now.

Prince Callum watched as the sombel soldiers rhythmically marched to gather the rats into a condensed, but sizeable group. With a loud trumpet call, the sombels followed Milo's orders and

directed the prisoners out of the campsite and towards the riverbank. Within a half an hour, they disappeared behind the rocks
and boulders, and only the sound of fires burning raged in the
distance.

Satisfied, the prince flapped his wings, lifting himself into the
sky, and flew towards the birch tree. He passed over the burning
embers of the now defunct campsite and what used to be the
flowering woodlands of Old Padley.

Closer to the birch tree, Tanwyn hovered over a high branch.
His wings fluttered slightly, balancing his tremendous body so the
sombels could disembark onto the tree. Prince Callum approached
the dragon and hopped onto the branch. He helped Tegan place
her feet safely on the tree limb.

Dermot and Moss, the fox soldiers, rushed over to the sombels,
aiding each one as they disembarked from the dragon's back.

"Tegan, are you alright?" Dermot asked.

"I am," she stated.

"Oh, but you are shaking!" Moss observed.

Tegan noticed it too. "I am...I am just tired," she replied, relieved
to now be surrounded by friends.

Dermot put a blanket around Tegan's shoulders and led her
inside a brightly lit room in the tree. And there, on a makeshift
cot, sat Lewis propped up on several pillows and covered with a
wool blanket. He appeared quite amused as a small fox tended to
his injuries.

Tegan searched the room for Beckett and spotted him talking
to a group of fox soldiers in the corner. As she approached him,
Beckett exclaimed, "Tegan! You will never guess who's here!"

Beckett swung Tegan around so his friend could see the stairwell. Two figures emerged into the ample lantern light. One
was Kenna, wearing a toothy smile; and she led the other figure
through the crowded room.

Tegan shrieked, "Papa!" She hopped over to her father and hugged him tightly.

"You did it, Tegan!" Arthur said, hugging her. He backed up and held his daughter by the shoulders to look her over. It took him a few minutes to gather his emotions before asking, "Are you hurt?"

Though weary with fatigue, and arms bruised and sore, Tegan replied, "No, no, I am perfectly fine." And she was. Those wounds would heal soon enough. But right now, Tegan could not believe her father stood there in front of her. How she had longed to see her family again! The sombel soaked in every second of this reunion. There would be much to talk about and share with her father...with everyone really. After all, it was a hike back to Haven. And she couldn't wait to get back home. *Home*; the sound rang fondly in her ears.

It had been days, maybe a week or more, since Tegan embarked on her journey. Time ran together and eventually became a blur. But in the short span, the sombel encountered many different creatures, helpful and dangerous; and she managed to escape several life-threatening situations. Despite all the walking, the hiding, the exploring, and the fighting, Tegan looked forward to the simple routine of joining her family again. Just washing the laundry seemed like a dream right now.

Lost in thought, the sombel heard a voice next to her and turned to respond. "Tegan?" It was Kenna. She ran up to the sombel with a troubled look in her eyes. "I need to talk to you. Something very important has come up."

Alarmed, Tegan returned to the present moment and replied, "Sure, Kenna, what is it?"

"I spoke with Dermot a few minutes ago," the little fox started, and then hesitated. "He told me that news just arrived from Chipping Farms...my father is missing! They think Reginald is behind it."

Tegan heard what Kenna said, but had trouble processing it. She didn't know how to respond. *Reginald--the fox king-- is responsible?*

"I need to find my father!" Kenna declared emphatically. "I have to know what's happened to him. And if Reginald is behind this, I swear he will regret every second of this takeover." She squinted her eyes and snarled her lips, baring her small white fangs in pure rage. Kenna needed all the help she could get. This job meant dealing with powerful creatures much bigger than herself. She pointed at Tegan, "You," she said, and pointed at Beckett, "and you. Come with me to find my father."

The sombel's heart pounded. *Me? Why does she want my help? I am done with so-called quests. All I want right now is to go home and see my family.*

The fox grabbed Tegan's paws in hers, "You have experience confronting enemies in ways I do not. I might be knowledgeable scouting certain terrain, but you looked the rat king in the eyes and lived! You're a hero!"

Tegan blinked again and again, listening to her words but unable to comprehend the information at hand. She only thought of home. "Shouldn't you ask someone with way more capabilities and skill?" she asked. "I just want to go home," the sombel muttered under her breath and tried to smile through her fatigue.

"At least you have a home," the fox responded flatly. "The last one I lived in crumbled into ashes, set on fire as part of the rebellion. My family forced to relocate and I'm scraping by just so I can help other families get back a touch of normality. I can't do that unless Reginald is dethroned." She took a step back and softened her tone a bit. "I understand about your family. Your father...he is here and he is safe. But I don't know what difficulties my father faces right now." Kenna continued, "You've seen what greed does to a creature. Reginald is no different. And I trust you, Tegan.

You can be discrete....the fox clan, you know, are a very suspicious bunch." It was Kenna's turn to impose a smile.

Tegan looked deep into Kenna's eyes, recognizing panic and fear in them. She knew this horrible feeling as well. Combine it with desperation and you have a nasty storm brewing inside one's soul, ready for any shred of events to ignite it.

The sombel knew what she had to do. It was the only thing she could do. Tegan squeezed her friend's paws in return and gently nodded. After all, tomorrow was a new day.

EPILOGUE

For hours, the group hiked back on the narrow footpath toward Haven. The sleepy sun had finally dipped its head behind the mountain range in the distance. Tegan and Kenna chatted to pass the time quickly. They conversed and speculated about the news of her missing father. Even Beckett, easily distracted by the sounds of the night, perked up and offered to help. He was foraging for another adventure.

While the reports of her father had startled the small fox, both Prince Callum and Arthur were the least surprised. As the travelers headed back to the village by moonlight, toting snacks and small lanterns, the prince and Tegan's father discussed the events leading up to the coup. The Redlan clan had been in shambles ever since Reginald overthrew Edwin.

"What more do you know about my father?" Kenna asked Arthur.

"I only received notice this morning. Your father was not at the pub, and your mother hadn't seen him either," he replied.

"Well, father doesn't always stay at the Boar's Nest. He sometimes sneaks back to our home off of Tunsdale....Ma makes sure he is hidden though," Kenna explained.

"Does Reginald know about any of this?" Tegan asked.

"Reginald knows my father works at the pub during the day. In fact, Reginald put him to work there once we moved back." She walked a few steps and then continued, "He isn't aware that father hides out there though. Reginald likes to keep an eye on him, in case Pa decides to talk."

"What does your father know?" Tegan asked.

"More than Reginald wants him to, I'm sure," Kenna responded. "He still has all the old documents and billing accounts from his employment with Edwin. He keeps those in a secret room in the pub."

"I bet there's information there that would make Reginald blush...figuratively speaking," Beckett interjected. Tegan and Kenna flashed their eyes at him and he cleared his throat. Then he asked, "Why can't your father be seen at home?"

"Reginald wants something that my Pa has. I don't know what it is. But until he gets it, my father is restricted to the pub. Reginald's lackeys make sure he stays there."

"Something in that secret room, no doubt," Beckett mumbled.

Kenna and Tegan continued walking in silence, each thinking about the same thing: Kenna's father. As Edwin's accountant, her father meticulously kept the business books for many years. What did he know, or possibly discover, that made Reginald take notice? Was her father in danger? Would Reginald take out his retribution on the former aid? All of these unknowns...no wonder Kenna was a mess!

Suddenly, a loud bang, and then another! The dark sky bloomed in color as fireworks scattered across the night sky. A stream of red, and blue, followed by white sparks twinkled like jewels in the night. The group hesitated, watching the bright lights hover in the distance.

"We're nearly there!" Tegan said excitedly.

"And just in time for the Midlands celebration," Arthur added. The group heard voices in the distance...happy voices, singing and laughing, and making merriment. It was such a contrast to the drudgery they had endured.

"Look there!" Arthur pointed in the direction of the fireworks and continued, "Prince Callum, will you be staying for the festivities? I insist."

The prince chuckled, "I think I can stay the night before returning home. Besides," he grinned, "I've heard the oat cakes are delicious!"

Arthur smiled, "I'll make sure you get more than enough."

"What about you, Kenna?" Tegan asked. "Can you stay?"

"I...I would love too, but—" Kenna started.

"Oh, please stay! You need a good night's sleep before setting out again. And I promise to send for news about your father first thing in the morning," Tegan replied.

"It really would be the best," Beckett spoke and rested his paw on her shoulder. "One night, to take care of yourself."

Kenna looked from Tegan to Beckett, and then back to Arthur and the prince.

"Stay, and you can start again in the morning, once you've had the chance to rest," the prince added gently.

Kenna sighed and took a deep breath. Then she replied softly, "Alright, one night."

Tegan knew it wouldn't be an easy task. *Locating Kenna's father? Does she realize how difficult this kind of quest can be? And what if her father doesn't want to be found?*

Tegan was confident about one thing—she needed her friends' help to navigate the harsh world she now found herself in. Baptized by these trials, Tegan's eyes had been opened to both the good and the evil, battling for dominance throughout the country. Safety and the comfort of home became nostalgia, and she tucked it away in her heart; a refuge from danger, a slice of heaven--her own haven.

JENNIFER WHIDDON

But storms of all kinds raged on in this world. Some she would fight, and some she would leave to others. Tegan was chosen, but could not let that cloud her judgment. On the side of peace, her anthem would be maintaining stability throughout Fellnore. Whatever it took.

Beckett, Kenna, Tegan, and Prince Callum had fought the good fight, and their trust and friendship now reflected their camaraderie. This new alliance had endured the trials, and surely there'd be more to come.

Could Tegan conquer the world? She laughed to herself and thought, *"With the help of my friends, I can do anything."*